TO
PROTECT
AND
TO **SERVE**

GOODING

Order this book online at www.trafford.com
or email orders@trafford.com

Most Trafford titles are also available at major online book retailers.

Print information available on the last page.

ISBN: 978-1-6987-0262-9 (sc)
ISBN: 978-1-6987-0264-3 (hc)
ISBN: 978-1-6987-0263-6 (e)

Library of Congress Control Number: 2020914381

Trafford rev. 07/31/2020

 www.trafford.com
North America & international
toll-free: 1 888 232 4444 (USA & Canada)
fax: 812 355 4082

Ever since he'd been assigned Drone as a partner they were sending him on these strange escapades. No more strolling through the entertainment district at night, keeping the Normals in line, usually just by looking at them. Now they had him trying to bust up a satyr or, worse yet, stumbling along in the dark through the old city in search of Deviants. It was her; he knew that. She was the reason he'd suddenly become such an adventurer—through no fault of his own. She was what the other cops called a Crusader, a cop who was fanatical about their work, and Crusaders were dangerous, all of them. Crusaders got their partners killed, if the partners weren't careful. There was no way this turn of events could be considered a promotion. What it should be considered, he had decided, was an ugly twist of fate. Or else it was somebody's idea of a joke. Or revenge.

"Shh!" she said to him, and he wasn't aware he'd been making any noise. She had her pistol drawn, and she was peering ahead of them into the darkness. He had his pistol drawn too, only because she had drawn hers, and he stood just behind her and watched, more like a spectator than a participant in … whatever it was they were involved in. He wasn't sure what they were involved in; he was just following her lead. His breathing was constricted and his chest was tight. His heart pounded in his ears. Whatever was going to happen, he wished it would happen soon.

And then the light appeared again, a tiny point of light perhaps fifty feet ahead of them and closing slowly. It traced the pattern again: straight down to the alley floor and then across, in the shape of an L. Then it winked out again.

They waited, and soon footsteps were audible on the cinder floor of the alley. They came nearer, and nearer, and still nearer, and Duda felt more than saw Drone tensed in front of him. Then the light came on again and traced the pattern again, slowly, and Drone's gun cracked—a deafening sound like a small rock hitting a tin barrier at very high speed—and almost simultaneously Duda heard a startled gasp, and then, very shortly after that, the sound of a body hitting the alley floor.

"Cover me," she hissed. "Cover me!" And they advanced in the darkness until they came to the sound of labored, rhythmic gurgling on the alley floor. He was still just behind her. "Careful!" she seethed at him. "He might not be dead. Get your light on him. *Get* your light on him."

He was too slow (he was *always* too slow). She found her own flashlight before he found his and used it to locate the dying man's face. The gurgling had already stopped.

Duda stared. "He's just a boy," he said sickly. Nausea swept through him.

"Hold this." She gave him her flashlight. "Keep it on his face. *Keep* it on his face."

"He's dead. Look at his eyes."

"*I* know he's dead. You think I'm blind?"

She bent beside the corpse and felt for a pulse, though she knew she would find none. "Keep the light on his face. *Keep* the light on his face."

"Why? He's dead."

"There might be more of them."

"And they'll come out of his face?"

"Shhh! Listen!" She looked up and away from the corpse, down the alley whence the dead man—the dead boy—had come, before he was dead, of course. "Did you hear that?"

"No."

"Listen!"

"There's nothing to hear. He was alone."

"They're never alone."

"There's nobody out here with us."

"He made their sign. He wouldn't do that unless there was somebody out here to see it. Go down the alley and check. At least go down to the end of the block. And keep an eye on the rooftops. They could be up there."

He was not her subordinate, but he obliged her, the way he usually obliged her. He crept along the alley to the next cross street and found only more darkness, and more silence.

When he returned she was standing over the body, wiping her hands with a cloth she must have ripped from the dead boy's clothing. "Some shot," she said, and she didn't seem pleased. "It hit him in the throat and blew the chip right out the back of his neck."

"That's impossible."

"Go ahead; look for yourself. There's a hole back there the size of a tiny fist. And no chip."

"What about the spinal column?"

"It's intact. Maybe the bullet grazed it. I can't tell in this darkness. Maybe it hit him at a weird angle. See what the medical guy says."

"I don't believe it."

"Look for yourself."

"I'll take your word for it."

"Can't stand the sight of blood? There's sure a lot of it. I'm guessing the bullet completely severed the carotid artery. He bled out so fast.

"Damn it. I aimed for his chest. Where I thought the chest would be. I could barely see. It's so dark out here."

"You got the job done."

She didn't like the way he said it. "I did my duty," she growled, as though she were swearing at him. It took very little to make Drone angry, especially coming from him, and the least it took was to imply that she hadn't acted professionally.

"He looks so young," Duda said. "He's a boy. A teenager—at most. A boy that age doesn't even understand. What could he possibly know at that age? What was he even doing out here—by himself?"

"He knows enough to listen to their foul lies and be persuaded. It's all propaganda; don't you know that? A kid his age is exactly the right target for those monsters. He's impressionable. He listens to their lies and believes them, and the next thing we know we've got another terrorist to deal with."

Duda offered nothing in response, and she added, "And now we've got a dead terrorist. I hope that chip is all right. Otherwise this will all be wasted." She shook her head at her own incapacity to hit her intended target—even given the darkness in the alley she would not make excuses for herself.

Maybe she was looking for reassurance or validation, but Duda gave her nothing, and she finally said, as if reading his mind, "Would you rather that be you on the ground there?"

"Was he armed?"

She hesitated before answering. "No."

Now it was his turn to hesitate. The nausea persisted, and he looked away from the boy's face. "Did you call this in?"

"They're on their way. Bigger wants us to search the whole area. At least four square blocks. We'll expand the search once they get here."

"All right," he said. But he didn't feel like searching anything. He felt like calling it a night.

For the next few hours they searched, with help from their backup, but they found nothing—nothing but deserted streets and alleys and mostly deserted buildings. They searched in pairs because this was not a neighborhood that could be safely searched by individuals. During their search they rousted a few Deviants, but they were not the dangerous kind. Not terrorists. They were wandering strays who failed to appreciate the benefits the magnanimous State had to offer them. Magnum, one of the officers who'd been sent in as backup, shot one of the strays more or less for sport, after ensuring he was nobody important and was not dangerous. The other officers were angry, but all they did was chastise Magnum for his trigger happiness. They were not angry enough to be bothered with the paperwork that would accompany such an incident, so they heaved the dead man into a dumpster and did not report his death. He would not be missed by anybody except perhaps a few of his fellow Deviants. No recrimination would follow his death.

Daylight was breaking by the time they arrived back at the compound. Like the rest of them, Bigger was near the end of his shift, and he was not happy. "And all you found was a few bums?" he snapped at them during the debriefing.

"Besides the kid, that was it."

"That's impossible. So you're telling me this little terrorist was just out there wandering in the alley by himself. Walking alone in the darkness and flashing their sign just for fun."

They looked at each other, but none of them said anything. They knew how ridiculous their story sounded.

"That's what I thought," Bigger said. "We're going back out there tonight. There's something out there, and we're gonna find it."

Before they went off-duty that morning Duda and Drone stopped by the Medical Examiner's office, downstairs—all the way downstairs, beneath street level. Edgar was in charge down there and seemed glad to see them. "Gets lonely down here," he chuckled. "I can talk all I want, but nobody talks back. The only time I get any company is when you guys keep me extra busy and they put somebody else on to help me." He looked at Drone. "You need to kill more people."

"We're doing our best," she said, but she had only the slightest sense of humor and didn't care much for small talk. Nor did she care much for Edgar, or for anybody else at the compound who didn't work the streets with her. They were cowards, all of them, for remaining in the safety of the compound. "Did you look at the one we sent you tonight?"

"Right over here." There were three gurneys in the room, all three of which were occupied by shrouded corpses. It was cold in the room, almost as cold as it had been outside that night, but the corpses were undisturbed by the cold. Edgar took the two officers to the last gurney and drew back the sheet that covered its occupant.

Duda felt sick again. The nausea that troubled him before had finally subsided but now it abruptly returned. "He looks younger here than he did out there."

"Fifteen, sixteen," Edgar shrugged. "Old enough to get himself in trouble, apparently. Definitely old enough to get himself shot. And killed."

"He had it coming," Drone said tersely.

"Did he?" Duda said.

"He's one of them," she said. "He gave their sign. He bears their mark. He had it coming."

"I hate to interrupt your lovers' quarrel," Edgar said, "but it's almost time for me to end my shift. I'm hungry; I'd like to get some breakfast. What did you two need to know?"

"The chip," Drone said.

"What about it?"

"Was it intact?"

"Funny you should bring that up." Edgar reached down and grabbed the deceased's head, tried to turn it to show them a different angle, but then almost immediately gave up trying and let go of the head. "Anyway," he said, "you took out the artery but completely missed the endoskeleton. Not a bone broken in this boy's body." And with that he bent down, strangely, and kissed the boy's forehead. "A magnificent shot," he said, straightening up again. "One in a million. Straight between two narrow columns of bone through an aperture no bigger than that." He demonstrated with thumb and forefinger. "Incredible shooting."

"Enough sarcasm," Drone said. "What about the chip?"

"I sent it upstairs already."

"I thought sure I destroyed it. I was so worried about that."

"Impossible." Edgar shook his head. "You would have had to shoot our friend's head off. Wouldn't happen. The spinal column is perfectly intact. Look. I can't even twist his head around. If the spinal column were severed I'd have him looking at my toes now."

"Stop it," Duda said.

"Whatsamatter?"

"He has a weak stomach." Drone shook her head. Then she said, apparently in all seriousness, "How did you ever get to be a cop?"

"Shut up," Duda said. He didn't often lose his temper with her, or at least he tried not to lose it. He did his best to keep it in check—for his own good. He truly feared she might shoot him in the back some night. She'd call it an accident, say he stepped in front of her when she was taking aim at a Deviant. He'd be killed in the line of duty. What a shame that such an accident should occur.

"It was dark out there," she said to Edgar, ignoring her partner. "I couldn't see with all the blood, especially."

"An honest mistake," Edgar said. "You have to be a trained professional." And with that he playfully removed his latex gloves and turned to look for the contaminants receptacle against one wall. "You can cover him up again," he said to Duda. "Wouldn't want him to catch cold."

They were exiting the stairwell on the main floor and ran into Bigger on his way out of the building. "You paid a visit to the basement?" he said.

"We wanted to find out about the chip," Drone said.

"We'll know what's on it by tonight. Nice work," he said. Then he looked at Duda. "What the hell's wrong with you?"

Drone answered for him. "He has a guilty conscience," she said. "He doesn't think we should shoot poor innocent little terrorists."

"A guilty what?" Bigger looked Duda up and down. "Conscience is for cowards," he said. "Conscience just stands in the way of duty."

He turned to walk away but Drone stopped him. "Wait a minute," she said. "Did you hear that somewhere?"

"Here what somewhere?"

"'Conscience just stands in the way of duty.' What you just said."

"What? No. I didn't hear it somewhere. It's the damn truth."

"I love it," she said. "I have to write it down."

"You do that." He looked at both of them. "We'll be back there tonight. I guarantee it. That kid wasn't out there taking a stroll for his health. There's a terrorist cell out there somewhere, and we're gonna find it."

For two reasons, the State required its citizens to live in groups of four. First there was the environmental reason. Four citizens sharing the State's valuable resources, such as power and water and waste disposal facilities, was obviously more cost-efficient than three or two or one citizen selfishly squandering those resources. Citizens were frequently reminded that their world's resources were scarce and had to be carefully guarded to ensure their fair and efficient distribution among the world's populations. The thoughtful, generous government employed many experts to be stewards of their planet's resources and relied not only on their expertise but on the cooperation of the masses in seeing that the experts' imperatives, based of course on the most sophisticated scientific analyses available to humankind, were properly carried out. When the occasional shortage or disruption in service occurred, citizens were promptly and publicly reminded, repeatedly reminded, just how difficult the experts' job was—and therefore just how valuable the experts were. If such problems occurred even in spite of the experts' hard work and diligence, just imagine the chaos that would roil the land and destroy the ordinary citizens' security and comfort without the experts there to guide them! The State never tired of reminding its citizenry of the experts' value to them all.

Then there was the more important reason for the government-mandated living arrangement. The State's mental health experts had determined it was psychologically better for citizens to live in small groups, the better to keep each other company and, more important still, the better to keep an eye on each other. The State relied very heavily on its citizens to police each other, as it were, and report aberrant talk or behavior to the authorities as necessary. It was all for the health of the State. The State counted on the cooperation of its citizens to maintain order, as it counted on those citizens to shepherd its scarce resources. Four was as large as any family was permitted to get—the parents and two children—so every small apartment in the re-birthed country, the country that was brought to life in the State's Great Society rebuilding program, could accommodate four people. It was a means of assuring not merely equality and convenience but proximity. Citizens kept in close quarters were citizens easily kept track of. They could also be moved around as necessary in the service of the State.

The State had tried to do away with the family altogether, as that ancient and archaic contrivance distracted the citizens, taking their attention away from their larger, shared purpose, which was to serve the State that served them. But the effort to dissolve the family had failed, though of course the State would never admit it had failed. The State admitted to no mistakes, and no miscalculations. The State made no mistakes, and no miscalculations. The compromise over the family was, it informed its citizenry, required for their collective mental health. State mental health experts produced charts and graphs and tables and used mystifying technical language to explain *why* the family should still be permitted, if on a radically modified and limited basis. As part of the compromise it separated the families when the children were still young and sent them off to the State's learning centers. All children of the State, whether they were born into families or outside them, were predominately reared in the State's learning centers. For it was vital to the welfare of the State that they be properly reared, and the only way to ensure that was to place trained experts in charge of the child-rearing process. When they reached the age of eighteen they were dispatched to various parts of the country where their services were required. The children born into families were always dispatched to places where contact with each other or with their parents would be virtually impossible. It served the interests of the State to ensure that family ties were irreparably broken.

Those who were not born into any family besides the glorious family of the State—and they were the vast majority—were also separated, at age eighteen, from the other children they had grown up with and assigned employment and living quarters where their services were needed. Their roommates were chosen for them by skilled mental health experts—for the State employed many, many mental health experts, even more mental health experts than soldiers or cops, and it employed many of those. By using their expertise to determine living arrangements, the State could ensure appropriate groupings to protect its own interests. The State cared greatly for its citizens, and to protect its own interests was to protect their interests—a fundamental truth of which they were repeatedly and sometimes forcefully reminded.

As a police officer and hence a highly valued servant of the State, Duda naturally earned special privileges. He was permitted to live with just one roommate, in his case generally a fellow police officer. His latest roommate, Depacote, had been a depressive type whose bouts of intense sadness and occasional unchecked violence were hard to tolerate, though the violence could be an occupational asset, and it was for that asset that Depacote had been trained and employed as a police officer. However, the strategy backfired, though not of course through any fault of the State. One morning Duda came home from his shift and found Depacote dead from an overdose of one of several antidepressants he was taking. They had been used to check his violent impulses and were dispensed in carefully measured amounts, but it was always easy to blackmail a State pharmacist, and the black market for drugs was a thriving enterprise, perhaps the biggest single industry in the entire country and a great boon for the police because it kept them busy and made them appear quite important. Also, police officers made great black marketeers themselves, for they were in constant close contact with both the demanding consumers and the ready suppliers. Quite an efficient working relationship had developed among the three groups over time.

Duda had been tempted to put off notifying the authorities of his roommate's demise just so he could enjoy a bit of privacy, but he knew the State would quickly discover Depacote missing and search for him, and besides, there was the problem of the decomposing body. Before serious decomposition set in, he did his duty and saw to it that the corpse was properly disposed of. It was sent to the recycling center for reclamation. The workers at the recycling center had a saying: ashes to ashes. Duda's reward was that the State was slow in assigning him a new roommate, and for several months now he'd lived the life of a solitary citizen. It was blissful, and he wished it could last. But of course it would not last. The State would never permit it to last, for the State had to protect its own interests, and in doing so protect Duda's interests. Any day now he could expect somebody to show up at his door and announce himself as Duda's new roommate.

He had been on the night shift for his entire career as a police officer, nearly five years, but nonetheless sleep during the morning hours was nearly impossible for him, and all the more difficult this particular morning because he kept thinking about the boy they had murdered in the alley the night before. Duda just kept seeing the boy's lifeless face—the vacant eyes especially. They were so washed out, so etiolated and cold, and yet so accusatory! He tried many different methods for falling asleep and staying asleep, but none of them ever worked very well, and this morning none of them worked at all. He listened to the radio. He watched television. He masturbated. Finally he drank, and by noon he was drunk but he was still not asleep. He lay on his bed for hours, counting every second, then diverting himself with thoughts of various things, then trying to think of nothing at all (which never worked), and finally counting the seconds again. About three o'clock he may or may not have drifted off. It was hard to tell because he seemed to lose consciousness for a while, and yet when he regained it, around six o'clock, he did not feel as though he'd slept. So he could not be sure whether what he'd experienced was sleep or something else, something in between waking and sleep.

He got up and took a shower. The hot water ran out after only a couple of minutes, but he stood and soaked in the tepid remnants of it and did not yield to the cold for a long minute or two more. It was a war between him and the cold water. Finally the cold water won. He could no longer stand it and had to get out.

In an odd way the shower had helped him, for it had braced him. He was not drunk anymore though the taste of the liquor was still in his mouth, and he shivered uncontrollably for several seconds as he was toweling himself off. When he was dry enough he scurried back to bed and curled up this time between the sheets. "It's freezing in here!" he said aloud, angrily, and then he pulled the bedding tightly around him, his head still damp, and tried again to sleep. But he was no more successful than before, and this time his mind went back to the face of the boy in the alley. He stared at the face, tried to pull his mind's eye away from it, succeeded temporarily, then failed. It was dark in the room now, and he knew this exercise in futility would go on for hours if he let it. Moreover, his tiny apartment was cold—they were keeping the heat down low in all the buildings to save energy—so there was no comfort in it. He might as well be outside in the cold as inside in it.

So he got up and dressed in the same uniform he'd worn the previous night. He dressed quickly and took quick care of his hygienic needs, worrying very little about his appearance and not a whole lot more about his health. His mind was disheveled and he felt a sort of recklessness, a careless disregard for the world and for himself. This must come from murdering somebody, he thought. He saw the dead boy's face again and then put it out of his mind. Then he saw Drone and put his hands tightly around her throat and choked the life out of her. This fantasy pleased him. Apparently there was some satisfaction in murder after all.

Then he was out of his apartment and down the stairs and into the street. The street was cold and dark, and there was some comfort in the darkness, but there was no comfort in the cold. Many people were out in the street— many people like him, no doubt, who'd had the same idea about getting out of their cold habitations and milling about, at least—and because of the darkness his uniform was less conspicuous. He did not stand out as much as being a cop, and passersby seemed less wary of him. They barely seemed to notice him, in fact. He moved along the street and turned here and turned there, and then he saw a familiar café ahead and ducked inside.

3

I t was a tiny place—four tables and a counter with six round, swiveling stools—and only three people occupied it at present. A man sat at a table back in the corner, another man sat at the service counter, and the girl behind the counter was the reason Duda had chosen this place. She was tidying up, moving a few things around on the rear counter along the wall, the supply and storage counter. The television on the wall above her head was playing—naturally—and the president was on the screen, talking about the shortages of meat though nobody in the place seemed to hear her. Few people paid attention to the president's speeches. Few people paid attention to any of the politicians' speeches. It sufficed to know that the State was always right. What was even more significant, the Sate did what it damn well pleased anyway, so there was never much point in listening to it justify itself, no matter what it said or did.

Duda sat down at the counter, leaving two stools between himself and the other man at the counter. Just as he settled onto his stool the other man said, apparently to anybody who felt like listening, "It's those damn Deviants. They're responsible. The bastards are destroying the food supply."

"It's not the damn Deviants," the other man spoke up, the man over in the corner. Both men were middle aged and to Duda, who had paid very little attention to either of them, they seemed interchangeable. One was just a copy of the other. They both sat hunched over and spoke in gruff, guttural tones and seemed angry at the world, or at least some occupants of the world, but obviously not the same occupants. Each had his own faction to be angry with. "It's not the damn Deviants," the man at the table repeated. "It's the damn government."

"You just heard what the president said," the man at the counter countered.

"As a matter of fact I didn't. I didn't hear a word she said because I don't pay any attention to her. I never pay any attention to her because she never says anything worth listening to. Everything she says is a lie."

Neither of the complainers had looked at the other. The man at the table sat staring into the dark corner of the room, and the man at the counter seemed to be staring at the wall behind the counter.

"Did you hear what he said?" The man at the counter was speaking to Duda now, having stolen his gaze away from the wall at last. Duda didn't think the man had even noticed him, but apparently he had. "Did you hear what that guy just said?" Duda looked his way, and the man pointed. But Duda's eyes did not follow the man's pointing to its intended target.

"No."

"Well maybe you should pay some attention then. That guy over there is speaking treason and here you are a cop and you're not doing a damn thing about it."

Duda didn't even move, and the complainer grew irritated with him. "Did you hear what I said?"

"I heard what you said"—still not moving.

"Do you believe this? Do you see what's going on here?" Now he was complaining to the girl behind the counter—or maybe he was just complaining to the air. "What kind of a world is this? No wonder it's such a mess."

He turned on his stool to complain to Duda. "You're a *cop*," he said.

"I know that."

"Cops are supposed to maintain order. What's the job of a cop?" he said, as if he hadn't just explained the job of a cop.

Duda didn't answer, didn't even look at him, and he repeated, "Cops are supposed to maintain order. Maintain order and serve the public good. That's your job. Every citizen knows it. And you're a cop and you *don't* know it?"

"I do now that you've explained it to me." He still hadn't looked at the man.

"This is unbelievable," the man wailed. "This is why the world is in the mess it's in." He leaned toward Duda fiercely, and if he had been closer, instead of two stools away, Duda may have popped him one right in the mouth and then perhaps whacked him with his nightstick for good measure. But because he was too far away Duda didn't even react to him.

His failure to react only piqued the man's anger. "You have a *responsibility* to see that your fellow citizens maintain a proper attitude," the man growled. "That's part of your *job*. It's not optional; it's your obligation. It's part of serving the public good."

Duda finally turned his head just enough to look at the man. "You're right. I'm thinking right now that somebody in this room has a bad attitude. I'm thinking I may have to knock him around a little to shut him up. Maybe that'll adjust his attitude—and serve the public good."

"You want some more rice?" the girl behind the counter said. Apparently she was talking to the man with the bad attitude. "You're entitled."

He ignored her. "I don't *believe* this," he said, and he stood up suddenly. "That guy over there talks treason, and a cop sits here and listens to it and refuses to do his job?

And then he *threatens* a law-abiding citizen to boot? This is an outrage.

"Let me see your badge number. Let me see it."

Duda had made no pretense of covering it up, and now he turned slightly on his stool to let the man get a good look at it.

"I'll remember it," the man said. "Don't think I won't. I'm going to the authorities about this. If you think this is over, think again. You don't know who I am, but you'll soon find out."

"You want some more rice?" the girl repeated.

The man's response was to turn and storm out of the café. "You're entitled to it," the girl said to his departing backside.

"It's cold in here," Duda said.

"You want some rice?"

"I thought you'd never ask."

"There's some bits of onion in it, and some bits of carrot, and maybe even a few peas. A real bonanza. I had potatoes before, and for a while there was even some ham, but you're way too late for that. Don't even think about asking for beef or pork or poultry. There's some fish—little bits of it."

"Fish it is," Duda said. "Fish and rice."

"A real bonanza." She peered through the service window into the kitchen and placed the order. Duda couldn't see the cook, but he knew there must be one back there.

The girl turned to him, still hovering by the service window for his order to come up. "That guy is a facilitator at the learning center down at the corner," she said. "He means what he said. He'll turn you in."

"You have beautiful eyes," Duda responded. It was illegal for women to paint their faces, or to make other shows of ostentation, but this girl didn't need to paint her face. She was beautiful even without trying to be. Duda wanted to see her with her hair down, but she had no hair to let down. Nobody did. Everybody's hair was cut short to maintain equality—the appearance of equality, at any rate. "Did you hear what I said?"

"I did. You say that every time you see me. Did you hear what *I* said?"

"I did. You said that guy's going to turn me in. He thinks I'm a bad cop."

"A cop with a bad attitude, apparently." She grinned and brought a bowl of rice and set it before him. "Look," she said. "I'm even wiping your silverware. Not everybody gets clean silverware."

"I feel privileged."

"It's because I like your attitude," she said. "Consider it serving the public good."

"Anna," the man called to her from the table in the corner. "Please be careful. He is a cop."

"A cop with a bad attitude," she said.

"But still a cop. Sorry, officer," he said without looking at Duda. "But a person must be careful these days."

"I understand," Duda said. "I'm afraid I do understand."

She let him eat his rice with bits of fish in it. Before he set to it, though, he complained about the television. "You know I can't do anything about that," she said. *"You* could, though. With that thing you've got on your belt."

"Anna," the man in the corner reminded her.

Duda attended to his evening meal and tried to ignore the endless stream of government authorities and "scientific" experts who came on the television, educating the public about one thing and another. There would be entertainment later, government-approved entertainment, but for four hours every evening there was only educational programming. Duda blotted it out of his mind by trying to focus his thoughts on other things. For some reason his mind fell on an incident that had occurred two years before, when he was working the streets with his old partner, Mattock. One evening very much like this one they had come across three boys smoking cigarettes in the street. It was illegal to smoke at all though many people smoked discreetly, out of public view, as they did many other illegal things discreetly; and Mattock, a surly man with a violent temper, had first elicited sarcasm from the teenagers and then felt himself provoked to beat one of them in the interest of serving the public good. He had beaten the boy with his nightstick until the boy begged him to stop, and then he had strolled away, telling Duda he had just taught him an important lesson about maintaining order and serving the public good. It was best, he said, that Duda learn this lesson well and learn also when to apply the knowledge effectively. He would be doing himself and all his fellow officers a favor. Mattock had later been killed in a terrorist bombing when they were called to an alleged disturbance in one of the city parks. It was only fate that had kept Duda from being killed in the same bombing— he was investigating a different area of the park when the bomb exploded. He reckoned it was the shooting in the alley the night before that had brought the incident with the three boys in the street, and Mattock's subsequent obliteration, back to mind.

"Do you?" the girl was saying.

"Do I what?"

"Want some tea? Do you want some tea?"

"Yes. Please. But what I really want is to see you again."

"I would also like more tea, Anna," the man in the corner called. "Am I entitled?"

"You know you are, Austin." She poured a cup of tea for Duda and then excused herself and went to pour more tea for the man at the corner table. They chatted briefly while she was over there, exchanging words Duda could have deciphered if he'd wanted to, but unlike many of his fellow peace officers he was no eavesdropper. He ate his rice and waited for the girl to return.

She went back behind the counter, though, and stayed at the far end of it, away from him. "This hits the spot," he said.

"I'm sorry? Did you ask for something?"

"I said, 'This hits the spot.' This rice. Believe it or not."

"I'm glad," she said. "It's all we've got."

"My mouth was dry," he said. "And my stomach was empty. I needed this."

She said nothing. She appeared to be tinkering with something behind the counter.

"I really want to see you again," Duda said, finally.

"At least they're bombing the right people now," the man in the corner said loudly. He was responding to something on the television. The parade of authorities droning on about affairs of state had been interrupted by a breaking news story. Some senator's limousine had been ambushed on its way to the Capitol. More and more of the national politicians were traveling with armed escorts these days, but this senator's car was fired on by a rocket launcher from the roof of a nearby building, and the armed escort had no time to react to the attack and no means to repel it. The news video showed only the badly damaged shell of the limousine and did not say whether the senator had been seriously injured or even mortally wounded, only that he or she had escaped the scene. Duda didn't hear the senator's name and didn't care, as all government officials were the same to him. But the man in the corner seemed pleased. "We need more of this," he said, and he seemed not merely willing but eager for Duda to hear him.

"You know, they used to just bomb people randomly. It seemed random, anyway. They'd go after those groups of True Believers, the young kids who were such ardent supporters of the government. Rat finks, every last one of them." He said this bitterly, as if he spoke from personal experience. "Punks. Stooges. They were little terrorists for the government. You say one thing out of line and they'd have the government down on you. Bastards. That's what I grew up with.

"Now at least they're getting after the source. Get the higher ups. The decision makers. Corporate bigshots and politicians. Probably some of the same assholes who used to rat on us in the streets. These are the people who lead the way. They make the policies. They make the rules we end up having to follow. They tell us what we can have and not have, what we can say and not say, what we can do and not do. I say kill every last one of the bastards."

"Austin," the girl cautioned from her end of the counter. "Now who's being indiscreet?"

"I would like to see you again," Duda said loudly, abruptly. It was his turn to command attention. He knew the man in the corner was trying to get a rise from him, and he wanted to make it clear he wasn't bothered by anything the man had to say. He was interested in the girl—Anna—and only in the girl.

"Right here you'll find me," Anna said dryly. "Where you always do. Four evenings a week."

"You know what I mean."

"I do. And I've told you before, I don't date cops. Even attractive ones."

The compliment was not lost on him. He wanted to see her again. He wanted to see her somewhere else, away from the café. "We're no different from anybody else," he said. It was an attempt at genial sincerity, an attempt to connect with her.

But it drew an unanticipated response. Over in his corner Austin sputtered noisily with laughter. Then, turning in his chair and seeing Duda's expression, he feigned surprise. "Oh," he said, "you were serious? I thought you were making a joke."

"I'm not sure I like you, Austin," Duda said.

"Beat me with your nightstick then. It won't be the first time."

But Duda didn't want trouble with these people, not even with Austin. He returned his attention to his rice and finished it quickly. Then he stood up. "You still have beautiful eyes, Anna," he said.

"Mr. police officer," Austin said to him.

"My name is Michael," Duda said. He looked from one to the other of them when he said it. He wanted Anna to start calling him by his name, which, so far in their brief acquaintance, she had never done. He withdrew his ID card and handed it to her so she could run it through her little machine.

"Well, Michael. You don't really think you cops are just like everybody else, do you?"

"No, Austin, I suppose we're not. Does it make you happy to hear me say that?"

"It tells me you might be honest, at any rate. The same can't be said of most cops."

"The same can't be said of most people."

Austin appeared impressed at the quick parry. Maybe this cop was one of the smart ones. They were not numerous, but they did exist. He made a slight gesture at Duda as if to salute him.

Anna handed Duda his ID card, and he put it away. Austin said, "I'll bet you spend a lot of your own time checking ID cards, don't you, Michael?"

"It's part of my job."

"It's part of Anna's job, too. But she doesn't do it to spy on people."

"All right, Austin, you're right. I don't want to get into a philosophical discussion with you. But you're right."

"Pity. I was hoping to do exactly that with you—get into a philosophical discussion, I mean. I just love having philosophical discussions with representatives of our beloved government. They're so ... enriching."

"Austin—you realize the government really isn't interested in the information it collects on you. It collects a million pieces of data a day on every one of us, and it hardly ever uses any of them. *You're* the one listening to the crap on television. How much power does the government really have? The government can't put meat on your table, much less spy on you because you're complaining about it."

"You're the one who's deceiving himself, young Michael. You're a police officer—and you seem to think I'm just some old fool. Are you going to tell me you've never once used the data from an implant, or from somebody's ID card, to incriminate a fellow citizen?"

Duda could not bring himself to tell such an obvious lie—on that night of all nights, when he was on his way to find out what the government knew about the boy his partner had just killed, with him standing behind her offering his implicit approval. He moved toward the door without answering Austin's question. "Good night, Anna," he said to her. "I'll see you again soon. Good night, Austin. It's been interesting." And then he was out the door, out of one cold—the drafty cold of the poorly heated café—and back into the drier, more penetrating cold of the street.

4

Bigger assembled his squad and gave them their assignments for the night. Six officers, three sets of partners, were assigned to the same district Duda and Drone had covered the night before. It was a deserted and dangerous section of the city, technically off-limits to the public, that harbored Deviants of all kinds, most of them harmless. It was the ones who *weren't* harmless who interested the police.

At one time the neighborhood had been a fashionable area of a thriving metropolis. When the government had taken over all business activity in the country and the economic decline (or economic improvement, depending on your vantage point) had commenced, this neighborhood, along with other commercial and residential zones, had gradually deteriorated. Residents had fled the area as the businesses left and the gangs and the cops took over, and the government's plan to save energy by "modernizing" its citizens' living arrangements, moving them into densely packed "urban islands" where they enjoyed more "communal" accommodations—that is, they lived and generally worked in bland, monolithic, clustered high rises—had completed the zones' abandonment. The plan was to return these abandoned neighborhoods to Nature, razing the buildings and ripping up paved surfaces. Expert planners envisioned spacious parks where citizens could enjoy Nature under government supervision. Indeed, the experts generated magnificent renderings in which contented citizens intermingled with happy fauna in rejuvenated pristine environments. But the plan had bogged down as the government's resources dwindled and had to be diverted to other purposes. Many of the abandoned areas were now simply rundown versions of the neighborhoods their former inhabitants left behind. Criminal activity was rampant in them, and neither the police nor the military could muster sufficient force to control or eliminate such activity. For one thing, the criminal populations were transient; they moved around to avoid easy detection. Much more important, though, the criminals received protection from certain high-ranking government officials. It was the criminals who maintained the flourishing underground economy on which the populace depended for many consumer goods that were either illegal or simply difficult to come by. The cigarettes mentioned earlier, for example, could not be legally manufactured in the commonwealth because of their documented ill effects on health; hence they had to be supplied by the underground economy. Many other products similarly deemed unhealthy for public consumption were similarly provided by the underground economy. And many government officials augmented their entitlements by participating in this economy. Moreover, the underground economy provided goods and services the nation's citizens insisted on having and without which those citizens may have become unruly. The underground economy, in other words, helped to maintain order (and serve the public good) in a way the police could not.

But the dangerous Deviants were terrorists. They had no respect for the government or its tireless efforts to build a better world and provide a better life for them all, and they had made it their own mission to undermine the government's efforts and eventually vanquish the government itself. They operated in secret, most of them living among their fellow citizens—some even holding prestigious positions in the government they were trying to destroy. These were serious malcontents who could not be ignored or tolerated. Participants in the underground economy supplied goods and services the populace demanded; the terrorists, on the other hand, were destructive and therefore must be destroyed themselves. Special task forces had been formed for just that purpose, but occasionally ordinary patrol officers such as Drone and Duda had to be pressed into service as well.

Hence they found themselves being briefed for an excursion back into the dangerous neighborhood they had visited the night before. On the big screen in the briefing room Bigger showed them data culled from the chip extracted from the young terrorist Drone had killed, and from other sources. Some of these artifacts they had already seen, and Duda found himself daydreaming through much of the presentation. It was entirely immaterial to him whether they captured or killed any Deviants. He did not regard the Deviants as a threat to him. He did not care what they did to the government. In fact, whatever they did, the government probably had it coming—and that included the assassination, or at least the attempted assassination, of the senator earlier in the evening. Government officials and their government media machine churned out endless messages about the valuable protection the government provided its citizens, without which they would be at the mercy of sinister forces; but in truth Duda did not regard other forces as more sinister than the government itself. That impression had been amply reinforced by the events of the previous night, when, assured by his partner they were confronting a murderous terrorist, he had stood by and watched as she shot and killed a sixteen-year-old boy. Who was more "sinister," after all, the boy or the cop who shot him? Bigger had publicly commended them both for providing another data source to be mined. It didn't matter that the boy carried no weapon. What mattered was that his corpse could be mined for information about people who *might* carry weapons, and who might use them against the government. Therefore, his death clearly served the public good. But Duda was not so sure.

His mind was wandering along this very track when something occurred that did interest him. Some of the data Bigger was showing them consisted of pictures of known Deviants associated with the deceased boy, whose name, it turned out, was Caleb Brewster. First one photo, then another, seized Duda's attention with such force that he was afraid he might betray his surprise to others in the small room. The first photo was of Austin, the middle-aged man he'd encountered in the café just an hour or so before. The second was of Anna, the girl with the striking green eyes he'd been pestering for a date for the last couple of weeks. Their photos were part of a series, and Duda was attentive enough to ascertain without asking that neither of them was a known Deviant. They were, along with most of the others in the photos, simply known associates of Caleb Brewster. In itself that fact was not incriminating. Had Duda's own microchip been examined closely, it would have revealed information about associations with various fellow citizens of questionable repute. For that matter, Bigger's chip, or Drone's, or any other citizen's chip, would have revealed potentially suspicious entanglements. After all, every one of them came in daily contact with fellow citizens, and the nature of these associations was not always readily apparent. The reason Duda had been so blasé with Austin about the data mining was precisely that: Tracking every one of its citizens' contacts with every fellow citizen would have required more time and resources than the government possessed. In fact, both Austin's and Anna's records might now conceivably be indicated in a search of *Duda's* microchip because he had made personal contact with them—simultaneous contact, no less. The three of them had all been in the same place at the same time. So the mere fact that two fellow citizens had been in contact with a known Deviant was not a guarantee they were terrorists.

But the government's intelligence personnel had devised screening mechanisms that would winnow out those whose incidental contacts with a suspected terrorist could immediately be discounted as mere incidental contacts. Therefore, it was significant that Austin's and Anna's photos were among the twelve or so that Bigger showed them that night. It meant something—but what? Duda didn't know and could only guess. What he knew for sure was that they were on the list of people he was being advised to look out for. And that knowledge both startled and troubled him.

In the troop carrier that conveyed them into the target zone, along with a dozen or more of their colleagues, Drone chattered away with a few of their fellow officers. Duda was mostly silent—no surprise, as he was subdued by nature, and also because he detested Drone. The feeling was mutual. They tolerated each other only because they were required to tolerate each other, and both had begun requesting transfers within months after they were assigned to each other. Sooner or later Bigger would surely tire of reviewing the requests and grant one of them. For now, though, they were stuck with each other.

The truck drove through semi-dark streets and briefly through open countryside littered with the detritus of a dead civilization. Then it crept among the hulking shadows of the deserted neighborhood where Drone had murdered a young boy the night before. It lurched to a stop behind one identical truck and in front of two others, and the police officers quickly and quietly disembarked without waiting for the order. They knew better than to linger around the vehicles. They wore no armor—the State could no longer afford armor for its police officers every time they entered dangerous territory—and it wouldn't have mattered that much if they had worn armor. Armor was by no means sure protection against the kinds of heavy weaponry the police had faced in these situations. Their surest protection was to leave the vehicles and disappear into the darkness, to employ stealth as their armor.

They split into pairs as they followed one dark street after another, and finally, according to their preconceived plan, Duda and Drone were on one side of a dark street while two of their associates were more or less parallel with them on the other side. They combed the entire neighborhood, one empty building at a time. Every now and then a shadow or cluster of shadows cropped up in the darkness and then disappeared, and the searchers could not be sure if what they'd seen was an apparition. In the darkness the imagination could easily play tricks, and the only way to distinguish fantasy from reality was to remain perpetually alert and proceed with relentless caution. Warily, they went on to the next building and then the next, guns drawn most of the time, and their intense focus took a toll on their energy and their nerves. With several hours remaining in their shift they were already exhausted.

Finally they entered an eight-story brick building and ascended one floor at a time. Prowling the building interiors was even more stressful than prowling the streets because the spaces were tighter. They were under constant strain. Moving quickly they verified that one floor after another was deserted. Using his flashlight Duda indicated to Drone that he was moving on alone to the eighth floor while she finished searching the seventh. She nodded assent. They had been searching for hours and found nothing, and complacency was becoming a threat. As dangerous as this activity was—all the officers in their detail had heard the horror stories of fellow officers who'd been ambushed and brutalized on these forays, sometimes brutalized even to the point of dismemberment—there was still the threat that the hours of finding nothing, nothing, nothing could lead to complacency. Drone was rarely complacent, but even she was not immune. She succumbed to complacency on this night and sent Duda ahead on his own.

Halfway along one dark hallway he heard subdued voices just as he reached for the doorknob of what he assumed would be another empty room. Readying himself for action—which included having his pistol ready at his side—he hit the doorknob and swung the door open and entered a candlelit enclave occupied by six people, four sitting, two standing, their faces ghostly shadows in the weak light. The room was sparsely furnished but Duda saw that it contained several sets of shelves laden with books. The exterior window was covered with a heavy curtain. The occupants of the room abruptly lapsed into startled silence upon his entrance, and then several of them stooped reflexively and blew out the candles. There was a long, extraordinarily intense lull as Duda scanned their faces with his flashlight, spotlighting one of them at a time in quick succession, and they watched him expectantly. They didn't know it, but he was every bit as anxious as they were. He felt precisely as he had felt the night before, watching Drone calmly go about her business in the prelude to murder. But now he was alone. Now he faced a decision that was his and nobody else's. And the "correct" decision was one he dreaded making.

Then his flashlight paused on one of the faces, and then another face next to it. The faces belonged to Austin and Anna.

The lull continued. Nobody spoke. The people in the room all waited on him, but he gave them nothing to react to. Instead he froze, standing for a long moment with the beam of his flashlight resting on Anna's face. He wanted to speak to her but did not know what to say. Then he heard a noise behind him, somewhere down the long hallway, and finally jarred himself into motion and withdrew from the room and closed the door behind him. "All clear here," he called to Drone.

She shushed him, but without much vigor. The building was deserted. She waited for him to join her at the head of the staircase and they descended the stairs together.

5

The next night he visited the café much later than he had stopped in the night before. She was there alone, and he startled her. She seemed uncertain whether to wait on him or flee. She finally decided to wait on him, but she watched nervously as he sat down. "Something to eat?" she said.

"No. Just some tea—if you've got some."

Her hand shook as she poured the tea. The television on the wall behind her seemed to shout at them both. "I wish you could shut that damn thing up," he said.

"You know I can't."

He sipped his tea, and neither of them looked at the other. The television kept blaring its inanities.

"I suppose I should thank you," she said, finally.

"No need to."

"Well thank you anyway."

He sipped his tea, and she leaned on the counter. "Why did you do it?"

"I think you're beautiful," he said.

"That's no reason, and you know it."

"It's as good a reason as any, as far as I'm concerned."

"Don't you like your work?"

"No."

"That answer didn't take long. Why do you do it then?"

"Why do you do yours?"

"It's what they gave me to do," she said. "You know how it works. I'm serving the public good."

"Each one a servant, each one a master," he said. It was something they all learned very young. "It's what they gave me to do. You said it yourself."

"But you must be suited to the work. You know all those tests they give us. You have to be suited to the work."

He spoke to her as though he hadn't heard what she just said. "You have a beautiful smile. I can't decide whether your eyes are more beautiful, or your smile, or just the combination of the two."

And she in turn pretended she hadn't heard. "We all take what they give us," she said. "What choice do we have? But you have to be special to be a cop. You have to have a certain aptitude. An attitude about things."

"I have an attitude all right," he sighed.

"You wanna know what I think?" she said.

"Will I get to see you smile again?"

She obliged him, and he said, "All right, tell me what you think."

"Maybe it's what I thought," she said. "I thought cops became cops because they like to terrorize people. They're sadistic by nature, and that's why the State trains them to be cops. Being cops lets them take out their anger without fear of punishment."

"Until somebody blows us away in the street. It's not safe being a cop anymore."

"It's not safe being an ordinary citizen, either."

"It's not even safe being a bigshot politician," he said, glancing at the television to remind her.

"I suppose not."

"Look," he said, "I'm a cop. It's what they gave me. All right?" He wanted to divert her attention—he wanted, in fact, to change the subject completely, so he removed his sunglasses from the case strapped to his belt and put them on. "It has its perks. Do you get to wear glasses like these?"

"Nobody does. Just cops. The rest of us have to keep our eyes visible."

He removed the glasses and put them back in the case. Then he snatched something else from his belt and held it up in front of her. "Do you know what this is?"

"It's a communication device; I don't know what they call it. But everybody's seen them. We've all seen you talking on them."

"That's right. I can contact people all over the city in an instant with this thing."

"So you're a cop who can talk to other cops through a little box. I have no desire to talk to cops."

He returned the communication device to his belt and threw a heavy sigh. "And here I thought I was getting to see your sense of humor."

She smiled at him again, but it wasn't much of a smile. "I've always hated cops."

"I know, I know," he said. "But we take what they give us. You said it yourself. We take all those tests. I took the tests too."

"The sadist test?"

"Sure," he shrugged, "whatever you say. You can call me anything you want, as long as you keep smiling at me like that."

"You know the flattery won't get you anywhere. I don't date cops. I told you that before. I've told you several times."

"Not even cops who look the other way?"

"You can't expect me to believe you looked the other way just because you find me attractive."

"I looked the other way because I don't have the stomach for arresting people who aren't criminals."

She looked at him very intently. He knew he had said something that intrigued her—really intrigued her. "You don't think of Deviants as criminals?"

"No. Not most of them." He sipped his tea and then replaced the cup in its saucer. "A lot of them are just bums. They don't like the government's system so they get out of it. I don't care about that. Why should I?"

"Everybody's supposed to serve the community," she said. "Each one a servant, like you said before. You know that."

"I know what I said." He paused. "What were you doing in that room?"

"Talking. Talking and reading. You saw the books."

"I saw the books."

"The books are dangerous," she said. "The books are against the law."

"They didn't look very heavy, most of them. I don't think you could really hurt somebody with them." It was supposed to be a joke, yet another attempt at humor, but he knew it wasn't very funny, and it did not make her smile, so she obviously agreed that it wasn't funny.

"I have seen people like you—people in that black uniform—harass and physically abuse people like me for reading books like those."

"All right," he said. "I'm sorry. It was supposed to be a joke, but I know it's not funny. I know people in this uniform have beaten people for reading certain books. I've seen it happen."

"But you haven't participated in it?"

"No. I swear to you I haven't."

"You surprise me again."

"I'm full of surprises. But you still won't date me."

"I believe people should be free to read any books they want," she said. "What do you think?"

"I try not to think," Duda said. "It always seems to get me in trouble."

"I guess you're in the right profession after all, in that case."

"What was Caleb Brewster doing in that neighborhood? Where was he going? What was he up to?"

"Damn it! I was starting to trust you. To believe you. But you're one of them after all."

"I'm not. But I'm curious. I can't help it."

"Don't you have to be at work soon? I'd like to close; I know that. Now I'd like to close."

"What time are you supposed to close?"

"I close when I feel like it. Like everybody else. I'm supposed to be here until nine, but I hardly ever stay that late.

"Don't you have to be at work? Isn't it time for you to go out and terrorize some people? Maybe kill some poor boy?"

"I wish you hadn't said that."

"I wish you hadn't killed that boy. It *was* you, wasn't it? I didn't know that when I said it—I didn't even suspect it—but it *was* you. Please leave. Please. I have to close now."

"What was he doing out there? Just tell me. Tell me that. Tell me he wasn't just on his way to read a book."

"I'd really like to close now, mister cop. Please."

"He bore the mark," Duda said sharply. Then, "Do *you* bear the mark?"

"If I do, you'll never see it," she said tersely.

"Why would you do it? Why would you mutilate yourself that way?"

"Why would you become a cop?"

"I already told you. I'm a cop because it's what they made me. Why did you become a Deviant?"

"It's what they *made* me." That was her reflexive answer. But then she looked at him very hard again and gave him her serious answer. "There is freedom that comes with being a Deviant."

"Freedom from what? The State gives you freedom. Didn't you pay attention in school? The State gives you freedom from stress and worry. It gives you a life of security and all you have to do is dedicate your life to service in return. Serve the community that serves you."

"You remember all the platitudes. Everything they taught us. *That's* why people 'mutilate' themselves, as you put it. *That's* why they're willing to bear the mark."

"Was Caleb Brewster a terrorist? Are *you* a terrorist?"

He did not get to hear her answer, for she had no time to make one. The door of the café opened and a young couple entered. They looked like kids who would frequent the bars, or maybe even the satyrs, not a glum little café like this one. Duda was suspicious of them just for being there. "She's closing," he said.

"Are you?" The young man looked at Anna.

"I was getting ready to. As soon as he leaves." She nodded at Duda. "But I've got some tea and coffee if you want that. I don't think there's anything else left."

"We'll sit over here," the young man said, and they moved to the table back in the corner, where Austin had sat the night before.

"That's a popular table," Duda said loudly, to all three of them. "It's popular with the Deviants."

The cook's face appeared in the pass-through window and stared at him. "We can leave if we're bothering you," the young man said.

"No," Duda said. "I have to go. It's time for me to get to work." He glanced at the cook, then at Anna. "I have to go out and murder some people. Good night," he said.

And the only ones who bade him "good night" in return were the two who had just entered the café.

6

He could think of nothing else for most of the night—nothing but the dreary little café and the beautiful girl who worked there and the couple who came in and sat at Austin's table, the Deviants' table, and the cook glaring darkly at him through the serving window. All the way to the police compound, hoofing it along the dark and mostly deserted streets, he had been wary, waiting for the cook to come at him out of the night. And even after his shift started, when he knew he would not be ambushed—at least not that night—he kept running the incident through his mind in bits and pieces, like clips from a scene that he was editing for a movie. He examined a clip, discarded it, moved on to another clip. Snatches of dialogue sounded in his ears. The scene reassembled itself in various ways in his mind, as if he were a director trying to piece together a narrative that would satisfy him. None did.

They were assigned to the street that night, but to a beat in another edgy sector of the city, where a lot of young people were known to collocate to look for unseemly activities to amuse them. Drugs and alcohol flowed freely in such places, and the constraints of life in a closed society relaxed and sometimes disappeared. Young people smoked cigarettes openly and drank bootleg alcohol and used various drugs, many of them fashionable homemade concoctions, often synthesized from legal drugs dispensed by the State's doctors to enhance the mood of its citizens. If the groups of these young people were small, they could be fairly easily dispersed, often without violence. If they were large, they could be problematic, for there was strength in numbers, and more important there was courage, sufficient courage to incite acts of foolhardiness or bravado, depending on your perspective.

There was moreover a rumor floating about of a satyr, a big one, and a large number of beat cops were sent out ahead, but as they were assembling, another group, larger, was also assembling, in body armor and full riot gear. The SWATs. They were out every night, but only rarely did they convene in groups this large. Generally, they kept themselves less conspicuous, if still conspicuous enough to remind the public of their ready availability. They were always around in case they were needed, and any citizen who needed a reminder would very promptly receive one. To Duda they looked more like a military invasion force than a police unit. Drone seemed fascinated by them—she clearly *was* fascinated by them—in all their paramilitary splendor. In her mind they represented order, authority, the power of the State to assert itself when such assertion was required. She was not merely pleased to be associated with them; she was proud. They made her feel important. And one of the storm troopers (as Duda thought of them), a burly man with a round, heavily stubbled face, caught her eye and smiled at her, and she smiled back.

The beat cops went first, walking the streets in packs of four, alert to the possible threats around them. It was hoped that their appearance at the satyr would instill sufficient unease in the revelers to disperse them, to send them straggling off to other, even more remote locations to practice their illegal activities in smaller and less threatening numbers. That was what was hoped; it was not what was expected—hence the SWAT personnel whose more persuasive methods were likely to be required. In the meantime, the beat cops were vulnerable. Large numbers of young people roamed the streets with surly attitudes and disdainful eyes for the police. They flaunted their cigarettes and alcohol, there in the streets, some even appearing to taunt the officers who moved among them. "Hey," one kid called out, holding a pint bottle in front of his chest. "I need a job. Can I be a cop?"

"I should arrest that punk," Drone said fiercely, not quite under her breath.

"Shush," Duda said to her. "Do you wanna live through the night?"

"You're a coward," she said.

"He's a pragmatist," said Carver, who was with them. "There's no sense starting trouble here. We might not get the best of it."

"You're a coward, too."

"And you're a damn Crusader. Do we balance each other out?"

"You're exactly what's wrong with this country today," she retorted. "You let punks like these walk all over you. They have no respect for authority."

"They have no respect for anything, themselves included." Wesson said. He was the fourth member of their group. "They might have more of it if they could get jobs. They've got miserable prospects, and miserable attitudes because of it."

"You too?" She shook her head. "Disgusting. When we need strength the most, all we get is cowardice. What's become of the men of this country?"

"Come on," Carver said. "Let's keep moving. We have an objective here. Straight from our fearless leader. We have to get to the auto plant down the street. That's where the satyr's supposed to be."

"The government tries to make jobs for them," Drone said, as she fell in with the others. "They don't wanna work."

"Would you?" Carver said. "If you collected your entitlements either way, with or without working?"

"Don't you start this, Carver. You're talking like a Deviant. I can put you on report."

"I'm sure you would, too," he spat back at her. "Everybody knows your reputation, Drone. How does Bigger's dick taste, anyway?"

"I should—"

"You should what? Go ahead and try. If you want them to find your body in a dumpster."

"Are you listening to this?" she said to Duda. "Are you hearing this? You're my partner—"

"Shut up," Wesson said. "Shut up, both of you. And keep your eyes open. I hear music. The auto plant is just up ahead a few blocks."

They could hear the crowd now and see the flickering light of a large bonfire. The music blared from loudspeakers that were probably set up on the roof of some vehicle—that was the way it usually worked. The clusters of people heading both to and away from the satyr were more numerous. They also seemed even more brazen. Drone called Bigger and he said the SWAT group was already on its way. Somebody else had called into the compound and informed them a riot was likely. There were already far too many revelers present to disband them peacefully, and their numbers had been bolstered by workers from the auto plant, many of whom were older and even more inclined to resist the authority of the police. The auto workers had decided to take a break from their jobs that night, and they were showing their younger compatriots how revelry should be conducted. Drone and her fellow beat cops did not yet have a direct line of vision to the satyr, but the noise of the gathering grew louder and they could feel the energy from it.

Their original mission had been to disperse the revelers, but there was no chance of that now, and they were instructed to remain inconspicuous until the SWAT personnel arrived. As they drew within sight of the crowd in the parking lot of the auto plant, somebody in the crowd decided they were not welcome at the satyr and hurled an empty bottle at them. They ducked, and it sailed over their heads. "Halt here and hold your ground," Wesson said. "Let's just wait right here."

"You're not in charge," Drone said, and she thrust herself toward the raucous crowd just as the loudspeakers, mounted on the roof of a large truck, lapsed into silence. She had drawn her sidearm.

Somebody else in the crowd heard or saw her and there was a brief surge of revelers toward her. "Wait!" Wesson called, but it was too late. She fired into the crowd and somebody fell, and others exploded toward her. She fired again. The other three officers drew their weapons and fired shots into the air. The crowd checked its advance, but somebody threw a heavy object—a stone or brick—and it hit Drone in the shoulder. She shrieked and flew back, landing on her back on the pavement. Her gun flew away from her and the crowd surged again as if it had recovered its nerve. Duda and Wesson stepped forward and Wesson kept his gun trained on the advancing masses while Duda swept Drone up and threw her over his shoulder. She seemed to be unconscious. He fell back with her flung over his shoulder, flopping like a sack stuffed with sand. Carver hissed at him from an open doorway and he made for it, but the crowd was after him. Duda knew that the two of them, he and his insensate cargo, would be overwhelmed and probably trounced or pummeled to death. Two nights before, when he had passively witnessed the murder of

Caleb Brewster, his heart had beaten noticeably in his chest like pounding waves; but now there was only the rush of adrenaline and he was barely aware of the advancing mob although he knew that it was after him. He knew too that it would destroy him and yet he moved as if in a dream, as if he were watching himself move in slow motion. The crowd came at him, hurling epithets and physical objects, and yet he was barely aware of any of it. He moved toward the door where Carver was waiting for them and it was as if none of this were happening to him. Drone was light over his shoulder and he could not even feel her weight. Objects struck him and struck her and he did not even feel them. Then something heavy hit him in the back and though he barely felt it he went down to his knees just a few feet from the open doorway. He knew then that they would die. Carver reached for him and he reached out his arm and the world moved in slow motion.

Then came a thunder of weapons firing and the crowd screamed collectively in startled terror. Many in the mob froze, and all seemed to forget about the fleeing police officers. Instead they turned reflexively toward the guns that had fired on them. For a long moment they seemed frozen in their tracks, almost simultaneously assessing their predicament and then frantically casting about for an escape that they would not have time to find. Duda dashed through the open doorway as another fusillade rang out and Wesson collapsed behind him. The crowd screamed again in terror and, no longer frozen in its tracks, scattered helter skelter, seeking refuge in all directions at once. There was only bedlam in the street now, as all pretense of cohesion and solidarity was abandoned, and the mob became a sea of panicked individuals all trying to save themselves. More shots rang out, and more screams, and now some members of the crowd fell to the pavement while others fled. The music continued to blare from the loudspeakers on the roof of the truck.

"Is she all right?" Carver called over his shoulder.

"I don't know."

"Wesson's down. The bastards shot Wesson. The damn SWAT bastards shot Wesson." He stepped outside into the chaos and grabbed Wesson's body and dragged it in through the doorway. Somebody hit the doorway just behind him, a young girl, and he stood up and shoved her with both hands and she flew backward into the melee again.

A few more shots were fired, but then the craziness stopped. A SWAT guy in his armor, with his shield down over his face, appeared in the doorway, looking like a mechanical creature. He raised his weapon, but then he lowered it. "Is everybody all right here?"

Nobody else said anything, so Duda answered him. "Is there a medic with your team?"

"Somewhere, yeah."

"Grab him. We've got two officers down in here."

A long ten minutes later the medic came through the doorway, but Wesson had been dead even before the medic was summoned. Duda tended to Drone, who was conscious but seemed to be in shock. Outside there were moans and some crying, but the ruckus was over. The SWAT personnel were rummaging through the scene, searching for their colleagues first and then for the living among the other fallen. The SWAT member who had first discovered Carver and Duda and Drone returned for the medic, but when he saw the man hunched over Drone he turned and left.

Duda and Carver went outside and helped with the cleanup. They foraged through the bodies and helped tend to the wounded, seeing that they were safely removed. In a couple of hours the job was finished. Higher ups from the police department were there, and reporters were there, and a few other dignitaries were also there. One looked familiar, a politician Duda was sure he'd seen on television. He was talking to reporters, telling them what they must say. It was all a very unfortunate accident, he told them, and certainly regrettable. A few of the revelers had been injured, and perhaps even killed. No pictures were taken. Pictures might rouse emotions that need not be stirred. The politician told the reporters what to say, and they listened carefully. Both the politician and the reporters seemed oblivious to the others on the scene. The only police personnel the reporters spoke to were a few of the higher ups, who had only showed up when the rioting and shooting were over. Duda heard from an ambulance driver that thirty-four people, seven of them cops, had been killed. Scores of others had been wounded, some quite seriously. The area was cordoned off and the bonfire was allowed to burn down, providing some additional light for the evacuation and clean up before the flames died and the wood smoldered. The air was cold, and it smelled of smoke. But when the clean-up was finished, just before dawn, few traces remained of the satyr or the violence that ended it. Drone had been carted off and Carver and Duda were separated and did not reunite until they were back at the compound, where Bigger debriefed them. He asked them some questions, but primarily he told them not to talk about the incident. An official report would be issued to the media and that would be the end of it. The whole incident would be reported to the public in a politically expedient way. The politicians and the press would see to that.

Finally, Duda found himself sitting on a bench in one of the corridors of the compound, staring blankly at the opposite wall. He had been examined by a doctor, who told him the contusion he had sustained from being struck in the back by the heavy object, whatever it was, was not serious. "Your back'll probably be sore for a while," the doctor said. "Maybe a few days. But you'll live. You want some pain medication for it?"

"You got any whiskey?"

"You'll have to get that somewhere else."

"Forget about it then."

Now he was sitting in the corridor thinking about nothing at all when Carver happened along. "Are you leaving?" Carver said.

"I guess so. I hadn't thought about it."

"I know how you feel. You're in shock."

"Is that it?"

"I've got just the thing for you," Carver offered. "Let's go have a beer and shoot some pool."

They went to a place Carver knew that was dark as a cave inside even though it was daylight in the street now. The place served crude forms of food, and the two cops drank pitchers of beer. Shadows sat on stools at the bar, and a juke box played the whole time they were there. Nobody bothered the cops. They shot pool and drank four pitchers of beer. The beer made Duda forget about the pain in his back.

"I know where we can go now," Carver said. He took Duda to a sex shop and they sat in the lobby. When the manager of the shop came in, Carver said to him, "Can we see your girls?"

"We're not open yet." He looked up at the clock on the wall of the lobby. "Come back in half an hour."

"Don't be ridiculous," Carver said. "You see these uniforms, right?"

The manager looked at them but did not say anything.

"For a lousy half an hour you want to risk a terrible accident at your establishment? Come on. Be reasonable."

"All right," the manager said, finally. "I'm always glad to help out a public servant. Let me go talk to the girls."

They were in another room having breakfast or coffee or something. The manager came back with four of them, none of them very happy to be there at that hour of the morning. Duda gaped at one of them and she said, "You look like you saw a ghost."

"You remind me of somebody," he said.

"Oh, great. Just my luck. I remind you of your long-lost lover. That don't mean you can kiss me, asshole."

He took her upstairs and found himself trembling. "You really *are* in love," she said. Her tone was almost poignant when she said it, as if she were sentimental about it.

"No," he said. "No. But you do look like her."

They had sex, and it was like it always was in these places. For him it was anticlimactic. It would never be this way with Anna. "Where are you from?" he asked her.

She told him, and it meant nothing to him. "Where's your girlfriend from?" she asked him.

"I don't know." Then, "She's not my girlfriend."

"You're just in love with her."

"No. I barely know her." She was getting dressed again, and he said, "Why do you do this?"

"What? Why does anybody do anything? Why are you a cop?"

He thought about it for a moment. "I don't know."

"Well, there you go. Why does anybody do anything? Nobody knows. We all just do as we're told."

"Never mind," Duda said, sitting on the edge of the bed. "I just went through this with somebody else."

"Your girlfriend?"

"Yeah, sure. My girlfriend."

She smiled at him, a rare gesture of intimacy from a woman in her profession. Maybe Duda could develop a fondness for her. But of course she was no Anna.

"It seems like there's something I should ask you," he said.

"Ask away."

"I can't think of what it is."

"Let's go downstairs, then. Your card's at the counter. We have to get it back for you."

"Do you accept gratuities?"

"Forget about it, cowboy. You've already done enough for me. You've made my whole day."

"Really?"

She smirked at him. "I hope your girlfriend is good to you. If she's not you're in for a lot of heartbreak. Nice boy like you. I thought cops were never nice boys. How do you get away with being a cop when you're so naïve about things? Cops aren't supposed to be naïve. They're supposed to be assholes. Most of them are assholes."

Outside in the street Carver asked him how it went. "It was all right," Duda said. It was always all right.

"So was that what you needed?"

"I guess so."

"I'll see you tonight." But he probably wouldn't. Carver and Duda barely knew each other and almost never worked together. They would never be friends. They were friends momentarily only because they had survived a life-threatening situation together, a situation into which they'd been randomly thrown. By nightfall they would no longer be friends. They would nod hello when they met in passing, but there would be nothing more to their relationship than that.

7

He stopped at the café that night on his way to work. Anna wasn't there. A young man was behind the counter in her place. "Where's Anna?" Duda said.

"Who?"

"The girl who usually works here."

"How the hell should I know? I just started."

"You're sure you don't know Anna?"

"He doesn't know Anna," a voice came from the corner. "Austin. Where the hell is she?"

"She isn't here."

"I can see that, Austin. But you know where she is."

"Do I?"

"I'm an officer of the law."

"Oh, that's right. Have you been maintaining order lately? Were you maintaining order last night?"

"That's my job."

"So you were there at that little donnybrook last night."

"That what?"

"The scuffle. The fracas. The melee. The 'disturbance,' as our government has called it."

"With the Deviants."

"I wish you wouldn't lump us all together like that. Those merrymakers last night weren't Deviants. They were loyal citizens who got a little carried away. They couldn't contain themselves. Deviants have a purpose. It's personal with them. Deviants hate your guts. Take my word for it."

Duda turned to glower at him only to discover Austin had his back to the room. He was peering into the shadows in the corner. "Where is she, Austin? You haven't answered my question."

"Answer one for me, first. Were there fatalities last night? They didn't say on the news. They're careful about those things. They wouldn't want us to think there are malcontents in our midst. There are no malcontents here in paradise. Peace-loving citizens just get a little exuberant once in a while."

"My partner was almost killed last night," Duda said. He said it as though it were a great affront to him, a source of deep personal sorrow, but in truth he didn't care. "I don't want to talk about last night."

"Well, if it's such a sensitive subject. You can't get much from the news, though, you know."

"Are you having anything?" the kid behind the counter said. "Or did you just come in to talk?" He would not have been so bold had he not witnessed Austin's bravado. He hated Duda—knowing only what he stood for he hated him—but he also had the sense to fear him.

"Give me a hot tea."

"Sugar?"

"Yes."

"We don't have any."

"Then why did you offer it?"

"Habit."

"I thought this was your first night."

"I worked up the street before. Place just like this one. We always had sugar."

"You must have been special."

"We had special people come in. The Secretary of the Treasury, he came in. I wouldn't lie to you."

"I didn't say you would."

"You had a look on your face."

"The Secretary of the Treasury," Austin said. "Put him together with the Secretary of the Interior and you'd have half a brain between the two of them."

"Ju hear that?" the kid said to Duda.

"I did. It's prob'ly true."

"Well," the kid said. "Maybe cops aren't so bad after all." He was waiting for Duda to sample his tea. When he did, finally, the kid said, "Well?"

"It's bitter. Needs sugar."

The television was droning on, endlessly droning on, and Duda was sick of it. He hadn't been in the place more than three minutes and already he was sick of the television. He was irritated with Austin, too, for not telling him where Anna was. He was, in fact, just plain at odds with the world. "Tell me a story," he said to the kid.

"I don't know any."

"I know a story," Austin said. "It's about a cop who asked too many questions."

"I'll play along," Duda said. "Where is she, Austin?"

"She doesn't work here anymore."

"Do you know where she *does* work?"

"It could be anywhere. You know how it is. Anything to be of service to the State. She might not be working at all. She gets paid either way."

"She might be furloughed," the kid said helpfully. "Lots of people are."

"He's right," Austin said. "Did you know that almost thirty percent of the adult population is furloughed right now? Did you know that, Officer—did you know that, Michael?"

"I didn't. But that explains why there are so many kids out running around in the streets."

"Not this kid," said the kid behind the counter. "This kid is serving the State."

"That's the spirit," Austin said. "Isn't it, Officer ... Officer Michael?"

"It is. I guess."

"Serving the State with a smile," the kid said.

"Serving it bitter tea," Duda said. "Promising the people sugar it doesn't have."

"There's an analogy in that somewhere," Austin said.

"A what?"

"There's a ... let's say it's like a lesson. The State promises, but the State doesn't deliver."

"I know what the word means. Where is she, Austin?"

"You're persistent; I'll give you that. Even for a cop."

"Where is she?"

"I don't know, Michael. Maybe she was furloughed. They also serve the State whose hands are idle but don't cause trouble."

"I've never heard that one. I thought I'd heard them all, but I've never heard that one."

"I just made it up."

"You're very clever, Austin. I'll give *you* that." He turned to the kid behind the counter. "Did you know Caleb Brewster?"

"What?"

"You did. You almost choked on your own tongue when I asked you that. You knew him."

"You should be a detective," Austin said. "You might be good at it."

"I guess I know a Deviant when I see one."

"Give yourself a pat on the back," Austin said.

"You want me to warm your tea up?" the kid asked him.

Duda shook his head. "I wanna know where Anna is." He looked hard at the kid behind the counter. "You knew her, too, didn't you?"

The kid said nothing, and Duda said, "I bet you know her still." He turned to look at Austin over in the corner. "You know I'm not out to make trouble for her, Austin."

"Stay away from her, then. Any contact you have with her is going to make trouble for her. Go fall in love with one of your own kind. That partner of yours, maybe."

"How did you know my partner was a woman? I don't remember telling you that."

Austin turned in his chair to look at him. "Maybe you said it the other night." He paused. "Maybe you didn't. Maybe you're not the only detective in the room." He stared very hard at Duda, and Duda became uncomfortable. "I'm still not sure I like you, Austin," he said at last.

"And I'm not sure I like you, Michael. But here we are. Together."

"Yeah, together. It's lovely. I'm not sure I like it."

Austin had turned to face the corner of the room again. "You can always stop coming here, in that case," he said into the corner.

"But then I'd never see her again. At least I probably wouldn't. She'd never know the joy of loving me."

"Such a pity."

"You realize I'll keep coming back." He looked at the kid. "Don't worry; I won't make trouble for you. I don't care if you're a damn Deviant."

"Michael has a problem with his attitude," Austin explained. "He's not happy in his work."

"But I do my job, just the same," Duda said somewhat threateningly. "You can trust me on that." He was looking squarely at the kid when he said it. "So ... what was your connection with Caleb Brewster?"

The kid tried to stare back at Duda the way Duda was staring at him, but he wasn't very good at it.

"They knew each other casually," Austin answered for him. "Very casually."

"Let him answer for himself."

"All right." The kid cleared his throat. "I knew him casually. That's the truth of it. You know how it is with people."

"Yeah, sure. I know how it is with people."

The door of the café opened and in walked the same learning center facilitator who had been there two nights before. He was bundled tight against the cold. "Where's Anna?" he said. He sniffed haughtily at Duda as he passed by him on his way to the same stool he had occupied the night they met.

"She's not here," the kid said.

"For the love of—*these* are the kids we try to educate."

"You must not be very good at it," Austin said.

"We don't get the resources we need." Then, to the kid: "I can see she's not here. You don't know where she is?"

"I don't know *who* she is, mister. I just started here myself. They tell me to report for work, I report for work."

"A wise policy. At least you learned that much in the learning center. Be responsible. Do as you're told. Serve the public."

"Whatever you say."

"You can start by serving me a coffee. Cream and sugar."

"We don't have either of those things. We've got the coffee, but not the cream or sugar."

"Damn those Deviants!" He looked at Austin when he said it.

"Yes," Austin assented. "They need to learn to drink their coffee black. That way there'll be cream and sugar for the rest of us."

"You know what I mean. They've disrupted the economy with their instigation and their 'tea parties.' They should be shot, all of them. Shot as the traitors they are." He looked suspiciously at Austin again. "We can start with the ones in here."

Austin turned his head again, just his head, to look at him from the corner of one eye. "Your jokes aren't funny, mister."

"Who said I was joking?" He glanced over at Duda, who sat at the counter and pretended to nurse his tea, though he hadn't touched it in minutes. "For that matter, who said I was talking about you? I might be talking about one of our other fellow patrons."

"I don't feel welcome here," Duda said, and he stood up to leave. "People just don't seem to like me."

"You should know I've checked up on you, Officer Duda," the learning center facilitator said, wagging a finger at him. "I reported your badge number to a friend of mine in the police, and he did some checking for me. He had some interesting things to tell me."

Duda paused in his trek to the door. "I suppose you filed a formal complaint."

"No. But I checked up on you. After the way you behaved the other night I felt I had to."

"I'm sure you did." Duda started moving toward the door again.

"I felt I owed it to you to tell you," the man said to his back. "You're an officer of the law, after all. You must have done something right to achieve that."

"Don't count on it." Duda turned in Austin's direction, rather than the learning center facilitator's. He didn't even glance at the kid behind the counter. "Good night, Austin," he said. "It's been a pleasure as always."

"I feel the same way of course."

It was an odd scene: the learning center facilitator talking to Duda's back, Duda talking to Austin's back, Austin talking into the corner of the room.

GOODING

"You know I'll be back," Duda said as his hand hit the doorknob. "You can tell her that for me."

"If I see her, I'll tell her," Austin said. "But I can't promise you anything."

Duda said nothing more to the other two in the room, and in a moment he was out the door. There was a fairly long silence after that—except for the incessant drone of the television, of course—before the kid said, "I'm sorry about my reaction when he mentioned Caleb. I just wasn't ready for it."

"You learned a lesson," Austin said. He turned, finally, his whole body this time, to face the two of them. "It's easy to lose your life in our world, son. Just ask Caleb."

"I know. I said I'm sorry."

"And I appreciate that. But sorry might not be good enough next time. Try to be careful instead of sorry."

He looked at the learning center facilitator. "So what did you really find out?"

"Disgruntled cop," the man shrugged. "If that. There's nothing on him, really. No commendations, no complaints. He hasn't done anything that should arouse our suspicion; he hasn't done anything that should inspire our trust, either."

"Should we think about approaching him?"

"Not a chance."

"Why not?"

"I just told you why not: He hasn't done anything that should inspire our trust."

"I don't like him," the kid behind the counter said.

"Why not?"

"He's a cop."

The learning center facilitator grinned at him. "You've got great instincts, kid."

"Why did he ask me about Caleb?"

Austin and the learning center facilitator looked at each other. "That's a fair question," Austin said. "Why *did* he ask him about Caleb?"

"I can't answer that question," the other man said. "All I can tell you is his record doesn't tell you much about him. He's a nob, a nobody."

"The fact that there's nothing on his record doesn't mean he's not a snitch," Austin said. "In fact, they might recruit him as a snitch just *because* his record's clean. They know we have people on the inside."

"I don't like him," the kid repeated.

"I know," the learning center facilitator said. "I didn't tell you to like him. Or to trust him.

"I'll tell you what," he said to both of them. "Let him keep coming back. Just keep baiting him. Play around with him, the same way you've been doing. He'll ask about Anna—just keep giving him nothing. See what happens. If he's just a nob in love, he's harmless. He's all hormones. We can't fault him for that. At least I don't."

"I can keep him chasing his tail," Austin shrugged. "I admit he *seems* harmless. He's almost likable."

"At least he's not a True Believer," the learning center facilitator said. "True Believer" was what they called cops and others who took their work seriously, who were devoted to the State and believed in it. They believed in its goodness and righteousness. They believed in its authority and were happy to serve as its enforcers. Drone was a True Believer.

"He could be hiding it," the kid said.

"You're right; he could."

"But I don't read him that way," Austin said.

"And your judgment is infallible," the learning center facilitator grinned at him.

"He has one very important thing going for him. He didn't arrest us the other night. You weren't there, but I'm telling you, he had us dead to rights." He looked at the kid. "Just so you know, I'm not just preaching at you. We all make mistakes. And we all need to be careful."

He looked back at the learning center facilitator again. "I'm just saying, we were his for the taking ... and he let us go."

"Anna's his blind spot. We already know that. He saw her and was blinded by love. Didn't see anything else."

"Maybe," Austin conceded. "But there might be more to it than that. Imagine what could have happened. If he'd been a True Believer you wouldn't have seen any of us again.

"I won't approach him. If I decide we might be able to use him, I'll talk to you first. All right?"

"It sounds like a plan." The learning center facilitator looked at the kid. "Can I get that coffee?"

Before the kid could move, the cook came through the door to the kitchen with the coffee, hot and black. There was a small bowl of sugar on the side, and he carried a tiny closed pitcher of milk. He set the saucer with the cup of coffee on it, the bowl of sugar, and the pitcher of milk on the counter for the learning center facilitator.

"We're not sure about him," the learning center facilitator said to the cook.

"I heard you. Let's just continue to play it cool. But we can always use another cop if we can get one. Let's all keep that in mind. Nobody said we'd never have to take chances."

He looked at the kid. "The trick," he said, "is to take calculated risks. It's a risky business we're in. Like Austin said, be careful, not sorry. Be smart, but don't be timid. You can't afford to be timid. It's natural to be afraid. It's inevitable to be afraid. But don't let your fear paralyze you. Don't let it give you away."

He looked at the older men again. "You want my assessment? He's a nob. He's not that much older than this guy—" he nodded—"and he has needs, just like anybody else. He's attracted to Anna." He paused. "And I think he likes you, Austin. No, I mean it. I think the kid likes you. I think your rapier wit appeals to him."

"And I think Ben's right," the learning center facilitator said. "I think this cop sees you as a cynical type—just like he is."

The other men all looked at him and he quickly added, "But we'll be careful with him. We've all agreed to that. But Ben's right, too, and we can't forget that: We can always use another cop. They're very valuable people. They can really serve the public interest—if they're used properly."

8

Duda shuffled along the dim-lit street with his hands jammed deep in his coat pockets. It was getting colder, and when he removed his hands from his pockets his fingers began to sting from the cold. If he held them out long enough they began to ache. He jammed the hands back into his pockets and vigorously churned the fingers to speed up the blood flow. He ducked his head to get his ears beneath his collar and warm them. He was miserable.

Scattered couples and small groups, almost all young adults, scurried along the streets as well, careful to avoid him when they saw who—saw what—he was. He barely noticed them. The paucity of people in the streets, the dismal lighting, and the bitter cold conspired to bankrupt his soul—if one can believe in such a thing. He felt desolate inside, deserted, as empty as the dark streets and just as cold. Never in his short life had he known such despair, and he knew she was the cause of it, but he also knew she was not the sole or even the root cause of it; she was merely the proximate cause. She had disappointed him. The emptiness inside him had probably been there for a while, but he had never really felt it, never let it bother him, until she through her brief appearance in his life, and now her sudden departure from it, made him feel the void inside him was all there was to feel. There was nothing else; there was only the longing, gnawing at his soul the way acute hunger gnaws at an empty stomach.

A girl he had been with a few years before, the first love of his life, as he thought of her, popped into his mind. He saw her in her underwear, standing by the window in his room, one bare leg tucked behind the other in shyness. Her shyness only heightened his desire for her, made him want her all the more. It was one thing to be intentionally coy; it was another thing, and a more provocative thing, to be naively coy, coy out of genuine timidity. That, of course, did not stop him from having her.

But this was different. This was not the tenderness of longing waiting to be fulfilled but the desolation of a desire that seemed destined to go unfulfilled. This was not the sweet pain of anticipation but the numbing agony of something lost before it could even be found—something he'd never even known was missing until now. This was like waking up nearly thirty years into his life to find he'd never been alive in the first place. Maybe he'd only dreamed he was alive. But how could he dream if he wasn't alive to dream in the first place?

Steeped in this rumination he lost track of himself and crossed paths with somebody in the darkness. They nearly collided. Duda had to swerve to one side to avoid the collision, and the other young man uttered an epithet and then saw the uniform and his eyes widened in terror. He offered no apology but hastened off into the darkness, looking back fearfully at the law enforcement official he had cursed. But Duda wasn't concerned about that. He was thinking only that it was terrible to be a cop—he was suddenly sure there was no loneliness quite like it. And he realized he really meant it and didn't care that he was feeling sorry for himself. And he *certainly* didn't care that he was putting his own concerns above the concerns of the blessed State.

Inside the police compound it was warm and bright, and momentarily he felt relief from his despair. More so, though, he felt relief from the bitter cold, and the simple comfort of being warm improved his attitude. What helped his attitude even more was being around his own kind. In the assembly room, where coffee and some kind of dry, tasteless snacks were served, the cops were chattering and Duda felt an affinity for them he couldn't recall ever feeling before. They were the closest thing he'd had to family since his days in the dormitory at the learning center, where fast friendships formed only to be shattered when they were all dispatched to different places and different walks of life. He hadn't missed them before, but he missed them now.

Meanwhile the television droned on. The president was giving her nightly address, something that typically would not catch their attention, but when Bigger heard the topic of the address he vigorously shushed them all. "I want to hear this. Quiet! I want to hear this."

The room fell silent. Few of them cared what the president said—about anything—but they cared what Bigger said and what he thought because he gave them their assignments and evaluated them. He could make their lives relatively easy or relatively difficult depending on how he felt about them. For several minutes the room remained quiet enough that everybody in it could hear the president's speech.

"We understand that some citizens, especially young citizens, have a certain zest for life," she said. "We may even share their enthusiasm, even if we lack their energy." This was supposed to be a joke, and she smiled at it. "But there is a time and a place for celebration, and a proper manner in which to celebrate. The State makes available such occasions for celebration, and it instructs its citizens in the proper mode of celebration. For even in celebrating we must serve the public and maintain order. Our goals do not change just because we are happy; nor do our needs. We must know and remember at all times that we serve the State. We live for each other, not for our own selfish interests.

"I recognize that there are those among us who would see our harmonious lives disrupted; they would see our efforts to forge a better world together thwarted, our collective future ruined. The State works daily to see that these contrarians, these Deviants—these traitors to our cause—are stymied, that they are rooted out from among us and, when possible, educated, made to appreciate the cause we all represent and embrace it themselves. When education fails we must resort to exiling these Deviants, removing them from our midst. For like bad apples they have the potential to contaminate those around them—as, I suspect, was in part the case at last night's unfortunate incident."

The hoots and catcalls had begun to erupt from every corner of the room, and within a few seconds they had escalated until the president's eloquence was drowned in a cacophony of jeers and laughter and conversations that had been suspended but were now resumed. Bigger made a vulgar gesture at them all but he was not really angry. He had silenced them because he thought the president would say more about the previous night's incident—that she would tell more lies about it—and Bigger was curious to hear precisely what role his subordinates would be assigned in the State's official narrative of the incident. But the telling of the narrative was over already, and the propaganda had begun, the propaganda aimed at putting the incident behind them all as soon as possible. There was nothing of interest to hear. Bigger was no more interested in the propaganda than were his rowdy minions.

Partner-less for the time being, Duda was sent to the street that night with another cop whose partner had fallen in the previous night's chaos, only the other cop's partner had died. The cop's name was Plato—at any rate, that was what everybody called him—and Duda barely knew him but knew his reputation. He anticipated that his companion would be pleasant if quirky, for that was Plato's reputation. He was known to chatter a lot about things that were not directly related to their work, and he was said to be entertaining, if not particularly competent. He was a middle-aged man who had been a police officer for a long time and was regarded as harmless, if little else. One of his partners had complained once that he spent more time conversing with the common citizens than policing them.

He singled Duda out in the briefing and approached him immediately after it. "You're Duda, right?"

"I am."

"I understand I have the pleasure of your company for the evening."

"I don't know how pleasant it will be. But we're working together, yes. That's what I was told."

"On a very relaxed assignment in Sector C." Plato sat down. "I suppose it's our recompense for the trauma we suffered last night."

"Why do they call you Plato? That can't be your real name."

"I'm nicknamed for a philosopher. An ancient philosopher. They don't study those folks in the schools anymore. Too dangerous." He leaned in and spoke softly when he said it. Still speaking softly, confidentially, he said, "The irony is, 'Plato' doesn't suit me as a nickname. They should have named me for somebody else. A different philosopher. I could have offered suggestions. They could have called me 'Locke.' I would have liked that. Or 'Paine.' That might have been even better. But their range is limited by the poor education they received. Their ignorance is intended to augment their bliss. I suppose I should be happy they even knew the name of Plato to give it to me. I suppose I should be flattered."

"I'll take your word for it." Duda glanced around. He was not particularly fond of talking about such things in a room filled with cops. The next thing he knew they'd be calling *him* a Deviant.

"I see," Plato said. "You're apprehensive."

"You know you have the reputation of an eccentric, don't you? A nut? Somebody who's not exactly normal?"

"I never worry about my reputation. It is immaterial to me what others think of me. Besides, I have no desire to be 'normal.'"

"That's a dangerous attitude to have in a place like this."

"Be more specific. In a place like this room?"

"In a place like this world—from what I've seen of it."

Plato smiled at him. "I think we'll get along very nicely," he said.

"I'm not eccentric," Duda said. "And I *do* care what others think of me. Some others, anyway."

9

Bigger had hollered at them to end their conversation, and they were dispatched to Sector C, where they could walk the streets in tandem in relative tranquility. The city had been designed by highly educated urban planners in the new style, as a cluster of urban islands at close intervals. Each island was self-contained. It housed thousands upon thousands of people who lived in giant high rises and worked nearby, in factories, offices, or supply centers. Some worked at the agricultural facilities that were outside each urban center to supply it with food. The idea, of course, was that the State's citizens would have to travel minimal distances to work, supply themselves, or recreate. There were few occasions to leave one's urban island because there were few reasons to leave one's urban island—at least in the State's estimation. Permission was required to travel from one urban island to another, and to travel from one urban center to another—one city to another—required special State dispensation. Such travel was generally reserved for State officials whose commitment to the State required it. Most citizens could claim no such commitment. Their obligation, after all, was to serve the State, and they could best meet that obligation in the ways determined for them by the State. Those ways very rarely included extensive travel.

An unforeseen consequence of this arrangement was the gang activity it inspired. Nobody could be said to live luxuriously in the urban centers—their circumstances were, by the State's careful design, utilitarian—but the illicit subculture flourished, and gang rivalries also flourished. Young men, especially, joined youth gangs representing their respective urban islands, and at night, in the sparsely lit streets, and in the parks and fields that separated the urban islands one from another, the gangs met to battle for territory or other possessions that were not really theirs to possess. To make the combats more meaningful they sometimes fought for things that *could* be possessed, if temporarily: alcohol, drugs, weapons, clothing, certain food products. They fought to the death, and in the morning the survivors worked for the State, unless they were furloughed, in which case they amused themselves and prepared for the next night's combat. Many of them slept all day just so they could be ready for the coming night's fun.

But most of the inhabitants of the urban centers were pliant and apparently content. They worked for the State by day and took to the streets by night, drinking in the bars and dancing in the clubs and amusing themselves with various State-approved entertainments, from instructive lectures and art shows to State-approved cinema and theater and athletic competitions. The police could, for the most part, move among them without inciting ire or even suspicion. For they were the lowing herd, placid, content, unquestioning, serving the State by day and serving their own desires by night, but within legally and socially acceptable boundaries. There were no Deviants among them, and rarely would you find one of them at a satyr— and even when they did go they were cautious, fearful, for they all knew that attending satyrs could taint one's reputation with the State. Drone hated walking among the herd. They offered no challenge; she felt they were a waste of the State's resources when cops were expended to oversee them. They were not a threat to the government and could just be left alone.

But Plato of course felt just the opposite. He seemed in his element strolling along amid these law-abiding Normals, nodding agreeably when he caught somebody's eye, chatting amiably when the opportunity afforded itself. He seemed to feel as if the police officer's true job were to provide reassurance, comfort, a sense of security—and to do it implicitly, without any threat of force. Once, when he briefly detained a young man who'd had too much to drink, he did it without antagonism, as if his purpose were simply to care for the young man, to look out for his best interests. Drone would have cracked the boy over the skull with her nightstick; Plato propped him up and spoke to him as if his only concern was the boy's well being.

They spent much of the night just strolling along and talking. "It's a balmy night," Plato said.

"It's freezing."

"It's all in your mind. Fifty years ago they said the world was turning into a hothouse. Imagine it's a hothouse, and so it shall be."

"It's freezing," Duda repeated.

"So it is." Plato waved a hand back and forth at the empty storefronts all along the street. "If these were open the whole street would feel warmer."

"Would it? I'm starting to see how you got your reputation."

"In the old city the lights at night were bright in the city centers. Everything was brightly lit." He made a gesture as if to take in the whole night sky. "It's dismal now."

"You said it was—what was that word you used? Anyway, it wasn't 'dismal.'"

"It wasn't? Perhaps I misspoke."

"How the hell do you know about the old city?" Duda's teeth were chattering, and he wanted conversation just to warm him up. Plato was known for conversation, and at the moment Duda didn't care how crazy he was.

"People. Books. Film. There are ways of finding things out if you're curious."

"I must not be curious. But I've been to the old city."

"I know you have. But that makes you exceptional. Most beat cops never see the old city. It's where the freedom fighters do their planning. And we are sent there, some of us, to disrupt their planning. A futile endeavor, I might add."

"The *who* do their planning?"

"The freedom fighters."

"You mean the terrorists."

"As you wish." Plato nodded pleasantly to a couple who scurried by them on the sidewalk, clinging tightly to each other to form one huddled blob. The friendly gesture was probably wasted; it was very dark now, except intermittently where pools of white light spilled from open establishments onto the sidewalk. In the pools of light people bunched together like throngs of vermin, and the noise they made was like that from a gaggle of geese. Bicycles whizzed along the dark street, but not many of them, and occasionally a passenger bus or a limousine made its way among the bicycles, often impatiently. Those who had the privilege of riding in motor vehicles had little patience with those who did not share that privilege. It was an egalitarian society—but in name only, of course.

"I don't know how they let you be a cop." Duda shook his head. "You seem more likely to turn up in a rehabilitation facility—as a patient, I mean."

"Very clever. I enjoy your dazzling wit. Actually, I did spend time in rehabilitation facilities—several of them—as a juvenile. I was diagnosed with wandering attention syndrome. Later they found inappropriate irreverence disorder. Then excessive inquisitiveness. And finally ... deviant behavior disease."

"No. Nobody with deviant behavior disease gets to be a cop."

The State's youngest citizens were routinely examined by its mental health experts to determine their fitness for service to the State. Over time these examinations had revealed a startling array of new mental health disorders that afflicted a wider and wider portion of the State's young citizenry and required a wider and wider assortment of drugs for treatment. At one point more than a quarter of all youngsters under the age of eighteen were diagnosed as mentally ill and treated with various drugs, and the percentage of those diagnosed just continued to expand. An epidemic was announced, and the State's mental health facilitators petitioned government officials for more funding and pushed for a new program to train as many more mental health experts as could be trained as quickly as they could be trained. The need was dire. The situation veered toward the catastrophic. At first the government officials responded with zealous indulgence, diverting all possible entitlements to the cause of curing citizens' mental health. Enthusiasm gradually waned, however, as the national economy declined, and more and more young people seemed content with the diagnoses they received and even more content with the treatment they received, which frequently rendered them unemployable and kept them idle. Rehabilitation facilities had proliferated like feral felines, until there weren't enough trained facilitators to staff them, and there wasn't enough funding to support them. The Surgeon General had continued to appeal— loudly—for more, but in the end his cries fell on deaf ears. Somebody influential in the government had decided that the epidemic was going to have to stop, or at least slow down, before it consumed the entire State. There was still funding for the research and treatment of the most egregious diseases: aggressive personality disorder, violent outburst disorder, and, of course, the frighteningly prevalent deviant behavior disease. But the epidemic, the State proclaimed, was over. The government's mental health wizards had it under control.

"Nobody with deviant behavior disease gets to be a cop," Duda repeated. "You're lying to me. Or else you're just crazy."

"I'm cured."

"What? That's impossible. Nobody's ever cured of DBD. I know that for a fact. *Everybody* knows it for a fact. You're as crazy as everybody says you are, Plato."

"I cured myself," Plato responded blithely. "And without any drug treatments at all."

"You're crazy. How'd you do that?"

"Want a cup of coffee?" They had stopped in front of a shop that was filled with mostly young people who were as exuberant as the crowds that filled the bars. "We're entitled."

They went inside and found a table back in one corner of the room. The room was not large, but many tables were jammed into it. Any patron's entrance or egress was a public event. And they were cops, so of course all eyes were on them as they took their seats. They were accustomed to the attention and ignored it, though Plato nodded genially at a few of the gapers. Duda waited until they were served before he resumed their conversation. Then he said, curtly, "Nobody's ever cured of DBD."

"Suit yourself."

"How'd you do it, then?"

"Mind over matter." Plato sipped his coffee.

"What does that mean?"

"It means I looked at my options and cured myself."

"And became a cop. Or were you already a cop?"

"Nobody with DBD gets to be a cop. You said it yourself."

"But you did."

"Yes." Plato looked around the lively room and smiled at some of the other patrons. He seemed to be enjoying himself.

"You're crazy." Duda shook his head. He had first found Plato merely ridiculous, but now he was starting to find him amusing. He talked in riddles and sometimes contradicted himself. And yet he was entertaining, in a way. He kept you guessing, and there was something entertaining about that.

"All right," Plato conceded. "I'm not cured. I'm in remission."

"You're still crazy."

Plato looked around the room again, taking in the clusters of people who were out for the evening, enjoying themselves. Then he returned his attention to his temporary partner and companion. "Do you have a girlfriend?"

"No."

"No time?"

"No interest. They're too much trouble. The sex shops are all I need. Or once in a while I have a girlfriend for a while. Never very long though."

"I just figured a handsome young man like you would have a girlfriend. Maybe multiple girlfriends."

"You seem to do a lot of figuring. Maybe too much figuring. What about you, got a girlfriend?"

"I do not."

"Married?"

"No."

"No time?"

"No interest."

"Too many questions to ask?"

"I told you I was diagnosed with excessive inquisitiveness disease."

"And I can see why."

"But I'm in remission."

"You're in remission from a lot of things."

10

They left the coffee shop a few minutes later because it was time for curfew. They would walk the streets and ensure that all the city's law-abiding residents were safely tucked away for the night. Then the city would belong to the cops and the criminals. In this neighborhood their job would be easy. A few delinquents might be about, but most of the residents of this neighborhood were pliant and obedient and would willingly do as their government instructed them to do. Other neighborhoods in the city were not so pliant, and not so obedient. The residents of those neighborhoods required more coaxing, sometimes violent coaxing.

They came to a VRE, a virtual reality excursion shop, that was just closing up for the night. The few patrons who had remained until closing saw the two police officers and scattered in both directions along the dark street, stealing off into the night like bugs scurrying from a flashlight's beam. Plato mused on the history of the VRE. It had been hailed as a glorious avatar of the glorious future, a future in which the commonest of citizens could have whatever he or she wanted within a short distance of home, and essentially on demand. The VREs would provide any sensory experience the yearning Normal desired at a minute fraction of the cost and energy expenditure a real excursion would require, if such an excursion were even possible for most Normals. Few of them, very few, were entitled. Their roles in serving the State confined them to much narrower geographic parameters, and certainly much narrower resource parameters, than any elaborate excursion would entitle them to. The VREs were a cure-all for that dilemma, a fantastic substitute for an inaccessible sensory world, and a solution to the potential problem of civil unrest spurred by an unrealistic desire for things most Normals simply could not possess. With the VREs, they could have them. The State designed facilities, inexpensive facilities, wherein the entitled Normal could enter and be instantaneously transported to a fantasy world beyond anything conceivable in the Normal's own world. These facilities, certain influential government officials maintained with support from certain scientists, engineers, and other central planners, were the future of the commonwealth and of the world. They were the answer to the question "What will become of humanity as the world's natural resources continue to dwindle?" What would happen was that enormous portions of humanity would find themselves happily immersed in VREs during most of their waking hours. It was posited that VREs could replace drugs as the opiate of the people.

But like so many of the State's plans for its people, this one was undone by a conspiracy of circumstances. One was the State's inability to provide the variety of experiences it had imagined and promised. The State's technicians were only so competent, and their own resources were limited. They could imagine the merely conceivable, but they could not deliver it. Their offerings ended, finally, in a strictly limited set of "package deals" that produced not unique experiences for all who desired them but routine, predictable, and frequently malfunctioning scenarios of which audiences quickly tired—while at the same time their craving for ever-more-exotic experiences grew. This was the second participant in the conspiracy. The Normals wanted more—and more and more and more—and the State could not deliver more. Crowds at the VREs, large and enthusiastic at first, rapidly shrank and even occasionally became surly. Plato said he'd heard of instances in which malcontented VRE patrons had resorted to violence and had to be subdued. But the biggest factor in the VRE's decline had been the simple lack of resources to maintain it. State planners who hailed the VRE as the solution to all the government's problems had envisioned a facility on every corner in every urban center. What they were able to provide, in the end, was a few scattered facilities that the general public largely ignored. The VRE had deteriorated into primarily an alternative sexual experience for the socially inept, physically or spiritually deformed, or simply bored Normal who lacked the energy for dating and found the sex shops insufficiently stimulating. Such was the crowd that scattered at the approach of the two police officers and melted into the night.

"I'll give you one thing," Duda said. "You're curious. And because you're curious you know things."

"EID, remember? Excessive inquisitiveness disorder. It's brought me plenty of trouble in my life. But it has also brought me knowledge."

"And what has that done for you? You're a cop. You walk the streets at night, just like I do. Why do you stay on the night shift, anyway? You must have plenty of seniority to work days by now."

"Less conspicuous," Plato said. "I'm less conspicuous at night. People don't notice me."

"They still notice you. Everybody knows your reputation, Plato. Sorry."

"Let's just say the right people manage not to notice me. They don't notice me nearly as much as they'd be likely to notice me in the disinfectant light of day."

Duda wagged his head. "You're the strangest guy I've ever met. And in this job I've met some strange ones."

"In every job you meet strange people," Plato said. "And if 'strange' is the worst thing I'm ever called, I'll be fine with that."

"I think I'm fine with it, too, to tell you the truth. I've been doing this job for less than five years and you're my fifth partner. My first partner was an old guy—not quite as old as you—and he taught me plenty. So what happens? They transfer him after a little over a year.

"My second partner was a Crusader who got himself blown up in a terrorist bombing. I'd have been blown up too except that I was off doing my own snooping. Sheer luck kept me from getting pulverized.

"And then I got another good partner who naturally got transferred too—and then this last idiot, another Crusader, who came about that far"—he gestured with thumb and forefinger—"from getting me killed last night.

"I think I can handle 'strange' for a while."

Plato smiled his indulgent smile—a paternal smile, if Duda had known what paternal looks like. "Well, I imagine the Fates might honor your wish, at least for a while. Of course, it's not up to me to decide."

"It's never up to us to decide anything."

The streets were empty and quiet now, and their stroll around the neighborhood was almost without incident. At precisely eleven o'clock, as the curfew tone sounded repeatedly, they came across a quartet of young people on the sidewalk, one of whom was weeping disconsolately while her companions tried to quiet and comfort her. Her ID card had been misappropriated, and she feared reprimand from the State. Plato assuaged her fear, issuing a notice of indiscretion she could take to her local police compound and redeem for a replacement ID. "There'll be some red tape," he said gently. "You know how that goes. There's always red tape. They might ask you some questions, and you might feel like they're picking on you. But it'll be all right. They'll get you a new ID and program it for you."

They sent her and her friends on their way and continued patrolling the streets. The weather had turned colder still, and Duda complained about it. "Let's get inside someplace," he said. "There's nothing happening out here. If people don't have sense enough to get in outa this cold, let 'em freeze to death."

They turned a corner then, and suddenly it was as if they had stepped into a vacuum. A wave of empty cold confronted them, and in it was a strange foreboding, a palpable sensation that something was going to happen. But the sensation was short lived, so short lived they barely had time to notice it (though both would later swear they had felt it). Very suddenly the vacuum was displaced by a violent shudder followed immediately by a deafening thud and a shockwave that hit them like a stiff wind, full on and terrifying because of the force it contained. Both in fact staggered in the face of the shockwave, and then both fell to the ground to protect themselves. The ground shook beneath them. Immediately in the wake of the thud and the shockwave, as if tucked in behind them, came a deafening roar, and they covered up reflexively as the roar seemed to pass over them and then quickly subside, and the debris flew all around them. They heard it shattering windows and pelting the walls of the buildings across the street and the pavement on every side of them, and some of it hit them, prone on the ground and covering up, and they waited for some large piece of debris to fall on them and crush them. But it didn't happen. The roar of the explosion subsided and they smelled smoke, and now it was the returning quiet that was deafening. It was as if the same surreal vacuum that had preceded the explosion had swept in again behind it.

But the quiet lasted only a few seconds, certainly less than a minute, and then came the shrieks of the wounded and dying. "Are you all right?" Plato said to Duda, and it took Duda a moment to find his voice and answer that as far as he knew he was all right. They were both all right. They knew they would survive the devastation unless another explosion followed. So there was still reason to be frightened, if the prospect of what they would find up ahead in the cold darkness was not enough to frighten them; and they got back to their feet and advanced, cautiously, to the site of the explosion less than half a block ahead. The debris settled, particles still tapping lightly at all the surfaces around them, but the dust and smoke hung in the air and clouded their lungs and obstructed their view and slowed their advance. Plato reached out his hand to tap Duda on the shoulder and stop him. Then he called their dispatcher and reported the explosion and said they were on their way to investigate but that medical personnel would be needed on the scene. That was a certainty. There was only one scream now, though it seemed that there had been many screams just a few moments before. Now there was just a woman's scream, and it was coming from the street ahead of them. She was lying in a pile of rubble, and her escort, apparently, was lying a few feet away with a piece of splintered lumber running through his stomach like a skewer and one arm missing but his head more or less intact. He was dead. The woman had stopped screaming and gone into shock, or else she had lost so much blood that life had almost left her. Her torso was mutilated, and her left leg was severed just above the knee, and Duda couldn't see her right leg either but thought it might be bent back beneath her. Plato used a strip of cloth from her overcoat to try to make a tourniquet, but even before he finished applying it she was dead.

Duda listened hard for other sounds from the building in which the explosion had occurred, most of the front of which now littered the street. But he heard only the movements and the voices of other people, civilians, who had emerged from their residences and were scrambling into the debris. "Oh horror!" a woman kept saying, "Oh horror!" and finally Duda said, "Shut up! I'm trying to listen for other survivors!" and she understood and shut up.

"Let's look in there," she said, nodding at the building.

"Okay," he said, "but let's be careful. We don't know what we're getting into. We don't want to get crushed ourselves if something collapses."

She nodded. "Do you have a flashlight?"

He turned it on and illuminated a path for them to follow through the dust and smoke and rubble, but the going was treacherous and very slow. Plato and a couple of other people joined them in the search, and they picked their way into the building, working toward a light that was on in the back. The smoke and dust were still settling, but the rubble was deep, and it was as if they were tiptoeing through a pile of loose, jagged stones in a dense fog. Their flashlights picked up body parts and articles of clothing, and when Duda's flashlight picked up what appeared to be a severed and lacerated human head, the woman who was walking beside him screamed and then quickly stifled it. "Sorry," she said.

He had moved the beam of light away from the head and said, "Forget it."

Voices were coming from the upper floors of the building. The building was eight stories, and about halfway to the back of it, where the light was on, the voices grew loud and Plato shined his flashlight upward into a gaping hole perhaps four stories high. "This must have been where the bomb went off, right about where we're standing," he said.

A woman stood above them in what appeared to be a corridor near the top of the jagged cavity, and she called down, "We need help up here. We have people injured up here. A few are badly injured."

"We're coming," Plato answered her. "Is there an elevator?"

"Not anymore."

"Stairs?"

"Right about where you're standing."

"We'll get up there," he said. "But we'll have to find a way to climb up. We only have a few medical supplies. We'll do what we can."

"That's better than nothing," the woman said to him. There was resignation in her voice. "A couple of these people are in shock. There may be others on the other floors. I've checked most of this floor. Do you want me to see if I can get up the stairs and check the others?"

"If you can do it without taking too much of a risk. Are *you* all right?"

"I'm fine. I was on the eighth floor. All I got was a jammed ankle when the building shook."

"If you can check the other floors without getting hurt yourself, that's okay. The fire department is on its way. I'm calling my officer in charge to update him."

"It'll take the fire department forever to get here."

"I know."

Plato called the compound and spoke to Bigger to apprise him of the situation. Duda and a couple of the others were still picking their way to the back of the building. When they got there, they would find nothing to inspire hope. No human sounds save those made by the rescuers came from anywhere on the first floor of the building. Some moaning and occasional weeping came from the upper floors, but the more the air cleared and the dust settled, the quieter the building seemed to get. It was taking on the feeling of a mausoleum. The woman who had spoken with Plato from upstairs returned to her perch on the fourth floor just as the fire department arrived. "It took you long enough!" somebody called from an upper floor.

The firefighters said nothing in response, but they went to work setting up ladders, and a couple of them managed to use the ladders and long strands of rope to climb to the fourth floor of the building. Their cohorts on the ground floor rigged a stretcher and they used it to ferry wounded survivors from the upper floors, an operation that took several hours. Meanwhile the government officials and the government media started showing up, just as they had showed up at the site of the massacre the night before. Plato nudged Duda. "Time for them to start putting their story together," he said.

"They'll have a hard time disguising this one. Too many loose bricks and loose body parts."

"On the contrary, this one will be easier than last night's satyr. This one will be some kind of accidental explosion—you watch and see."

Plato was right, of course. As Duda would discover in their time together, he was right about a great many things. The explosion was deemed the result of a gas leak caused by an imperceptible subterranean tremor. It was no fault of the State's that such a leak occurred because the State was not responsible for every activity that took place beneath the surface of the Earth. Citizens were reminded that their own ancestors had abused the planet in their ignorant and neglectful misuse of its resources, and that misuse had resulted in consequences, unfortunate consequences, that could be felt to this day. Eventually this lesson would find its way into the learning centers, where the young would discover that an evil system of greed and exploitation called "capitalism" had prevailed in those long-ago benighted times, a tragic system finally overcome by the pioneers of the new socialism. Before it could be overcome, however, it had wreaked havoc on the planet and all its inhabitants. This gas leak, and the resultant devastating explosion it caused, were part of capitalism's awful legacy and a valuable lesson to future generations. Eventually a placard would be placed at the site commemorating the tragic event, and of course attributing it to its proper source.

"It was a damn bomb," Plato mused. "The smell of the accelerant is still in my nostrils."

"Mine too," Duda said.

"That was not natural gas. I know what natural gas smells like, and I know what the aftermath of a bomb smells like. That was the aftermath of a bomb."

"I know. I recognized it too."

"Horrible," Plato said. "Horrible. It was the worst thing I've experienced in my years on the force. It was the worst thing I've experienced in my life. I know I'll never get those images out of my head. Or that wretched smell out of my nose."

They were sitting together over coffee two nights after the explosion. "So much for your 'freedom fighters,'" Duda said tersely. And when he could see Plato wasn't going to reply he added, "You know that's who it was."

"I know they got their target, too. A very prominent diplomat was in that building. He had a drug problem he didn't want the State to know about—he was afraid it'd make him a liability, just when his star was rising."

"How do you *know* these things?"

"I keep my ear to the ground. I pay attention. That's all."

"There's no more to it than that?"

"Are you accusing *me* of the bombing, Michael? Is that what you're doing?" This was the closest Duda had seen Plato come to displaying anger.

"They're animals," Duda said. "Drone was right about them. I thought she was wrong about everything, but she was right about that."

"There are things you don't know, my young friend. There are very important things that you don't know."

"And I don't wanna know them. Not after what I saw the other night." Duda stared into his coffee cup, but what he saw was that disembodied head in the rubble. "I don't see how you can make excuses for them. Drone was right: They're animals."

"I'm not making excuses for them. You can explain things without making excuses for them."

Duda shook his head. "I'm supposed to go and see Drone tomorrow morning. Maybe I'll apologize to her for thinking so poorly of her. She was so insensitive about that Caleb Brewster kid. And I detested her for it. 'He was a terrorist,' she said. 'A damn juvenile terrorist.' She had no sympathy for him, and no qualms about shooting him. And I thought *she* was the animal. But now I'm not so sure."

"So you've changed your mind about Crusaders?"

"I didn't say that. I just ...," but his voice fell away. He was mulling the question over, and he already knew his opinion of Crusaders hadn't changed and probably never would. "If they didn't have to be so aggressive. If *everybody* didn't have to be so aggressive. Why the hell does everybody have to be so aggressive?"

Plato smiled at him in a way he hoped Duda would take as sympathetic, not patronizing. "And you say *I'm* not suited to be a cop."

"Because I just don't get it," Duda said. "I really don't. It seems like it should just be cut and dried. But it's nothing like cut and dried. Nothing about it seems cut and dried."

"Remember the obligation of a police officer. Our credo."

"To protect and to serve. None of us can ever forget that. It's drummed into our heads from the first day at the Academy."

"And whom do we protect and serve?"

Duda found the question baffling. He looked around him at all the Normals crowding the booths and tables. The din they made was an incomprehensible medley, a confused jumble of disparate sounds at varied pitches and volume levels that, taken all together, made no more sense than an idiot's garbled tale. Collectively, they represented an assault on his sensitive ears. And that's *all* they meant

to him. How about bombing *these* people? The whole
grinning, cackling, blubbering, stammering, howling,
mindless lot of them seemed deserving of it—just for
breathing his air and violating his space. He could only
imagine what Drone would have to say about them. She'd
find them barely worthy of her contempt. "The State," he
said. "We protect and serve the State. That's our mission.
That's our purpose in life."

"I thought you might say that." Plato took up his
spoon and stirred his coffee.

"What am I supposed to say?"

Plato put down the spoon and sipped the coffee. "We
really should be going. We don't want our fellow citizens
reporting us for loitering. How do you think that would sit
with the State?"

"All right then. Forget about it. Let's go."

They made their way through the crowd and back
out into the cold. It seemed pointless—to Duda it seemed
pointless. The deeper they got into winter, the less
crowded the streets would be. Unless some other calamity
awaited them, they'd spend hours patrolling streets that
were nearly empty, shooing timid Normals back into their
homes. The previous night they'd come upon a corpse
in an alley, a Normal who'd imbibed too much and then
paid the price of his drunkenness by freezing to death in
the cold—and that had been the highlight of their shift.
So what would it be tonight, a drug overdose? A minor
assault, perhaps? Another weeping Normal who had
misplaced her State ID? A part of Duda shared Drone's
disdain for these mundane streets and the deplorable
hordes who nightly roamed them. That same part of him
understood why she hated being assigned to these streets,
why she craved more stimulating locales to ply her trade
and prove her worth to the State. In the morning when
he went to see her, he might even confide in her his

revised judgment of her character. He even thought of a few phrases to tell her, to show her he'd had an epiphany and now saw her in a different light. At the very least, he had changed his attitude toward the visit he had been compelled by somebody else to make. Now he actually looked forward to the visit as an opportunity to establish some kind of rapport with her.

But when morning came he was tired, and his enthusiasm for the visit, and his newly discovered desire to commune with Drone, perhaps create something resembling a genuine kinship with her, had all but dissipated. By the time he got off the bus to the medical center he was back to wishing he didn't have to make this visit at all—and back to resenting the man who'd compelled him to make it. It made matters worse that the medical center was a dreary, colorless place where the energy level was low, and what energy there was did not inspire thoughts of hope or happiness. He found Drone in a semi-private room whose window looked out at the drab wall of another wing of the building just a few feet away. The winter morning was dull and dark, and the dullness and darkness from outside insinuated itself into Drone's room and dampened Duda's spirits even further. In a word, the winter morning and the venue were depressing.

Drone's appearance made things even worse. She did not look like herself lying in that bed. She looked smaller and more vulnerable than she'd ever looked to him in her police uniform. He had never really pondered the fact that she was rather a small person to begin with, and in her institutional gown, in that institutional bed, with her left shoulder and arm in a cast (the arm raised as if to salute him), one side of her face heavily bandaged, and her eyes purple and swollen, she looked not only small but feeble. It dawned on him that even though he'd seen on the night of the satyr how badly she was injured, he'd expected her to look more like herself.

"Bigger said you wanted to see me," he ventured. That was how he greeted her—even without bidding her good morning. What he had noticed first was that there was no chair for him, no place to sit down. He was glad of that; it would make his escape easier. He stood fidgeting beside her bed, already contemplating his getaway from the moment he arrived.

Her mouth worked fine, though her voice was muted. "I wanted to thank you for saving my life."

"Think nothing of it."

"I can't do that. And you know I can't."

"I know. But I'm just glad you made it through okay." He hesitated before adding, "Wesson didn't make it."

"I know. Bigger told me."

Had it been left entirely up to him that might have been the end of the conversation, for he had nothing more to say. After all the bluster he'd felt the night before, the great rushing wave of desire to make amends to her, he thought this visit might even be pleasant, and certainly easier than it was turning out to be; but now, standing over her like this, he had no words. He tried to smile a smile of encouragement at her, but he wasn't sure that even came out right.

"Bigger's recommending me for a medal of valor," she volunteered, and it sounded a little bit as though she felt as awkward about this visit as he did. "I told him he should recommend you for one too."

"Thanks. I appreciate that. Thank you for thinking of me."

"You deserve it. You performed heroically."

Again there was nothing but awkward silence. What needed saying seemed to have been said. Duda heard another patient complaining to a nurse in the next room.

The complaining irritated him. Please shut up, he wanted to say. Or else close your door so I don't have to listen to you.

"I probably won't be back for two months," Drone finally offered. "The doctor says I'll be in this cast for six weeks, and after that I'll have at least two weeks of rehab before I can return to the force."

"Well, you should take whatever time you need. Your injuries are serious."

"Bigger's recommending me for the new Special Ops unit. I don't know if you've heard about it."

"I heard rumors. Congratulations." It did not escape him that the one he was really congratulating was himself.

"It's not that I didn't wanna be your partner. Bigger just thinks I'll be well suited to Special Ops."

"Absolutely. I think he's right." He meant it, too. According to rumor, this new Special Ops unit was just made for the Crusaders on the force. It was being formed in response to the growing perception—the State's perception—that the police force needed to become more aggressive. The SWATs were no longer enough. They needed a specially trained complementary team to address the growing problem with Deviants. It was no secret that the government wanted the nettlesome Deviants subdued—exterminated, if necessary. Both national and local police and military forces were gearing up for the challenge.

"I'm sure we'll still see each other," Drone said. She sounded downright hopeful, now that she was leaving him. She sounded as though she actually meant what she said.

"Oh, I'm sure we will."

But he was not sure they'd be seeing each other, and he definitely *was* sure he hoped they'd never cross paths again. He left the medical center only a few minutes later, wondering what had possessed him the night before to believe he really felt some powerful affinity for Drone and elated that whatever had possessed him, it seemed to have dispossessed him as soon as night turned into day. He headed home grateful for the thoughtful if inscrutable Plato as his partner, even though he considered it unlikely he'd ever really understand the man. Given the other possibilities, he could live with that.

12

Sitting in what seemed to have become their usual spot, Duda observed his partner admiring two young women at one of the tables in the center of the café. "That will be next," Plato said mildly.

"Another riddle from the man of mystery," Duda said, taking the bait. "What is it you're telling me will be 'next'"? He tried to follow Plato's gaze to its resting point. "Are you telling me you're plotting a ménage à trois with those two girls over there? Plato, you never cease to amaze me. You're just one surprise after another."

Plato's response was to pull up one sleeve enough to expose most of his forearm and extend it in Duda's direction. "Compare," he said. And that was all he said.

Duda extended his arm, but Plato had to remind him to pull up the sleeve. "The skin," he said. "I want to compare our skin."

"All right," Duda said. "Mine's hairier. Yours looks more weathered though. Your advanced age is showing, my friend."

"Notice anything about the skin tone? The color? Now look around the room. What do you see?"

"I see a bunch of Normals in their usual habitat. They appear to be having a good time, at least most of them— but their chatter just blends together into white noise. They all look alike and sound alike, to me."

"Ah, now we're getting somewhere."

"Where are we getting? You'll have to tell me; I'll never guess."

"They all look more and more alike; they all sound more and more alike—because they're all *becoming* more and more alike. Call it 'breeding,' my young friend. Call it a shrinking gene pool. Our masters are working to make us more and more alike.

"And that"—he gestured toward the two young women again—"that will be next. Differences between the sexes are so troublesome. The cause of so much misunderstanding and conflict over the years, the generations, the centuries, the *millennia*. Can you think of one fact of human existence that's caused more trouble? Historically, I mean."

Duda just sat shaking his head. Shaking his head and grinning.

"You can't, of course, but then, who can blame you? Look at the way you've been educated. History for you began with a man named Hegel, I'm guessing."

"I've heard the name," Duda shrugged. "It was probably in the learning center. But right now I'm thinking about whether my partner, a man named Plato, is on some kind of medication. And if he is, I'm wondering if he'll share it with me."

"And I can assure you I'll never be more lucid. But you, my young friend, can't follow this discourse because you lack a frame of reference. That was deliberate on their part. For you, the true beginning of history was the twentieth century. Maybe even the twenty-first century. Am I right? And Hegel, or maybe Marx, was a mere prehistory starting point—covered on the first day of class."

"You could be right. I don't remember, Plato. I honestly don't remember. Those names should mean something to me, I'm sure. But they just don't. You're right; I'm not educated like you are. Sorry."

And then he thought of something. "Wait a minute. What about the dinosaurs? We learned about them. I remember learning about them even before the first level at the learning center. Weren't they before ... what was his name?"

"Hegel. Georg Wilhelm Friedrich Hegel. And yes, he did follow the dinosaurs. All of humanity did—has. But my argument still stands. You have a very abbreviated concept of history—dinosaurs notwithstanding—and it was very much by design.

"Tell me, my dinosaur-loving young associate, have you ever heard of an institution called 'slavery'?"

"*That* one I know. It was instituted by the capitalists in about the seventeenth century CE. It was part of their exploitation of the masses, owing to their greed. They built their evil empire on the backs of the masses. Until the socialists came along and vanquished them."

"Wonderful. You were paying attention in school after all. Bravo. And do you know what the slavers did with slave families? They split them up. They sent one family member here and one there, spreading them out far and wide."

"And now you're going to ask me why they'd do such a thing. Am I right?"

"You're absolutely right."

"To keep them from establishing firm ties. Without family, every individual was more isolated, more alone. They felt rootless, and that made them attach themselves to their plantations and their slave masters. It was all they had. Am I right again?"

"You are absolutely right again. It's becoming obvious that you were a much better learner than you've let on.

"So the slaves' situation was very much like our situation when the State separates us. It moves us around, hither and yon, making it very difficult for us to establish firm ties. It permits families—for now—but it discourages them. We're to give our all for the State. That's what really matters. Each one a servant; each one a master. Am I right?"

Duda was suddenly dumbfounded. The department's philosopher king had just led him to an epiphany—and he wasn't sure what to make of it.

"For more than two generations now they've been working to level us all out," Plato continued. "Conflicts among races were a source of endless misery for our ancestors. The State is working to eliminate those conflicts by eliminating the races. And since the State has control of the reproductive process, for most of us, it's having great success. We're all becoming one. What's left of the family will continue to deteriorate. The State has had to be more patient than it's wanted to be. But it's having success. Give it enough time and we'll be indistinguishable from one another."

"A nation of slaves," Duda said.

Plato shrugged. "And so I was thinking about the next logical step. Eliminate the sexes. Who needs them in a world of test-tube babies?"

"Let me sniff that coffee. Come on, let me. I know you're on something."

"It's small consolation," Plato said, "but their elegant theory has a hole in it—just as all their other theories have holes in them. We'll still be individuals, each one of us. Each of us will still experience and perceive the world in his own way. They may have more control than they have now—"

"But they may also have less. Imagine a world where everybody looks alike but everybody thinks differently.

Imagine the havoc those look-alikes can raise without getting caught. 'Who did it?' 'Who knows? They all look alike.'"

"You're mocking me. It's all right. I've given you food for thought. So think about it. We need to hit the street again anyway."

"Back out into the miserable cold. Hey, Plato, do you think I can send my look-alike and just sit here all night?"

When his shift ended he made a beeline to the café where he'd met Anna. The place wasn't open yet, so he went home, but after sleeping most of the morning and well into the afternoon, he got up, cleaned himself up, got dressed again, and rushed off to the café. The sun had set but it was actually a little warmer than it had been earlier in the day, and the snow had begun falling. On their beat that night he and Plato would experience the joy of new fallen snow. It was a joy that only lasted one night before the city turned the snow into ugly, blackened slush and ice; but it was beautiful before it was defiled.

Duda stamped the snow from his feet before he entered the café. There were six other customers in the place that early evening—a regular stampede compared with what he'd experienced at the café before—but no sign of Austin, the learning center facilitator, or Anna. The new kid was behind the counter, at which Duda seated himself on the same stool he'd occupied before.

"Coffee?" the kid said to him.

"Give me a hot tea. And some milk and sugar for it."

"No milk or sugar. Sorry."

"Do you remember me?"

The kid looked around, as if checking to see if any of the other customers were paying attention. "I remember you." He then gave a glance toward the pass-through window into the kitchen.

"She's not here."

"Nope."

"And you haven't seen her?"

"I told you before, I wouldn't know her if I did. We've never met."

"You're sure about that?"

"I'm sure about that. You gonna eat somethin'?"

"I have to think about it. Let me try this tea." He sipped it. "Hm. Bitter."

"Yeah, bitter."

"What about Austin?"

"What about him?"

"Has he been in?"

"Since you were last here? I don't remember."

"Try."

"I don't remember, Officer. I honestly don't. Maybe he has, maybe he hasn't."

One of the other patrons got up abruptly, grabbed his winter coat from the back of his chair, and headed for the front door. "Must not have liked the atmosphere," Duda said when the man was gone.

"Did you want something to eat?"

"I just wanna know where Anna is."

"He doesn't know," the cook's voice came through the pass-through window. It was a little surly. It had the effect of chasing two more patrons from the café.

"Must be expecting trouble," Duda said. "They don't wanna be here when it happens."

"I don't wanna be here either," the kid said.

The cook came in from the kitchen just as two more patrons were fleeing. The lone survivor was a man perhaps Austin's age, sitting at Austin's table but facing the room. The conversation with Plato the night before flashed through Duda's mind. The horror! he thought. They *do* all look alike. But this man was not Austin, though he could have passed for Austin's brother. And, in a very broad sense, it occurred to Duda, he *could* be Austin's brother!

He was still chuckling to himself when the cook addressed him. "Does it amuse you to hassle this poor kid, Officer?"

"That's not what I was laughing about—if that's what you're asking." Duda met the cook's brusque tone with a brusque tone of his own. One thing he would *not* be was intimidated. In his profession he couldn't afford to be intimidated.

"He doesn't know where the girl is, all right? And he doesn't know where Austin is. And to tell you the truth, neither do I."

"I believe you."

"Then why do you feel the need to torment this poor kid? Do you want something to eat, or do you just wanna sit here and bother him? Because I gotta tell ya, your bothering him bothers me. All right?"

"And I gotta tell you something, too. First, I don't want anything to eat. An' I don't want any more of this bitter tea." He slid the tea away from him across the counter. "Second, all I did was ask the kid a few questions; that's all. And all he has to do is answer them; that's all."

"He did answer 'em."

"Let me finish. And third, I don't give a good goddamn if my bothering him bothers you, all right? If you really have a problem with me, let's step outside and settle it. I'll take off my nightstick, my sidearm, and my badge."

"Not in this goddamn cold."

"In that case, since Austin's not here I have a question for *you*. I know you were here before when I was here, and I have a feeling you'll know exactly what I'm talking about. So listen up:

"Last night I had a little conversation with a friend of mine, and the topic of this place came up. I won't say how it came up, but I can assure you no names came up, not even Anna's, but my friend has an intuition about things. I don't know how he has this intuition, but he has it, and it's uncanny.

"So my friend told me I should ask you a question. He said I should ask Austin—no, he doesn't know Austin's name—but I have a feeling you'll do. You'll know the answer just like Austin would. So here's my question: My friend said I should ask you to explain 'natural rights.'"

13

Winter that year was brutal. It came in hard and lingered, and it left almost as hard as it came in. Snow would remain in bits and snatches until early April, disappear during two weeks of false spring, and return with a vengeance near the end of the month. The truly cold weather was gone by then, but it had stuck around long enough to leave a lasting impression on the people who lived it. It was not a favorable impression. In retrospect, that winter would be variously known as The Winter of a Thousand Hardships, The Winter of Endless Misery, and The Winter of Our Discontent. None of these appellations, of course, issued from the State itself.

What made the winter so difficult was that a time of severe weather conditions was also a time of shortages and service disruptions. A prolonged shortage of paper products in December continued into the new year and was joined by a food shortage early in January. Ordinary citizens were accustomed to shortages of certain products—meats, especially, but also occasionally dairy products, and of course luxuries such as sugar and alcohol—but in this round of shortages even staples such as wheat products and vegetables were in short supply. Citizens found themselves competing for scarce goods, and their attitudes suffered for it. As a result, communal good will also suffered a shortage. But what made things worse, far worse, was the power outages that started in late January. This frigid winter was no time for power outages, but the outages were even more frequent than normal, and more sustained. These outages placed most citizens in physical distress, imposed physical sickness on many of them, and drove some to madness.

Plato and Duda found themselves breaking up more fights than usual, chasing more people out of the cold bars and back to their colder apartments at night, and—the most morbid of their new duties—reporting more frozen corpses to be retrieved and disposed of by the reclamation centers. They also found themselves following up on more robberies, and a few times they happened upon burglars in the act. One night they wandered entirely by chance into a situation in which multiple burglars were simultaneously at work. A meat truck, traveling late at night in an attempt to enter the city and reach its destination undetected, had been hijacked and diverted to a side street, where a crew of four enterprising thieves went to work on it. They told the truck's driver, and his passenger who was there to provide security, to stand aside, and under threat of physical injury or even death, the pair quite willingly took the hijackers' advice. The thieves were hard at work unloading the truck and parceling out its contents to be shipped off to various other places for storage when the two cops spotted the robbery in progress and called for backup. By the time the backup arrived, the hijackers had disappeared. Neither Plato nor Duda really cared—which was why they hadn't intervened in the robbery while it was in progress, waiting instead for the insurance of backup. They knew the meat was likely to hit the black market and would still be available to Normals, but through a different medium from that provided by the State. The government would lose control of the process, but the meat would reach its appropriate destination just the same. The black market always worked that way, often much more efficiently than the State's own system, and the cops' attitudes toward their work—and toward the magnanimous State—had been adjusted in much the same way so many of their compatriots' attitudes had been adjusted. That is to say, they didn't care how goods got to the right places as long as they got to the right places.

At times, the apparatus of government seemed almost superfluous. People needed things, and the black market provided them. In fact, it seemed almost to have supplanted the apparatus of government. Official order in the commonwealth, the kind of order ostensibly secured by a formal system of government, the system of government that Plato and Duda represented, seemed to be disintegrating. The two police officers might soon have more to worry about than secure goods for their fellow citizens. They might soon become targets themselves.

State officials of course worked tirelessly both to explain the shortages and service disruptions and to allay their citizens' concerns. Most important, though, they worked to place blame where it needed to be placed, so that their citizens' rising anger would be aimed in the right direction (away from them). Official after official took to the airwaves to complain about the real perpetrators of the shortages and service outages: the Deviants, of course.

"These people are your fellow citizens," the Secretary of Health and Welfare fumed on one broadcast. "They live among you. They may work with you. They may be your next-door neighbors. And yet they have so little regard for your well-being that they'll gladly undermine it for the sake of a cause, their cause. I suspect most of these people—perhaps all of them—would claim to be interested in improving the general welfare of our society. But you must ask yourself: Who are they benefiting? Whose lives are being improved? We see rampant suffering all around us, at a time when everyday life is stressful enough for all of us already, and yet the deliberate efforts to interrupt supply chains and cut power lines continue. The majority of us must pay so that a tiny, tiny minority may achieve ... what? Are their objectives clear to you? Do you understand them? Their objectives certainly aren't clear to me; nor do I understand them.

"But you have the power, my fellow citizens; you can put a stop to this nonsense. 'How?' you may ask. 'The desire is certainly there, but what about the means?'

"You have the means at your disposal, good people. You need only put it to use. Keep an eye on that coworker or neighbor of yours. Is he being a good citizen? You are capable of judging, so exercise the power you have. If you see something, anything, out of the ordinary about a neighbor or coworker's behavior or attitude, report it at once to your supervisor at work or to the resident adviser of your building if it's something that's going on at home. You have been trained since you were very young to cooperate with others, and one responsibility of cooperation is to ensure that those others are also fully cooperating themselves. Ensure that they are doing their part, as you are doing yours. Use the power you have to demand that others shoulder their societal burden, as you are shouldering yours."

Perhaps the most curious consequence of Duda's association with Plato was that he'd suddenly started listening to these politicians on the television, if only because he was tired of knowing so little while his partner seemed to know so much. After only a week or so of attentive television viewing he said to Plato over coffee one night: "It's just amazing the way they manage to avoid taking responsibility. To hear them tell it, the State has never made a mistake."

"Never a miscalculation or misjudgment," Plato asserted. "They are truly impeccable human beings with truly impeccable intentions and truly impeccable judgment."

"I think most of us realize that," Duda said. "I think it's why we never listen to them. We never pay attention to them because they never tell the truth. Nothing they say can be trusted."

"I call it the 'circle of futility.' That's a name I came up with for it long ago. They lie to us, so we don't listen. Because we're not listening they keep on lying. And because they keep on lying, we keep on ignoring them. And on and on and on it goes."

"A perfect circle."

"Endless. Ad infinitum, I suppose. Certainly ad nauseum. And for many of us, to the point of ignoring them—however you say that in Latin."

At times the lies were so egregious, though, that the new, attentive Duda could hardly believe his ears. He could hardly believe, that is, that ostensibly respectable people, people considered worthy of holding high government offices, would have the gall to say such things to a potential audience of hundreds of millions. How many among those hundreds of millions would recognize they were being lied to, and in such a way as to insult their intelligence? Surely most of them realized they were being duped. They had to! Nobody could really be as stupid as the State seemed to assume. One evening, for instance, he was having an early dinner before going to work when a professor from one of the local universities appeared on the evening educational broadcast to add something new to the discussion of the crisis they were all experiencing—all "sharing," as the State's representatives liked to put it.

"We must all remember," the professor reminded them, "that the energy shortage we're currently experiencing, whose debilitating and even murderous effects are being felt throughout our ranks, is not of our own making, but results rather from the actions taken by our ancestors a hundred years ago. That's right: a hundred years ago! Capitalism ravaged our planet then, sapping its resources and destroying its atmosphere. And we are now paying the price of that abuse: extreme weather events and inadequate resources to address them. Lay this crisis at the feet of those who brought it on but did not have to experience it. Through no fault of our own, we are paying for the mistakes of our antecedents. There is an ancient anachronism about "visiting the iniquity of the fathers upon the sons to the third and fourth generation." Unfortunately, that saying is apt to explain our current circumstance. Our ancestors were indeed patriarchal, so it is appropriate to refer to them as our 'fathers.' And we are indeed paying for their 'iniquity' three and four generations hence."

Plato grinned when Duda related the anecdote to him. "What does it matter what you say if nobody's listening anyway?"

"I was listening."

"But you're one man, Michael. And you're not representative, believe me. You know I've been talking for a while now, fully aware that people take me for a quack. And yet I was listening too."

"I guess that's what you get for paying attention."

"Besides, you have to remember that even among those of us who do listen, there are differences in perception. The voices come at us in an endless stream. You recognized that even before you started listening to the noise because I used to hear you complain about it. You complained every time we got near one of these televisions—and you know these televisions are everywhere. Now you know the reason for that.

"So now you're listening, as I'm listening, and there are others who are listening—more of them than you probably realize; but not all of us hear the same things. No, the information is the same—I don't mean that—but we focus on different things. That's just human nature."

"Human nature?"

"Yeah. It means it's just the way people are. They don't tell us about it in the learning centers; we figure it out for ourselves. They really don't want us to know. They really don't want us to talk about human nature."

"Why not?"

"Control, my young friend. They want control. But let me finish making my point. You hear something, and I hear something else, and others hear their own things and focus in on them.

"You heard this professor talking, for instance, and it made an impression on you. That's what stuck out in your mind. I might have ignored him and then become obsessed with the next so-called 'expert' who came on. And every one of the millions who are actually paying attention is having the same experience: hearing things selectively, according to our own interests and priorities."

Duda was grinning at him the way he always grinned at him before he made some comment about Plato the "mystery man" or Plato the "seer" or Plato the "eccentric." It meant he still didn't see the point. Plato explained it to him: "It means we're a bunch of individuals. They're not. They're a group. They're organized. Their whole purpose is to be organized—to maintain control."

"The Deviants are organized."

"Yes, my young friend, I suppose they are. I suppose they are at that. At least you see my point."

14

From the State's perspective, things went from bad to worse even as the end of winter approached, and at last the beleaguered citizens of the commonwealth sensed that some kind of relief was near. They could feel and smell spring in the air. If they were to continue to suffer, at least they could do it without freezing to death. Spring when it finally arrived was virtually assured of raising spirits at least somewhat. They would be able to emerge from their cocoons, anyway, and to be among other people again. If nothing else, the coming of spring meant the end of shivering, of the agony of relentless, penetrating cold. It meant the end of cowering in their apartments, wrapped in blankets or extra clothing—or even old packaging material if that was all they had available—expending all their energy in the futile effort just to warm up. It meant they could go outdoors again—just go outdoors—without suffering. For the ordinary citizens, spring meant the rebirth of hope.

But late winter saw the rise of a new group, a mere mob at first but slowly it began to organize, and as it organized it acquired a name, the National Workers Alliance (NWA), and the National Workers Alliance meant more trouble for the State. The National Workers Alliance grew from the efforts of a single visionary young man, Hugo Lansky Long, whose previous career consisted rather more of unemployment and gang activity than of what might be termed "legitimate labor"—which is to say, labor for the State. He'd been one of those who, out of work most of the time, found fulfillment in the turf battles among urban islands, and in eager participation in the black market in drugs. He was a born leader (if the State had permitted belief in such things) who did not merely join gangs but organized and led them. Although he was not a particularly large young man, he was a particularly fierce, passionate young man who acquired the reputation of being both fearless and ruthless, and above all, of having an extraordinary ability to inspire others to follow him. Later rumor—for there were no current rumors about him because he was a nobody who came from nowhere—later rumor would have it he had always been an instigator, that he had intended from the time he was very young to lead his working-class compatriots into revolt against the State, but that he had bided his time because he was a nobody who came from nowhere, and he needed time not only to accumulate assets from the sale of drugs, but also to accumulate followers to join in his revolt. He had more luck accumulating followers than assets, but he accumulated enough of both that the fateful Winter of a Thousand Hardships, with all its deprivation and misery, afforded him an opportune moment to step out of the shadows and into the limelight. He meant to raise some hell.

He had begun his revolution long before he began his revolution—which is to say he had begun by questioning the authority of the State without ever suggesting that he meant to overthrow the State. What he meant to do was spread discontent and skepticism among those he daily came in contact with who already resided on the fringe of State society. They were not Normals; nor were they quite Deviants. Most of them lived between the two worlds, accepting the State's generous hospitality, for instance, by living in the quarters it provided and enjoying its entitlements, while simultaneously participating in the black market to enhance their existence. In fact, of most of them it could be said they lived *at* the expense of the State while they lived *for* the thrill and material rewards of participating in the black market. They were cynical by nature (if the State had permitted belief in such things), and they had rejected the grandiose vision, dogma, and promises of the State and all its "experts" well before they even matriculated from the various learning centers that produced them.

In secret enclaves and at important conferences that only the State's highest-ranking trustees were privileged to attend, the experts and their political patrons and cohorts renounced these fringe characters as "failures" of the State and a collective liability to the State; but they existed—there was nothing that could be done to change that, at least not yet—and some of them even performed a valuable function: They made the wonders of the black market available to Normals who otherwise might have become discontented and begun to question the authority of the State themselves. This was a useful if lamentable function, and the State's elite acknowledged it even as the most high-minded among them continued to theorize ways of eradicating it. They wanted a world of pure devotion to high ideals and the loftiest goals of socialism—their goals—but since such a world seemed impossible at the moment, they'd take what they could get. (It could probably be said at this point that some of *them* also enjoyed the pleasures of the black market, but that would impugn their character by suggesting their realities didn't measure up to their ideals—and we wouldn't want to suggest that).

Long thus had budding revolutionaries behind him even before he had a revolution. Those who were attracted to his personality and saw in him the possibility of continued prosperity and continued security—without the onerous obligations of the State, which also promised security but seemed less capable than Long of providing it—those who were drawn to him before he even became a revolutionary would mostly still follow him after he became one as well; but they were not the ones the State had most reason to fear. For while they detested the State as much as Long did, they also profited from its existence. It was the State that made possible the black market they thrived on, and they were far more interested in continuing their hedonistic pursuit of either pure pleasure or lucre of any kind than they were in fantasies of creating some new social order. Some, in fact, might even regard a revolution as *detrimental* to their interests. But even they would follow Long in revolution if there was enough in it for them personally; and Long, a very savvy fellow himself, knew just how to win over their mercenary hearts. He made and repeated continual promises of vast wealth if they would help him ensure the revolution's success.

But those who were the greatest threat to the State, and of the greatest interest to Long, were the Normals who could be convinced to follow him in the revolutionary struggle. The Winter of a Thousand Hardships' most significant accomplishment was that it shook the faith of a sizeable portion of the population of Normals. These were people who had always submitted to the will of the State, but not because they embraced the State's high ideals or shared the elites' sense of purpose or dreams of a better world. They had submitted to the State's will because it seemed like their best option. What they were interested in was providing for themselves, and going along with the State seemed the best way of doing it. They served the State, but only because the State in turn served them. When, during the Winter of a Thousand Hardships, the State began to appear incapable of keeping up its end of the bargain, these Normals became restless and were willing to entertain thoughts of a new and better means of seeing to it that their needs and wants were provided for.

That new and better means, it began to appear, might just take the form of the fiery young revolutionary Hugo Lansky Long, the slick young provocateur who began appealing to them with complaints against the State and intimations he could give them something better. He worked on them in small groups at first, plying them with his very appealing rhetoric about the need for change and his own potential for making it happen. He enticed them to indoor assemblies at which as few as twenty and as many as a hundred people might gather to hear him talk. The groups were small, but they left the gatherings impressed, and as warmer weather finally crept in, Long expanded his reach, sending his black market associates to pass out leaflets that summoned curious Normals to outdoor rallies, using the same means to disseminate short essays that raised questions about those who were in power, and even circulating among the Normals himself to let them make contact with him in the flesh. Many shunned him, but others were receptive, sometimes even enthusiastically receptive.

The State had always done an admirable job of suppressing dissent and punishing dissenters—it very strictly limited ordinary citizens' access to the Internet, for instance, and it had also managed to limit their ability to assemble in large, unsupervised groups. But Long, with his extensive involvement in the underground economy and his extensive connections in that economy, did an even more admirable job of using those connections to spread his fame beyond New Leningrad, the commonwealth's capital in which he lived, to other urban centers across the nation. By June of that new and hopeful year, the odds were good that his name was at least recognized in every city in the country.

Although the State had from its inception proclaimed itself one unified political entity, a nation united in pure devotion to a single common cause (that cause of course being the improvement of the whole world), numerous factions had always existed without the State's legal sanction but also beyond the State's capacity to stop such factions from forming. Time and time again, the State's experts conferred over this tendency toward social and cultural fragmentation and theorized ways of preventing it, but no matter how much conferring or how much theorizing they did, the factionalizing persisted. Factions could form along almost any lines, from the religious to the territorial (we have already mentioned the inexplicable conflicts among urban islands within a single urban center). In a nation that had officially eliminated all private ownership and all class boundaries and was doing its best to eliminate racial boundaries and even physical differences among individuals, divisions of all kinds stubbornly persisted. But the one truly dangerous division was the one Hugo Lansky Long was quite intentionally fomenting himself.

Long's program was simple. He argued that the State was permitting other nations to take advantage of it, and through it abuse its people. The commonwealth, by agreement with other nations of the world stipulated in the Association of Nations' founding charter, was built on the principle that all nations should share the world's valuable resources, prudently distributing those resources under the direction of an international committee of experts in many different fields. But China and Russia in particular, Long claimed, were deliberately violating their contract with the rest of the world, and the nations of western Europe (those that had formerly comprised what was once called the European Union) were complicit in this violation by their passivity, their refusal to penalize the cheaters. Hence the State's citizens were being robbed, and the State itself was letting the robbery continue. The suffering inflicted on them all during the Winter of a Thousand Hardships was but the most recent and most salient example of the State's failure to protect them from those sinister forces outside their own borders. Why? Long asked them. The State repeatedly claimed the world's resources were severely limited—there just wasn't enough of everything to go around—and yet the underground economy by its very existence refuted that claim. Plenty existed—the State just wouldn't give *them* access to it.

The elites, however, *did* have access to it. Long produced and distributed photographs of various elite representatives of the State living in opulence that ordinary citizens had only been able to experience through the disastrously inadequate VREs. Even before the near-compete failure of the VRE technology, the government had realized it didn't want ordinary citizens experiencing such opulence, even vicariously (didn't want them getting ideas), and withdrew those experiences from VRE circulation. Again, why? Long asked. What was the State afraid of? What was it hiding from the people it claimed to serve? He produced similar contraband photographs of opulence in Chinese and Russian urban centers, as well as in a major capital of Europe called "Paris" (of which few of them had ever heard). All of this demonstrated that the people were being duped by their government. And it was being done quite intentionally. Long concluded most of his presentations by demanding justice and then laying out a plan for achieving it.

In private, the State's top officials worried that the National Workers Alliance was a potential existential threat to the nation they were working so hard to preserve and perfect. In public, of course, they admitted no such thing. In fact, they denied the existence of the NWA, and continued to deny its existence even after public knowledge of the group was so widespread it was absurd to keep pretending it didn't exist. But the State still maintained its silence on the topic of the NWA. It also bolstered the ranks of its military and police forces. Among other things, it recruited more Special Ops forces and trained them to subdue unruly civilians, even in large numbers. Plato and Duda were unaffected by these moves, but they witnessed them nonetheless, and they wondered how long it would be before a major confrontation took place.

They would not wait long for an answer. In late July the NWA held a rally in the People's Central Park. Thousands attended a function that was strictly forbidden by the State. Other speakers took to the podium to prepare attendees for the appearance of that new shining star of the people, Hugo Lansky Long. With additional incitement from these prefatory speakers, the crowd buzzed with anticipation. Before Long could address the excited masses, however, a small army of military personnel, SWATs, and Special Ops officers began assembling at the end of the park opposite the stage. Most members of the crowd didn't even notice them until they started their slow advance, helmets strapped on, visors lowered, shields raised, so that they looked like a phalanx of robots creeping ever-so-slowly forward. The crowd yielded, except those who fell before the advancing force and were battered with nightsticks for their failure to escape. The speaker who was on the stage to introduce Hugo Lansky Long caught sight of the fracas at the back of the crowd, and the advancing army of soldiers and cops, and used the podium's microphone to plead with them to stop their advance and let the citizens meet in peace. His entreaties were ignored by the government's emissaries, but they apprised those closer to the stage of what was happening behind them and triggered a panic that sent citizens fleeing in terror in all directions—except backward, where certain punishment awaited them. Hundreds were injured in the melee, and seventeen were killed, but not a word about any of it was spoken on the State's television or radio stations. And Hugo Lansky Long managed to disappear, not to be heard from again, publicly heard from, until the time was right for him to reappear.

15

In a country in which security cameras were even more prevalent than televisions for public viewing, and every citizen had a microchip implanted at "birth," it was possible to record virtually every movement a citizen made. But it was *not* possible for even the most curious government to keep track of every movement by every citizen. That would have been just too much to ask of any security agency, for it would have required nearly as many spies as there were citizens to spy on. Still, speculation ran rampant when the Dev1 virus swept the nation. What role, precisely, did data collection play in the onset or spread of the virus?

The Dev1 virus was, the citizens of the commonwealth fervently hoped, the final injustice they would have to suffer before some semblance of normalcy returned to their land. After the ravages of a winter rife with shortages and service interruptions, a winter in which they lived for nearly three months in peril of freezing to death, they had felt they deserved more than just a few short months of welcome reprieve. But now this new terror besieged them, this unseen terror whose effects quickly came to seem even more punishing than those of the awful winter they'd so recently survived.

The Dev1 virus, according to the State's most capable virologists, was a new strain of flu, a relative of an older strain of flu but one with which the State's extremely able medical personnel could not claim familiarity and were not yet equipped to deal. Word leaked out from highly respected sources that it had been unleashed on the unsuspecting general populace, by none other than the infamous Deviants, as a form of biological terrorism. State officials were unwilling to confirm the rumor as the murderous virus began its rampage, but they were also unwilling to disavow the speculation. The source of the outbreak would be, for the time being, left open to question. But of course the suggestion that the Deviants were responsible had been planted.

There was certainly no question about the devastating effects of the disease. The Dev1 induced severe flu symptoms—nausea, fever, vomiting, diarrhea—rumored to lead almost inevitably to a death so hideous, so revolting, it sometimes prompted even the State's most seasoned medical professionals to pass out when they witnessed it. Special emergency medical facilities were set up to handle the deluge of Dev1 victims and isolate them from the public. Public access to these Dev1 patients was forbidden once they'd been diagnosed and admitted for treatment. And by order of the president the entire country was placed on lockdown. Citizens were to remain in their quarters until the lockdown order was lifted. The Dev1 virus was just far too readily spread to permit any kind of close interaction among citizens. Military and some police personnel were used to distribute supplies to the quarantined. The streets were deserted, so Plato and Duda, who were kept on their regular assignment, had the easiest duty they could ask for. They walked the empty streets together, keeping their eyes out for quarantine violators. In the three weeks of the siege, they encountered not a single violator on their beat. The Deviants were said to have taken entirely to the old city, or even to the wasteland beyond, and even the usually irrepressible black market struggled to operate. It was a bad time for the people of the most progressive nation in history to inhabit planet Earth.

It seemed odd that the disease afflicted mostly the young and healthy. Logic would suggest it would be more likely to strike the aged and infirm. But as the State's leading virologist explained on a national broadcast, this virus seemed to prefer to attach itself to healthier organisms precisely because they were healthier. The healthy body offered the virus a greater opportunity to proliferate—so the wise expert informed his fellow citizens. And what Normal would dare to question the wisdom, training, and experience of a seasoned medical professional? The general public learned everything it needed to know from daily updates on the television. Experts of every stripe made appearances to inform citizens not only about the physical effects of the virus, the extent of the infection, the fatality rate, and the progress toward containing and perhaps even eradicating it—but also about how to cope both physically and mentally with prolonged isolation. The State even brought on physical trainers to show citizens how to stay in shape in confinement and chefs to offer quarantine cooking advice. And the usual parade of government officials made their usual reports about the health of the economy, the news from other countries that were also hit by the virus, etc. They were often followed by popular entertainers who would tell jokes, perform musical selections, or just offer encouragement to their imprisoned compatriots, showering them with platitudes about how they were "all in this together." A popular saying was "As individuals we are fallible, but together, even alone, we're invincible." Another was "Stay home, for your own good and for ours!" And there were many others. Sometimes the entertainers who worked so hard to cheer up their comrades in quarantine even wept on air to demonstrate their compassion for both those afflicted with the virus and those quarantined because of it. And of course they saluted the "frontline workers," the medical personnel who dealt directly with the Dev1 victims, and the military and police personnel who distributed supplies and performed minimal required maintenance on the country's infrastructure until life returned to normal (if such a thing would ever be possible) and the workers who normally served this function could return to their jobs.

Duda was one of the few who never left his job, and he was likely one of the few who actually enjoyed the lockdown. His job was easier when there was nobody to protect or suspect, and there was ample time to stroll the streets on lovely summer nights and learn from his new mentor. In under a year he'd learned more from Plato than he had learned from all his learning center facilitators combined. He'd developed a sense of kinship with Plato he'd never felt for another human being. If he'd known how it felt to have a loving parent, or even a loving sibling, he might have better understood what he was feeling now. But of course he'd never known such attachments, so he was pleasantly bewildered by the attachment to Plato—and a little bit nervous about it. It could not possibly be good for him to develop such a strong bond with another person. At his time and place in history, such bonds could never last.

And he was right to be nervous, because this bond was abruptly broken, leaving Duda emotionally devastated.

He arrived at work one sticky August evening to be immediately sent to his new division commander, Hyde. Hyde had replaced Bigger, who apparently had suffered the same fate Plato had suffered—as Duda was just about to find out. Hyde was a man who wanted to be a woman. Sex changes had been fashionable for a time in the nation's past, but that was before the nation was reconstituted as the selfless socialist republic it had now become. Under the new constitution, sex changes, like cosmetic augmentations, were no longer permitted, as they were seen as both superfluous and inappropriately self-centered. Individual identity was to be suppressed to the greatest possible extent anyway, so the State saw no point in indulging its citizens' egotistical whims and expending valuable State resources to let them surgically alter their appearance, not to mention their physiques. Nor was Hyde or any other man/woman allowed to wear long hair or makeup, so he/she was forced to express his/her sexuality by wearing what looked like a pair of inverted round cups beneath his/her uniform to simulate a woman's breasts. This too was illegal, but for some reason Hyde had not yet been cited for it, so he/she continued the practice with an attitude that bordered on defiant. Hyde seemed not to like either Plato or Duda anyway, so their conversations with their new supervisor were never pleasant. The one that took place that August evening altered Duda's whole worldview.

"He's been reassigned," Hyde repeated in response to Duda's pestering. "Don't ask me where. I don't know. And why does it matter to you? You know how things work. People get transferred. If you're not used to that by now, I don't know where you've been. But I can tell you one thing: You'd better get used to it, because this won't be the last time you'll lose a partner, that's for certain."

Duda's new partner was Hooligan, and while Hooligan was agreeable enough, he certainly couldn't be called either introspective or enlightening. He wasn't likely to be labeled particularly bright, either. Nor was he very engaging, at least not to Duda, for they appeared to have no common interests to talk about. Hooligan had been moved to New Leningrad from Castro, a city in the southern part of the country. Duda had heard of it, but that was about all. He knew next to nothing about the place because it was in the State's best interest that he know next to nothing about the place.

Hooligan filled him in—and in an in and in. The southern part of the country had a warmer, milder, sunnier climate, and Hooligan ranted nearly every day about how much he missed his natal urban center with its palm trees and sunshine and, in his view, its superior culture. And of course its absence of frigid weather—how could he forget that? He couldn't, if his incessant chatter about the topic was any indication. He'd suffered through his first winter in New Leningrad and, he confessed to his new partner in apparent sincerity, contemplated suicide.

"No, I mean it," he said. "I thought about killing myself. How do you people stand such cold? I don't understand it. It's better now, but we have weather like this most of the year in Castro.

"I don't know if I can take another winter. I really don't. You might come in to work some night and find out I didn't make it."

"Let's hope next winter is better," Duda said hopefully. "Most winters aren't as cold as this past winter."

"Let's hope. I don't know if I'll make it, otherwise. I really don't."

Hooligan was a soccer fan, and he vowed to retain his loyalty to the Castro club even though he'd been relocated to a new city. "We were always at the top of the division," he said. "Every season. I went to every game. Man, I enjoyed that. New Leningrad—they were always terrible. Now I can see why. It's too cold for soccer here!"

When he wasn't complaining about the weather, though, Hooligan was tolerable, at least. Duda could feign interest and nod his way through a discussion of the soccer league, even if he didn't much care which team was at the top of the division and which team was "always terrible." He'd never even been inside the local soccer stadium. He'd also rather have a partner who was passionate about soccer than one who was passionate about busting young

Normals' skulls with a nightstick. In that regard, Hooligan was certainly better as a partner than either Drone or Mattock. He was no Crusader, by any means, and that automatically elevated him above those two intrepid fanatics. He seemed bent on doing as little as a cop as he could get away with, and that was fine with Duda. Much better a lack of ambition than a lack of restraint and an overzealous yen for violence and danger. Then again, now was a bad time for trying to judge. There was nobody on the streets to bother them, so it was impossible to tell how Hooligan might react when he actually had to deal with the public. But both Mattock and Drone had demonstrated their zeal in myriad ways even when they weren't being provoked by some Normal or tracking down Deviants. Hooligan showed no such aggressive tendencies or compulsion to order his partner around. It looked as though he was going to be content with this assignment as long as Duda let him rant about the weather and rave about soccer and didn't tell him to shut up. And Duda was willing and able to abide that arrangement.

So things could have been worse.

16

Unfortunately, things got worse, and they did so in relatively short order. The Dev1 outbreak was soon termed a "pandemic" at the recommendation of the State's top health officials, based on its being a worldwide phenomenon, not merely a local or national one. So its most ardent enthusiasts, who were fanatical about the disease in much the same way Drone was fanatical about Deviants, had themselves a global crisis to consume their attention and effort. There were even fantasies in some quarters about the Dev1's being an existential threat, and thus numerous small armies of humans of many different nationalities garnered notoriety, and significant television airtime, by walking around in hazmat suits for a while.

But alas, their fame was short-lived. A mere three weeks after the commonwealth's lockdown began, it was lifted when the Dev1 virus was officially declared no longer a health threat. Citizens could safely emerge from their cocoons for the second time in less than six months. They were certainly tickled pink about that.

The experts stopped short of calling the abrupt end of the pandemic a "miracle," but that was only because miracles were associated with religions and the State wanted no part of those. A perfectly rational secular explanation for the Dev1 virus's sudden demise had to exist, and it most certainly did. Because of the government's extraordinarily fast and effective response to the disease—its decision to put the entire nation on lockdown so that the virus could be isolated to those who were infected with it when it was first discovered, and perhaps a few other random exposures but only a *very* few—the virus had very soon run out of hosts and died out for lack of nourishment. Such was the explanation given the public by the State's leading virologist, who would soon be awarded the State's top non-military honor for his quick and incisive action in the crisis. The fast, effective response of the State was making it possible for ordinary citizens to return to their normal lives without fear of infection. The Dev1 virus had been eradicated. Not even a vaccine to ward off future outbreaks would be required, for the virus was no more. The people of planet Earth were saved. A monument would eventually be erected in the People's Central Park to the thousands who had succumbed to the merciless Dev1 bug before the virus itself succumbed, their tiny portrait photos posted in one enormous collage in commemoration, so that their compatriots might "never forget," but as far as most of their compatriots were concerned, those poor victims might as well never have existed. The survivors would most certainly get along just fine without them, and the vast majority were just glad their own ordeal was over.

For Michael Duda, however, the trouble was just beginning. Just as his compatriots were rejoining him in the streets—and they rejoined him in anxious droves—Duda got the news that he was being joined at home by a new roommate. The luxury of living alone was coming to an end. In the space of a few weeks he had lost his dearest friend and mentor, the man who, in Duda's eyes, had awakened him from intellectual slumber; he had lost his gravy duty patrolling deserted streets that posed no threat to his health, safety, or even his energy level; and he had lost the blissful solitude in which he'd been able to contemplate these other joys of living in uninterrupted quiet and tranquility. He'd gone from thinking deeply and satisfyingly about life for the first time *in* his life to being burdened in ways that once again made him question whether any satisfaction could in fact be derived from living.

The new roommate was a young man named Wing, a slight young man about the same age as Duda who kept mostly to himself. For that, at least, Duda could be grateful. Wing had no employment that Duda was aware of, he had no girlfriend or other friends or acquaintances that Duda was aware of, and he watched no television whatsoever except for a bit of the educational stuff Duda had so recently acquired an interest in himself. For the most part, Wing kept to himself, locked away in the tiny compartment that passed for a bedroom (we have already mentioned that the State considered space a commodity too valuable to squander), engaged in near-perpetual close interaction with a small laptop computer that never left his company. Wisecracks entered Duda's mind about that laptop's being Wing's love interest, but they never made it to his lips because he found his new roommate likable and didn't wish to offend him. As roommates went, he was absolutely an improvement on the temperamentally erratic Depacote. They hadn't conversed much, at least not yet, but what little conversation they had engaged in had been civil, if not particularly profound. But civil was always preferable to uncivil, and conversation with Depacote had often been impossible, much less civil. More than once, the two of them had come close to fighting. Duda couldn't imagine raising his voice with this new guy, much less coming to blows with him. His overall assessment of his new living situation after a week or so was that it wasn't as good as being alone but beat the hell out of some of his past experiences. He could live with it—and anyway, it wouldn't last. Nothing ever did.

Wing too seemed content with the arrangement. One of the first things he said to Duda on moving in was, "Well, this is a refreshing change. I've never lived with just one roommate before."

"Never let it be said there are no advantage to being a cop," Duda said. "I haven't lived with more than one roommate since the dorm at the learning center."

"Then it's an agreeable arrangement for both of us."

"It's starting off that way."

Wing did have one habit that bothered him, though it was nothing he would ever take issue with because it was just a personal idiosyncrasy and not something he felt he had a right to complain about. It clearly was not intended as an affront, even though it did constitute an assault on the police officer's olfactory sense. Wing was several generations removed from an ethnic tradition that practiced a particular form of cooking that could be somewhat malodorous, to put it bluntly. At any rate, those who were not accustomed to the smells produced in the preparation of that cuisine might be prone to find those smells at least mildly "noisome." Wing liked to practice that form of cooking himself, presumably as a remnant of his heritage that had somehow snaked its way down through the commonwealth's experts in child-rearing and into his culinary repertoire. Duda wondered if Wing would even be able to explain where his culinary habits came from, given that the smells his cooking produced were the sort of smells one might associate with "Grandma," or some other such archaic entity (Duda wouldn't have had an inkling what kind of food his own ancestors must have consumed—he came from a damn breeding room in a damn medical facility). Anyway, it didn't matter. He would tolerate the smells for a long time before he'd make a fuss about them. If he were ever going to complain about one of his roommate's behaviors, it would have to be something done purposefully to offend him. He would put up with a great deal of bother if it was unintentional bother—if it was not done with the intention of offending him. Michael Duda appreciated the fact that all individuals, himself included, have characteristics that others might find irksome. It was, in his view, a view amply reinforced in his conversations with Plato, simply part of being human.

He did, however, make an effort to escape Wing's cooking smells when innoxious escape was possible. In the last days of summer, and then in early autumn, it was relatively simple. Duda made an excuse to take to the outdoors and then left for a couple of hours. By the time he returned the cooking smells had dissipated, though traces of them always lingered, and he noticed that the stove and other appliances in the kitchen were starting to acquire a surface film that, left uncleaned long enough, would have to be dealt with one way or another. But he'd decide what to do when the time came to decide—whenever that was going to be. In the meantime, he would continue to put up with the cooking because it was the only thing about Wing that bothered him.

He was curious about how the man spent his time, though. All he'd been able to learn about his new roommate's past was that he'd "worked with computers," and that left room for a lot of possibilities. He was also curious about why Wing had *stopped* working with computers, but not curious enough to pry. Perhaps he was *still* working with computers but just doing it from home. That might explain why the laptop was always with him, and it would explain why he spent so much time on it. But Duda didn't ask. He went off to his job every night, slept when he could during the day, and conveniently left again, almost every evening, about the time Wing would start making the preparations for dinner. He would take his own dinner out somewhere and then go on to work. It most certainly didn't beat living alone, but it was an arrangement he could live with, at least for the time being.

One of the things he did when he was out and about was drop by the café. She was not there; he'd discovered that on his first visit after the Dev1 virus was conquered. But what surprised him was that nobody else was there either. The café was closed and dark. On subsequent visits he discovered it was still closed and dark. It had become one of the numerous storefronts in the urban center that was *always* closed and dark, apparently permanently closed and dark—the places Plato used to indicate with a sweep of his hand and talk about how desolate they made the city feel. Then he'd launch into a discourse about "the old city" and how it had been well lit even at night, and the streets were crowded with people who didn't all wear the same drab tunics; and the women wore dresses (he'd had to explain those to Duda) and heels (he'd had to explain those to Duda) and long hair and makeup and jewelry (he'd had to explain all those things to Duda too) and the bars and restaurants were crowded with people and the State was nowhere in sight. And everything was different then. And when Duda had asked how he could possibly *know* all these things, he'd tapped his temple with his index finger and said, "I pay attention, my young friend. I pay attention."

Now Duda was the one who paid attention, and he too felt desolate. He felt empty inside, and he knew he just wanted to have Plato there to counsel him. He thought, as he had sometimes thought when Plato was actually with him, that the man could be making it all up and it wouldn't matter. Even if it was all fantasy, it had made him feel alive in a way he had never before felt alive.

After that day he gave up on the café and started taking a different walk, the goal of which was in part purgation, to get the recent past out of his system. He would find a new place, perhaps meet new people, and his life could get on to its next phase, whatever that was going to be. Perhaps he would even meet another young woman like Anna, and she would take Anna's place in his heart and he would be happy again. It wasn't what he really wanted—down deep—but what he really wanted down deep wasn't going to be available to him. He had to move on.

Before he resolved to move on he had also made another trip to the prostitute who had served him the morning after Drone's injury. At that point he was still trying to recapture the magic of Anna. The prostitute didn't remember him. "Do you know how many guys I've had sex with in the last year?"

"Forget about it," Duda said. "I'd really rather not find out."

"Fine with me," she said. Let's just say it's in the hundreds."

"I'm sure it is."

"Hey, it's my job, all right? Don't act superior, pal. I can get you another girl."

"I wasn't acting superior. I didn't think I was acting anything at all. I was just—"

"You were just in love with your girlfriend," she cut him off. "And you wanted to pretend I was her. But I'm not, all right? I'm me. *Me*!"

"I understand that. I'm sorry. I didn't mean anything at all; I really didn't."

"Maybe we should get you somebody else," she said. "I'm starting to get a headache."

"Me too. Let's just forget about it."

"I'm sorry I'm not your girlfriend." She was softening up, trying to be more understanding.

"It's all right," he said. "Really it is. I'll just ... I'll just come back another time. Is that okay?"

"You can come back any time," she said. "I like you. I'm just ... I'm not your girlfriend, all right? I don't wanna be your girlfriend. I wish you wouldn't *pretend* I'm your girlfriend."

He stopped trying to explain to her that he really didn't want her to pretend she was his girlfriend—largely because he realized that's probably exactly what he *did* want her to pretend. But he wasn't going to tell her that. Now he just wanted to get the hell out of there. He couldn't get to the street fast enough. And when he did get to the street he felt worse than he felt before he entered the sex shop; and the whole miserable experience was part of what motivated his decision to move on. He sure as hell wasn't dropping in at that sex shop again. He needed a change of scenery.

The difficulty in finding a change of scenery was that, in the interest of fostering equality, the State wanted all the neighborhoods in an urban center to look alike. Bland apartment building after bland apartment building confronted him no matter which way he traveled. But the State didn't much alter the topography of the city—there were still some hills and valleys, and the river ran through the center of the city fairly near the police compound, and there was the People's Central Park, of course, and also Stalin's Bluff. Stalin's Bluff was a river bluff that overlooked the river and part of the city below. It had been off-limits to residents of the urban center when Duda was young, but the citizens kept climbing it because they liked the view from the top. They also liked the hike to the top of the bluff.

It was invigorating. So many of them kept climbing the bluff that eventually the State relented and turned Stalin's Bluff into another park. In nice weather it was common to find dozens of people up there at any given time, sitting on park benches or at picnic tables that the State grudgingly supplied, often just gazing out over the urban center and the landscape beyond. They could spread out, too, so they didn't feel hemmed in by other people, or for that matter the concrete boxes that constituted their homes.

It wouldn't have been inappropriate to suggest that Stalin's Bluff made the State nervous because it afforded ordinary citizens the chance to get a broader view of the world, to look out over the panorama of the urban center stretching all the way to the wasteland beyond it, the illimitable wasteland, and the last thing the State wanted was to have its Normals getting too broad a view of the world. Being able to see off into the distance that way might just stimulate the imagination to think inappropriate thoughts. Duda could finally understand just why, because looking out over the river and the world beyond it was a bit like having a conversation with Plato: It seemed to open him up, expand his horizons. He hadn't been to Stalin's Bluff in many years, but he suddenly realized it might be just the place to lift his spirits when they needed lifting—as they most certainly needed lifting now.

He sat alone on a park bench and looked around to ensure he was alone. Then he pulled a pack of cigarettes and a lighter from a hidden pocket in his tunic and lit a cigarette and inhaled deeply and exhaled slowly, savoring the taste of the cigarette and also the mere activity of smoking. Smoking was of course illegal in the commonwealth, though of course many people did it anyway, just as they did many other things that were illegal, and sometimes the State looked the other way, and sometimes it didn't. As a cop—though he wasn't wearing his uniform at the moment; it was his day off—he didn't want to get caught smoking by another cop, who might turn out to be a Drone who took her work seriously. But he enjoyed the cigarette for all it was worth. And he enjoyed the view and was thrilled with himself for having rediscovered this place. It didn't make up for the loss of both Anna and Plato, but it certainly improved his mood.

He sat there for a long time. It was a glorious fall afternoon, widely scattered clouds and just the slightest hint in the air that winter was again approaching, and the time was now to enjoy this experience because he might not have any more of them before winter set in again. So he sat on the bench and contemplated the view and smoked another cigarette, and then a third. Nobody bothered him. He sat there until he realized that sunset was only an hour or so away, and then reluctantly he stood up and stretched and started back down the hill.

On the descent he fell in with other people who were also making their way back down into the glum city. They trooped along at intervals, individuals or else clusters of two or three, and even one group of four, and then they reached the bottom of the hill and scattered and all went their own ways. Duda saw a bus up ahead and thought about taking it because it was a route that would take him near home—but before he made a decision about taking the bus he saw somebody who very abruptly made him change his mind. He would not be taking the bus after all.

18

Wing had seemed to appear from nowhere and started up the street in the other direction. Duda decided to follow him. He didn't feel strange or guilty about it; he was a cop. Following people was something he did fairly often. It meant nothing to him except the chance to learn something more about the young man who was sharing his abode. Well—it *might* also explain why the hell his new roommate happened to be in this same neighborhood, so far from where they lived.

Wing walked purposefully along the main street, paying little attention to the shops or the people he passed along the way. He did not seem to be in a hurry, but he wasn't dawdling either. Duda followed him at an easy pace and had no trouble keeping up with him. Nor did Wing suspect he was being followed. That was obvious from the way he kept a relaxed, easy pace and didn't even glance back. Duda noticed he was carrying his laptop at his side.

They turned on to a side street and the tail became slightly more difficult because there were very few people on the side street, and they were spread out. He had to drop back fifty feet or so to make himself less conspicuous. There were few storefronts now, and that meant few places he could either pretend to be going or duck into if Wing happened to look around. He had to be a little more careful now.

When Wing turned into a narrow alley, the tail grew more difficult still. Duda had to wait at the mouth of the alley, ensure that Wing kept plodding along, and then creep along the side of the alley himself. He and Wing were the only two people in the alley, so he had to be as quiet as he could be and keep his eye out for places to hide should hiding become necessary.

They made it to the next street. Wing turned and followed that street, and Duda knew now that something was up. Wing either knew he was being followed or was taking precautions not to be followed. This realization piqued Duda's interest. He started to ponder the possibilities: Was Wing meeting a love interest? Probably not. Was he involved in the black market? A strong possibility. Was he trying to lose a tail? That very real possibility made Duda uneasy.

But they made the next alley, Wing turned into it, and the "chase" continued. Duda crept along behind him again. They made the next street, Wing turned onto it, Duda made the corner and ... Wing was nowhere in sight.

The street was a side street, deserted except for perhaps three people in the entire block, none of whom was Wing. Duda was experienced enough at this business to remain calm on the outside, but on the inside he had tightened up. He looked around casually, trying to decide which way to turn. Wing had gone to the left—but had he somehow doubled back to the right? Had he ducked into an opening? Had he vanished into thin air?

Before Duda could decide which of these possibilities was the most likely, he felt a muzzle jab him in the back and a low voice said, "Stay calm ... calm. No sudden moves or you will have moved your last. Don't look back! Good. Keep facing forward or the last thing you'll see of this world will be this grimy street. Good. Now, turn down the sidewalk to your left and begin to walk, slowly, toward the next street. Don't look back! Good."

Duda knew the voice, but he was not about to look back and confirm his suspicion. He moved forward at what he felt was a relaxed pace, though no part of him felt relaxed.

"Good," the voice said. "You're doing fine. Keep going about twenty more feet. To that car right up there on your right. I want you to get in on the passenger side. Front seat. Good. Hold the door open and ... good."

Duda recognized the man behind the wheel as the cook from Anna's café. Austin climbed into the back seat directly behind Duda. "My gun is still pointed at the back of your head, Michael. Do I need to touch the muzzle to your skull?"

"No."

"Very good. I didn't think I would." To the driver he said, "You know where to go."

The car pulled out and drove slowly down the street. Duda felt his pulse pounding the way it had done the night Drone murdered Caleb Brewster. But at least he knew both of these men. There was some kind of comfort in that—or at least he thought there might be. "So what happened to Wing?"

"So what's it to you?"

"I just ... he disappeared."

"I have to say I'm very disappointed, Michael. I didn't expect this. I honestly didn't. I can't say it was the last thing I expected, but I had hoped for better from you."

"I don't know what you mean."

The driver was pulling on to one of the urban center's main streets. There was never a lot of automobile traffic in this city—or for that matter anywhere in the commonwealth—since private ownership of cars, like private ownership of anything else, was forbidden. There was a decent amount of bicycle traffic, though, all in the lane to their right. And of course the buses. There were always the buses.

He expected the driver to talk to him, since they were old acquaintances, but he just kept driving and didn't even look Duda's way. "Where are we going?" Duda said.

"You'll see."

"What about Wing?" Duda said. "Won't you at least tell me that? You're going to kill me anyway, aren't you?"

"It looks that way. You don't need to know about Wing. At this point, the less you know, the better."

"So why was he assigned to live with me? Just tell me that. You're going to kill me anyway—what difference does it make?"

"The less you know, the better. Just in case we don't have to kill you. But I'm disappointed, Michael, I truly am. This is not what I had hoped for."

"Well it's not what I hoped for either. I seriously doubt you feel worse about it than I do."

The car kept going. The driver remained silent. They got on the main highway that would leave the urban center and curl around toward the old city. By his reckoning Duda had perhaps a half-hour more to live. It was getting dark outside and he wondered—strangely—if it was a comfort to die at night. How had Caleb Brewster felt? Could Duda ask Austin to surprise him with the bullet? "Will you at least tell me who you are? What you are?'

The two of them were silent. "Are you the government?" Duda asked.

Finally, he got a reaction from the cook: a hearty laugh. "*You're* the government," he said.

"I'm a street cop. That's all I am."

"Then why were you following Wing?" It was Austin who asked.

"I was curious."

The driver shook his head. "Sure. We're curious too. Everybody's curious. The State is very curious."

"Don't think about jumping out, Michael," Austin said from the back seat. "Your death warrant hasn't been signed yet. Give yourself a chance. You still might talk yourself out of this. But please don't lie to us."

"I haven't lied to you. I was out for a walk, and I saw him on the street. I was curious, so I followed him."

"You were five miles from your apartment, Michael."

"That's a lot of curiosity," the driver added.

"And that's exactly why I followed him. 'Cause there he was, out of the blue. We were in the same neighborhood, far from home. Can't you understand why I'd be curious about that?

"Are you guys the secret police? I've heard about you. If you're thinking about torturing me, I beg you to reconsider. What I've told you is all I know."

"Who do you work for, Michael?"

"I'm a damn cop, Austin. You know that. You *both* know that. I came into the café to see Anna. You know how I felt about her. You were both there. That's all there was to it.

"Look, if you're gonna kill me, I guess there's nothing I can do about it. But what I've told you is the truth. And it's the whole truth. There's nothing else I can tell you."

The highway was nearly deserted. It wound through barren countryside for ten minutes before the old city came in view. Duda had not been this way before—they'd taken a different route when they went to the old city. But he knew more or less where they would end up. "I don't understand any of this," he said. "I'm a cop. You guys are not cops, I guess. That's what you say. So who are you? What are you?"

He still didn't get an answer. They rumbled along in complete silence for three or four minutes. Duda's mind was racing as he contemplated his options, but he was inclined to take Austin's advice and stay right where he was. If he had to make a desperate move, he'd wait until they were out of the car. He'd probably have a better chance that way. But there was a strange little part of him that just wanted to know who they really were before they killed him. He even heard himself conversing and then pleading with them: Please, just tell me who you really are. Then you can blow my brains out.

The old city was nothing but shadows this late in the evening. He would not have been able to distinguish it from the empty countryside if not for the buildings which loomed like silhouettes in the darkness. Even though he'd been to this place before, he didn't like it here, it felt otherworldly to him, and this was not where he wanted to die. But it appeared he wasn't going to have a choice. He had another perverse little conversation in his mind, and it ended with him pleading again: Can you please take me down to the ocean, at least? I'd like to smell the ocean breeze before I die.

"Days are getting short," the driver said suddenly, matter-of-factly. "Winter's on its way again. Let's hope we don't have another one like the last one."

Duda felt his life was running on an hourglass. There wasn't much sand left in the top bulb. "How come I let you go that night I caught you here, Austin? Explain that. Do you remember? I could have busted all of you and I let you go. Surely you remember that."

"I remember."

"You were setting him up for later spying," the driver said. "The time wasn't right to arrest him yet—or kill him."

"That's ridiculous. Think about what your friend here is saying, Austin. Does it make sense? Think about it. Think about it hard, please. Somebody's life is at stake here."

Then, "Wait a minute. If you were out here with those other people—with Anna and those others—what were *you* doing?"

"Over there," Austin said to the driver.

They pulled into a side street and crept along very slowly. Duda thought he saw shadowy figures creeping around in the dusk that was lowering like a dark film. "Are those people with you?"

"Keep going," Austin said to the driver. "We don't need trouble from them."

The driver kept going, but he said to Duda, "Why the hell were you following Wing today?" And then to Austin: "It doesn't make sense. We can't trust him."

"Keep going," Austin said. "I don't think it's safe to stop here."

"We can't take him you know where."

"You can if you're going to kill me anyway."

The driver looked at him sharply, and Duda said, "Hey, I might as well help you out. If you're going to kill me anyway, what difference does it make?"

"Do *not* trust this man," Austin said. Then, "You know that big open space down by the pier? That old parking lot or whatever it was?"

"I know it."

"They won't be able to sneak up on us there. Go there."

"What about cops?"

"We have to stop somewhere. We can't just keep driving around."

"Sure we can. Shoot the sonofabitch and shove him out the door. Let the Deviants have him." But he kept driving.

They came to a big open space near the water's edge. There was enough of a moon that they could see a few hundred feet in all directions. They couldn't see much, but it would be hard for the Deviants to sneak up on them.

"Right here," Austin said.

They got out, all three of them, and moved about twenty feet away from the car. Both Austin and the driver had their guns out now, looking around, making sure nobody was coming. This might be the time to make a break, but he sure didn't stand much chance of surviving the escape attempt.

"Watch him," Austin said. "I'm going to make a phone call. If he tries to run, put him out of his misery."

Austin went away from them, about twenty or thirty feet on the other side of the car, and the cook stood apart from Duda and kept looking around, but he also had his gun trained on Duda the whole time. He seemed nervous. They said nothing to each other. They could hear Austin's voice but could not make out his words. His voice was a low mumble, and they couldn't even really distinguish the inflection in it.

After about ten minutes, a very long ten minutes for Duda, Austin came back over to them. "Damn," he said. "It's starting to get cold again. I'm not ready for another winter."

"I'll take one," Duda said. "But Austin?"

"Yeah?"

"Remember how I said I wasn't sure I liked you?"

Austin laughed. "It's your lucky night, kid. You're gonna get to see another sunrise after all."

"You're kidding!" the cook/driver said. "Seriously, you've got to be kidding."

"Nope. We're supposed to take him home and drop him off."

"He's been cleared?"

"Not necessarily, but he wants to do some more snooping around before he decides."

"I can't believe this. I really can't."

"You sound disappointed," Duda said. He was afraid he might lose control of his bladder, the sense of relief was so strong. And his legs were weak. He could easily see himself collapsing into a puddle of his own making. "Are you still mad at me because I gave that kid trouble the last time I was in the café?"

"Get in the damn car."

They all got back in the car in their same places, and the cook, clearly angry, took off somewhat recklessly. "He better hope this doesn't bite us in the butt," he said to Austin.

"Just try not to have an accident out here. You've made your point; is it necessary to keep driving like this?"

The driver slowed down. He guided them back toward the highway. The car's headlights picked out more shadows in the night. Duda hadn't been here in a while—not since his days with Drone as his partner—and he was reminded just how dangerous this assignment had been. A cop could get killed out here if he wasn't careful—or, apparently, if whoever was on the other end of that phone call didn't say the right thing.

"Just remember that my weapon is still trained on the back of your head, Michael. So don't get any ideas."

"My only idea is to get home, Austin. I swear to you that's all I'm thinking about—except I'm still wondering just who you guys are."

"Don't push your luck," the driver said. "I'm in a bad mood anyway. I'm sure you'd hate to see my weapon discharge accidentally. That would be a shame."

They were back on the highway before anybody spoke again. It was Duda who broke the silence. "What about Anna?" he said.

"What about her?"

"Don't tell him anything," the driver said. "I mean it. Don't tell this bastard a thing."

"Is she all right?"

"Don't *tell him anything.*"

"All right," Duda said. "All right. I think I'm starting to make up my mind about whether I like you, Austin. I don't know if you'd like the answer."

"Are we really supposed to take this bastard home? We could dump his body right here beside the road and nobody would miss him."

"Take him home."

"I don't get it."

"So who'd you call back there? Was it that kid? That little punk revolutionary? Hugo "What's-his-name?""

"Blow his head off," the driver said. "Blow his damn head off."

"It'll make a mess of the car. You don't want that any more than I do."

"It'll be worth it just to shut him up."

"Don't you dare lump us in with that guy," Austin said. "Little populist punk. He's not with us. He doesn't want the same things we want. Don't put his name in the same sentence with ours."

"So what *do* you guys want? Aren't you the guys who go around blowing up politicians? Is that you guys? Or is that the guy you can't stand? All this terrorism stuff is very confusing to a simple street cop."

"We don't even have to bury his body," the driver said. "Any spot along here will do just fine. Let the maggots have him. Rats. Whatever else is out here. Hell, let the damn Deviants cannibalize the sonofabitch."

Duda was unfazed. He believed he was actually going to survive the night, and this conversation took him back to his days of verbal jousting with Austin in the café. He liked Austin. "I happened to be right on the scene when you took that guy out back in November. Last winter, remember? Secretary of Something-or-other. Hell, I don't know. They're all the same to me. I was right there when it happened. Me and my partner. Beautiful work, fellas. Body parts everywhere. People screaming. Innocent people murdered. Death and destruction everywhere. Beautiful work."

"Nobody's innocent," Austin said.

"Don't say anything more, Austin. This guy is just pushing your buttons. I think he's a damn spy. I think we'll rue the decision to let him live tonight."

"I'm not a spy. I'm just a damn cop—and I'm not even fanatical about that. I'm no Crusader."

"I wish we could trust you, Michael; I really do. But it's only because you have friends in high places that you're still alive."

"Austin, god damn it. You tell this guy anything more and I'll turn my weapon on *you*."

"Why were you following Wing today?" Austin asked him again.

"Just curiosity, Austin. I'm sorry, but that's all there was to it. So he works for you?"

"Oh hell," the driver said.

"That's all it was," Duda said to the driver, and he surprised himself with the firmness of his tone. "He's my new roommate. I'm curious about him."

"Not anymore he ain't your roommate."

It was the driver who had disclosed this tidbit of information, surprising both Austin and Duda. "Discretion is the better part of valor," Austin advised.

"You're one to talk."

"I'm not a threat to you, Austin," Duda said. "Even if you're the ones going around blowing up these government people and corporate hotshots and celebrities, I'm not a threat to you. I don't care about them; I swear. I only care about Anna."

Neither of them would tell him anything more, though, and they rode along in silence for a while. They were sweeping around and then into the urban center when the driver broke the silence. "Look at this," he said, contemptuously. "Imagine what these cities must have looked like. And look at them now. Encampments. Big, hideous concrete encampments. No majesty here now. Just big utilitarian rockpiles. That's what humanity has come to. *Reverted* to."

Maybe he was just talking to himself; it was hard to tell. Then to Austin he said, "We should kill this guy just for working for them. I don't care what he knows."

After that there were a few more minutes of silence. They were getting close to Duda's building when he spoke up this time. "I really don't care if you guys are the ones killing all these bigshots. I truly don't. I'm sure they have it coming. I just don't see what it accomplishes."

But they offered him no explanation, only more silence. They were down the street a block or so from his building when the driver pulled to the curb. "Consider yourself lucky, son. 'Cause you are damn lucky to be alive. If I had my way, you *wouldn't* be alive."

Duda climbed out of the car and was ready to walk the rest of the way home when Austin called him back. "Get back in the car—just for a moment," he said. "I need to tell you something."

Duda obliged him, though he might be committing suicide. But he trusted Austin. "Anna's dead," Austin said.

The driver glowered but did not speak. Duda's insides curled up in a ball.

"She was killed a few months ago."

There was another long pause, and he continued, "People in our line of work take chances," he said. "I'm sorry."

Duda nodded in appreciation or just acknowledgment but couldn't find words to speak.

"I just thought you should know," Austin said. "I don't know if we owed it to you, but I wanted to tell you."

The driver said nothing. Duda nodded again. "Thank you," he said. "I do appreciate that."

He was out of the car then and walking along the sidewalk with his hands stuffed in his pockets. He had dressed warmly enough for the day, but not for the night. He did not turn his head when the car he'd just been riding in passed him and moved on up the street. He was suddenly quite painfully aware, though, of how bleak and dismal this city was. He didn't know if he felt worse than he'd felt earlier in the day before he climbed Stalin's Bluff, but he certainly felt desolate inside. The elevator in his building was broken—still—and he climbed the stairs as if he were walking death row. This was not the first time he'd noticed things—he'd been noticing them for a while, ever since Plato started bringing them to his attention—but he was suddenly more acutely aware of certain things than he had been before: the dim lighting in the staircase, and then in the hallway to his apartment; the austere, colorless walls; his footsteps scuffing the concrete floor; the spartan light fixtures that were like metal cages; and his door, his door that made him think of the entrance to a storage locker. It could not have been less inviting if it had been branded with a skull and crossbones.

Inside was no better. It occurred to him suddenly that he should do some decorating—except that he had to get the State's permission for that. The State only permitted certain embellishments to the living quarters it provided its citizens, and those embellishments were minimal, and so dreary as to make it questionable whether they deserved to be called "embellishments" at all. But that was how the State had to be. It had to promote uniformity, sameness. They were, after all, all in this together. Their homes, like their dress, their grooming, and everything else in their world, must remind them of that.

Wing's tiny bedroom was empty, as were the bathroom and kitchen. The only trace of him that remained in the apartment was a very slight odor of his cooking.

20

Hooligan had spent the first hour of their shift complaining about the previous day's soccer game. His Castro team had fallen to the lowly New Leningrad team in what he perceived to be a fixed contest. His evidence in support of that claim seemed to be that his team was simply too good to lose to a team that was barely clinging to the First Division and stood a very good chance of being demoted the following season.

The game was played in Castro's balmy late-fall weather, Duda wanted to remind him, even though that was practically all he knew about the game, and the only reason he knew it was that he'd heard something about it on the radio. The only reason he'd paid attention to the radio story was that he knew Hooligan would talk about the game.

He did not, however, remind his partner of that very salient fact (at least Duda reckoned it was a salient fact—it would have been a salient fact in Hooligan's view if the game had been played in New Leningrad). Instead, he listened patiently to the complaining about the egregious fouls that were not called. "That tackle right at the beginning of extra play should have been a penalty kick. Did you see it?"

"No."

"It should have been a penalty kick. Plain and simple. Those referees clearly had it in for Castro. Clearly."

The game was played in Castro, Duda wanted to say. But again he refrained from saying it. His role in these conversations was generally just to nod his head at intervals and say "Hm" or "Wow" or "That's amazing." That was probably the quickest way off the subject and on to the next subject he wasn't interested in.

"I know you'll say the officials favor the home team," Hooligan continued with his analysis. "But that's not always the case. This is the capital city. There are political ramifications of calling a soccer game. No, I absolutely mean it."

"Hm."

"Better believe it. Most of the important government officials live right here. It pays to take care of the important government officials."

"Wow. I never thought of that."

"Well it's true. Politics is in everything—as awful as that sounds, it's true. Believe you me, it's true."

"That's amazing."

"Amazing but very believable. Think about it. The seat of our national government is here. The end of the season is two weeks away. The last thing those political bigshots want is to see the capital city's team demoted."

At some point in these conversations Duda's mind usually began to engage in a practice it had taken up under Plato's influence—but only after Plato abandoned him (as he saw it), leaving him with *this* guy. Without conscious effort, his mind took off on flights of fancy. He had the strangest visions, fantastic visions, like VRE experiences that didn't quite *feel* real because they were confined to his mind. But they looked real all right. They looked as real as anything he'd ever seen up on a movie screen, 2D, but in full color and with a soundtrack that was crystal clear.

In one fantasy he was sitting at an elaborately set table with Plato and several other people. The most important of those people was Anna, who looked resplendent in a form-fitting blue dress and blue heels. She wore a very dignified-looking necklace, and she had long, beautiful reddish hair that fell to both sides of her lovely face and swished gently but seductively around her bare shoulders when she moved her head—and she was always moving her head, telling stories and laughing. Her arms were bare too, and she wore red lipstick and blush and eyeliner and when she looked at him, he could only think about how beautiful she was. Then he focused on her teeth, which were very straight and very white and made Duda realize he'd never had much of a chance to examine the real Anna's teeth. Maybe he'd never really had the chance to see her smile. Everybody else at the table wore colorful clothing too—himself included, he presumed, though the fantasy occurred from his perspective so he didn't see himself in it. But he assumed he was like all the others, who wore attractive, colorful clothing and attractive hairstyles and ate and drank alcohol and smiled gaily as they chatted.

There was another fantasy in which he and Anna were arm in arm in the People's Central Park, and the park looked pretty much the way it did now except more colorful. The common citizens running around the park wore distinctive clothing, not the uniforms the State made them wear, and there were colorful flowers and trees and other things he hadn't ever really paid attention to in the real park. Duda came to realize that the difference between the real park and the place he saw in his fantasy was the people. The colorful people made the park seem more colorful too. The real park felt institutional, just another thing the State had fabricated for some social purpose (one that Duda didn't understand), but the fantasy park was a place where people went to relax and have fun and, in

Duda's case, to be in love. In this fantasy he always ended up staring at Anna again, who was the star of all his fantasies; but she made the park a better place that didn't feel institutional in the least.

There were other fantasies, too, other things that had no place in his real experience of the world: There was one in which he and Anna took a drive in the countryside in a car with a convertible top, and nobody arrested them. There was another in which they flew together in an airplane on a trip to Castro, of all places (maybe Hooligan's constant chatter about Castro had actually triggered this fantasy), and yet another in which they were at some kind of outdoor concert at which a band played raucous music that the State as they knew it would never permit.

And there were other fantasies, all lifelike and in color, all of them very real when they occurred, and it felt as though he were living in them. And it was always so dispiriting when they ended, always suddenly, and there he was strolling down the street in the entertainment district with Hooligan complaining about a damn soccer game. He always felt like a balloon, a very colorful balloon, that had just been abruptly deflated. All the color had just rushed out of him. He wasn't sure Hooligan was actually in color; he didn't seem to be. Hell, he wasn't sure Hooligan was even real. Maybe *Hooligan* was the fantasy. One could always hope. But it never turned out that way. At the end of the fantasy he came back to life as it was, and life as it was was awful. Damn you, Plato, he would say to himself.

A small part of him wondered if perhaps he was losing his mind. He remembered when he was a teenager at the learning center, being taught about people who had strange delusions and needed help that only the State's experts could provide. For those people were mentally ill, he had learned. They needed counseling and medication, especially medication. But he and Plato had talked about that, about mental illness, and about the thinking of things that weren't real but imagining them just the same, as if they might really happen in some world (apparently not the world of the VREs, as it turned out), and Plato had assured him it was normal to dream, that such fantasies were not a sign of insanity. But of course Plato was gone now, and Duda was actually having the fantasies, and he could no longer be sure. He needed Plato to explain things to him, but Plato was gone. Damn you, Plato, he would say to himself again.

And all he had now was Hooligan, who droned on, oblivious to his partner's daydreaming, as he seemed oblivious to many other things. He seemed aware only of the soccer games and the foul weather in New Leningrad, and apparently of cheating soccer referees and corrupt politicians who concerned themselves with the outcomes of soccer games. Perhaps Hooligan was lucky in that regard. Life for him seemed so uncomplicated. As long as Castro won its soccer games, and the weather was decent, he was happy. Or at least he seemed to be.

"And New Leningrad's defense was so porous, I couldn't believe we couldn't score more than one goal. It was ridiculous. There was a goal just after halftime that was called offsides and it clearly wasn't, but the goal was waved off and it changed the whole momentum of the game. I'm telling you, it was terrible. I've never seen anything like it."

"Wait a minute—look at that."

Two young men were scuffing on the sidewalk outside one of the clubs up ahead. Obviously, they hadn't seen the cops approaching or they wouldn't have been scuffling. Most cops were more than happy to take a nightstick to a reveler's head, and most revelers knew that. There was a general rule that Normals behaved when they saw cops around. They behaved because they feared for their safety. The State's means of dealing with civil disturbances was to let their cops beat the living hell out of whoever was causing the disturbance, and that was the end of it. There were few civil disturbances when the cops were around.

These two young scufflers must have known the rule, for they abruptly stopped their scuffling and were prepared to let bygones be bygones rather than have their skulls cracked. But it was too late. Hooligan grabbed the nearest one by the shoulder and struck him sharply across the side of the head. He dropped to the pavement, and in a moment he was bleeding from his ears. Others in the crowd winced and hollered. "Hey!" one young woman shouted. But that was all she said. The whole bunch of them, probably twenty or so young people, started to inch their way back inside the club. They were not about to risk getting clubbed themselves, so they retreated as meekly and as inconspicuously as they could. Duda even saw one young woman wiping lipstick from her lips, just in case these cops decided to enforce laws they might normally overlook.

"Call for an ambulance," Hooligan said to Duda, leaning to examine, from a distance, the young man on the pavement. The young man wasn't saying anything, but he now seemed to be coughing up blood.

"Clear on outa here," Hooligan said to those few gapers who remained too close for his comfort. They appeared to be friends of the distressed young man on the sidewalk.

"You called 'em?"

"They'll be here in ten minutes—if we're lucky."

"I'm in no mood for this nonsense. Damn it. Now I'll have to write a report on this."

These young men should have known better than to trifle with a cop whose soccer team had just been foiled by a corrupt government in an important game. Duda was thinking about how Plato would have handled the same situation—as Duda had seen him do several times—separating the two combatants, then quizzing them on what they thought they were accomplishing by fighting. In the end, they invariably promised to do better in the future and went back inside to have fun. Plato had written no reports in the time they'd been together except on the one devastating incident that had nearly killed them both. Duda had also written about that incident. Remembering what it had been like walking the streets with Plato, he smiled, and Hooligan of course misinterpreted it. "You like that?"

The kid was prostrate on the ground for twenty minutes before the ambulance arrived. He had moaned at first, but the moaning stopped after about ten minutes, and he lay with his head in a spreading pool of his own blood, the light in his eyes slowly fading. He would die on the way to the medical center.

He was not dead yet, though, and as the paramedics were examining him Hooligan stood off to the side and mumbled. "He caught me at a bad time," he said. "We should have won that game yesterday."

They were loading the kid on a stretcher into the back of their van, and Hooligan shook his head, watching them. "Damn it. I shouldn't have hit him so damn hard. I hope he's all right."

Duda and Hooligan were on duty when the bomb went off that killed the Secretary of State, but they were nowhere near the explosion and just heard about it through their fellow cops. They certainly got caught up in the aftermath, though. Not the physical aftermath of the explosion itself; the aftermath of politicians and legal authorities running around like chickens with their heads cut off. Never had Duda seen such commotion over one of these bombings, but he understood it. The Secretary of State was an important human being, where the government was concerned, and way too close to the top of the government hierarchy for his assassination to be taken lightly. If they could get him, who else could they get? And who else would they *want* to get?

Hyde convened the whole squad and gave them the kind of lecture Bigger had been fond of making. "There's an awful buzz over this one," he/she said. "We won't hear the end of it. They'll be breathing fire down our necks until we crucify somebody in public. It won't even matter if we get the right guy; we gotta get somebody. And since I'm just a little closer to the top than you are, the fire breathing is getting me first, so I'm gonna turn and send it right on down your way."

What that meant, exactly, in terms of real actions taken, wasn't clear, at least at first. It just seemed to mean there was suddenly a lot of anxiety in the compound, and they would all likely have a lot of leeway in their exercise of brutality on the general public. Beatings like the one-blow beating Hooligan had administered outside the club could occur without rhyme or reason, and nobody in the system would bat an eye. It was time to remind the public who was in charge—which really meant it was time to show the Deviants who was in charge through the vehicle of public brutality. The beatings could now commence.

And commence they did, though neither Duda nor Hooligan had much stomach for them. Poor Hooligan was unmanned when he discovered the boy he'd cracked over the skull outside the club had died. He felt terrible about it, and he wished he could take that night back. The incident robbed him of his taste for violence—whatever taste for violence he'd had, which didn't seem to be much—and he had no appetite for arbitrary displays of force that would show the Deviants the State wasn't to be trifled with. He stopped short of outright condemning the State, but just between himself and his partner, he was not about to turn into a thug. But others on the force took their charge more seriously, and a reign of terror commenced that almost certainly, when all was said and done, would prove to be a strategic error. Normals who had been indifferent to the police before began to develop a resentment of them. The reign of terror engendered fear, but it also engendered anger. The State of course had to compensate by ensuring that the fear remained greater than the anger. The citizens could hate all they wanted, but as long as they were more scared than angry they could be controlled. But it was a perilous balance to strike. If it shifted, it could mean disaster—probably for all concerned.

The State worked to maintain the balance in its favor using the valuable medium of television as much as public displays of force in the streets. They were complementary strategies, both necessary to foster the proper reverence in the State's citizens. One night a large force of SWATs and Special Opers, Drone quite possibly among them, was sent into the old city to raise havoc. The night produced a long line of body bags laid out neatly, side by side, in one of the old city's streets. Seventy-nine of them in all, and the SWATs and Special Opers milled around them, mugging for the video camera as the newscaster intoned, "The Deviants were members of the terrorist group that killed Secretary of State Chavez last month, a group headed by the notorious P. Henry."

Duda was having breakfast in a café when the news program aired, sitting in the back where he could be inconspicuous. There had been whispers among a few of the eight or ten other patrons of the café when Duda entered, but this news report elicited more audible hissing and catcalls. "They were just damn homeless people," one of the patrons said loudly. "Who the hell does the government think it's fooling?" There were other sharp comments, and sharp looks issued in his direction, and a woman at the counter started cheering when P. Henry's picture was shown.

It was Henry's picture that prompted a reaction from Duda, too, but it was not the reaction he would have expected. It went through him like a lightning bolt. He latched on to the edges of his table to steady himself, and then without even thinking he stood up abruptly to leave.

"Let me see your damn ID, officer," the man behind the counter barked at him, placing a very unflattering emphasis on "officer." "There ain't no free meals here. Cops pay like everybody else. Maybe more."

Duda mechanically extended the ID and waited while the man took his time running it through his reader. Finally, he handed it back and Duda turned. He saw nothing and heard nothing now. It didn't matter what they said to or about him.

"Have a great day out there, killer," the woman who had applauded P. Henry's picture said to his back. But Duda wasn't listening. He had to get to the street to get some air.

It was a gray morning, and damp—it felt as though snow might be in the air—and he reeled along the sidewalk heedless of where he was going. Nobody was at home, but he would not go there. He couldn't go there, for he would not sleep, and there was nothing else to do to pass the time productively. He found himself boarding a bus that would take him near Stalin's Bluff, and when he got near the base of the hill he jumped off the bus and walked to the base of the hill and started his slow ascent. There were a few people going up the hill that day, but not very many. He wondered how much he'd even be able to see from up there with the gray skies and the low cloud cover, but he didn't know where else to go. He ascended to the top of the bluff and found himself a park bench that looked out across the urban center. He saw all the concrete monoliths jutting up like a gray stubble on the face of Mother Earth, an unflattering stubble that didn't do her beautiful face justice. Then far off in the distance he noticed the old city. He hadn't noticed it when he last climbed the hill because he'd been looking off in the opposite direction. But he noticed it this time, and for some reason even though it was ancient and decrepit, it looked better to him, far off in the distance, than the hideous new city in which he'd spent his whole life so far.

He felt as though this place and this view gave him a different perspective on himself. It dawned on him as he was sitting there, looking away into the gray afternoon, that the entire extent of his life so far had been lived within this spot he was occupying and that spot out there, that spot out there in the distance. What lay beyond? He knew the sea was out there—he'd smelled and even heard it one night not long ago, when he felt his young life was about to end. But that was not the end of it—not the end of the world. There was a world out there beyond the sea that they could visit on television or in the movies, but they could not go there in person.

He felt small, even smaller than he'd ever felt before in his life. He couldn't even visit Castro, much less the land far off beyond the sea. When first Anna had left him, then Plato, he'd felt a hole inside him that seemed to fill up his whole being. And now the hole expanded, wider and wider and wider, but he did not expand with it. Instead he shrank, he kept shrinking until he thought he might disappear. He was going crazy all right. Forget about what Plato said. Plato knew so much, but he didn't know everything. And now Duda knew something he was sure Plato didn't know: that he was losing his mind, and that one of these days it would be gone with no hope of recovering it.

He sat on the bench and stared off into the distance. The day was leaden and gray, the sky and the earth seeming to merge far out at the edge of his range of vision. The sky and the Earth are becoming one, he thought. They're merging, one being absorbed into the other. The gray line of absorption was advancing toward him, gliding toward him like a wave. He waited to be absorbed by it. Take me, he thought. Let it happen.

But then it reached him and it was only rain. The rain came down softly at first, but then harder, and then much harder, and though he had been impervious to it at first it soon penetrated him, and that was the end of the bizarre trance that had seemed to possess him. He was soaked to the bone already, and the rain was coming still harder. He scrambled up from the bench and scurried like hell down the hill.

22

It was only a few days later that he was walking to work when a State limousine swept up alongside him. It pulled to the curb and he recoiled, wondering why it would stop so close to him. A man jumped out of the front passenger seat. "Get in," he said. "Damn it, get in. We're not going to hurt you." Using his finger and thumb, the man made the sign, *their* sign, the sign that had set Drone off the night she murdered Caleb Brewster.

Still, Duda hesitated, and finally the man said, "Are you Michael Duda?" And when Duda nodded he said, "Get the hell in the car!"

Duda climbed into the back seat and could not believe he was riding in such opulence. The seat, the upholstery, the metal appointments from the ashtray to the door handles. The smooth, steady ride and the quiet. The car seemed to be speeding along through city streets, if the scene outside was any indication, and yet he heard almost nothing and felt even less. They might have been standing still at the curb.

He was separated from the two men in the front seat by a tinted window. The window slid open on one side and the man who had hustled him into the car reached through and handed him a piece of heavy black cloth. "Blindfold. You'll have to put it on within the next five minutes," he said. "I'm afraid you're not permitted to see where we're going."

He put the blindfold on and snugged it up. He saw nothing now. A few minutes later he heard the window slide open and felt the man looking him over. "I'm sorry I had to be gruff with you back there. But this car is a target. I'm sure you know that. This is exactly the kind of car the Secretary of State was riding in when he was blown to smithereens. I'm sure you can appreciate that."

"Where are we going?"

"Please, Mr. Duda. Didn't I just have you put on that blindfold?"

"Aren't you the people who blew the Secretary of State to smithereens?"

There was a catch in the man's voice that told Duda his perception was right on the money. "This car is a target, Mr. Duda. We're not the only ones blowing them up. It pays to be careful.

"We'll be there in about forty minutes. If you need anything in the meantime, lean forward and rap on the glass. But please don't remove the blindfold. I'll be watching, and that would be a fatal mistake. He wants you alive and in good health, of course, but if I told him you tried something, he'd take my word for it."

Many different things went through Duda's mind in the ensuing forty minutes, but none of them was a guess as to their specific destination. He could barely tell when the car was turning, much less which streets it was taking. He could feel the car speeding up, slowing down, climbing, and descending, but that was as close as he could come to getting a read on their location. If he was going to try to figure out their destination, he'd be better off thinking of it in terms of people. The first name that came to mind was Austin's. After that there was the notorious P. Henry, whose picture on the television had jarred him. He even considered Hugo Lansky Long, another notorious figure, as a possibility. But he was riding in a government limousine.

How could any of those three have managed to secure such transportation? He felt helpless, but at least he was comfortable. If he had to be kidnapped, he supposed there was at least some merit in being kidnapped in style.

The car stopped, and he thought he heard somebody outside the vehicle talking to the driver. Then they were in motion again. They drove for another ten minutes before they stopped again, and he was again sure he heard the driver in conversation with somebody outside the car. They drove a few minutes more, and the next time they stopped he heard and felt the car's motor shut down.

The man who had hustled him into the car took him out on the passenger side. "Just a few more minutes," he said, "and we'll have you out of that blindfold."

The man steered him by gently pressuring his elbow. They went up a long walkway, and the man's voice said, "Steps. A bunch of them. There are twelve."

Then they entered a building of some kind and the man guided him across an open area with a wooden floor and into another room on the left, also with a wooden floor. The man closed the door to the room and finally removed the blindfold. Duda was in a very large room with books on shelves on three of the walls. There were hundreds of books on those shelves. There was a large desk in the room, too, and several places for sitting: a leather sofa, a pair of high-backed straight chairs, a captain's chair in each of two corners of the room. The only light in the room came from a floor lamp in one corner next to one of the captain's chairs. "Will you sit down, please?"

Duda sat on the sofa. "Would you care for a drink?" the man asked him.

"Uh ... I suppose."

His mannerisms told the man he was unprepared for the request. "I can get you a glass of water. But you're welcome to a bourbon or Scotch. Or a glass of wine, if you'd like."

"Whiskey?"

"I'll get you a bourbon. On ice. If you don't like it, I can get you something else.

"He'll be in in just a moment. You won't wait long; I promise."

After the man left, Duda surveyed the room. It was like no room he'd ever been in before. A number of times he'd been in various public buildings in the urban center—to carry out various and sundry duties associated with public life (to replace his ID card once, for instance); but they had been cold and austere compared with this. This place was rich and warm. It bespoke an elegance he would never have dreamed existed—except, perhaps, in the fantasies Plato had inspired in his head. And even then he wouldn't have been certain what to picture. He'd never seen anything like this even in the movies or on television. Plato had told him the commonwealth was careful to screen out images of wealth and luxury, but Duda in his ignorance had not known how to picture them. Seeing this room, he understood the kind of things Plato had been referring to.

As if to reinforce the notion of luxury the room had imparted, the man returned and handed him a glass so thick and ornate he thought it must belong to royalty. Then it dawned on him that he had no idea what kind of glass royalty must have—but it must be something like this. The glass was filled with a light brown liquid and contained several large ice cubes. He had sampled ice a few times before in his life, but never in these big cubes.

"Sip it," the man said. "It will bite. But once you acquire a taste for it, it will taste very smooth."

Somebody else came into the room, and when Duda looked, he saw that it was P. Henry. But in these clothes, and with a head of hair, he was almost unrecognizable. "Thank you, Dan," he said to the man who had kidnapped Duda and then brought him a bourbon. The man left the room.

"I thought I'd never see you again," Duda said.

23

The clothes and the hair suited Plato. Duda saw it right away. Even when he'd been learning from Plato on the street, he'd always felt their black police uniforms were somehow wrong. If he'd known about ancient Greece, he might have imagined his mentor in a long white robe; but even knowing only that Plato did not comport himself like a typical cop had made their police attire seem misplaced. This evening he was dressed in a light sport jacket, a collared shirt, and a pair of casual slacks, and he would have looked professorial had Duda known what professorial looks like.

"How's your bourbon, Michael?"

"I'm not sure. Your ... friend who brought me in here said it 'bites.' So I guess it must be good because it does bite."

"It'll do more than that if you drink too much of it. We'll have wine with dinner."

"I'm having dinner here?"

"You are. I'm afraid you don't have any choice in that matter. Later on we'll see."

"I guess I'll have to wait to find out what you mean by that."

"I guess you will."

"You didn't have hair in the picture of you they showed on the news."

"It wouldn't be productive. The State doesn't want to prompt any more questions than it has to."

"Did you kill the Secretary of State?"

"We'll be having dinner in just a few minutes. Are you hungry? I think you'll be pleased with the meal."

"Where are we?"

"You're asking a lot of questions, Michael. I need to talk to you before we go in to dinner."

"Is this the Forbidden City?"

"Didn't you once tell me the Forbidden City doesn't exist?"

"I told you a lot of things that weren't true. And then you told me the truth. At least I think you were telling me the truth. I've believed in you for a long time now."

"And you can go on believing in me. I've never lied to you."

"Who are you, Plato?"

"A little over a year ago, you met a young woman who led you to a certain small café in Sector C, very near your apartment. At that café, you met several men who were either café patrons or workers."

"You're talking about Austin."

"All right. Along with those men, and that young woman, I belong to an informal organization that is trying to free the people of the commonwealth."

"By bombing politicians."

"All right, Michael, by bombing politicians. Your meeting that young woman was an accident, a stroke of fortune. But the attempt to recruit you has been quite deliberate."

"Why? Come on, Plato, you know me. What possible interest can you have in recruiting me as a spy ... or a subversive, or whatever it is you people call yourselves?"

"We were all recruits at one time, Michael. I was a recruit. In fact, I was recruited in exactly the same way we've tried to recruit you. I was a police officer, just like you. My mentor decided that I had, shall we say, the right attitude, and over a period of time he educated me—just as I've tried to educate you. Just as I'd like to continue to educate you."

"Why?"

"Because I believed you have the right attitude. I might still believe it. That's why you're here tonight. I tried to tell you there's another possible world besides the one you're living in. I tried to show you. And I think you believe me. But I'm not sure."

"So you brought me to the Forbidden City—is this the Forbidden City?"

"Yes."

"But if the rumors were—are—true, the Forbidden City is the seat of the government. It's the home of the State."

"Correct."

"And you're here, right in the middle of it?"

"And I'm not the only one. Almost a million people live in the Forbidden City, Michael: politicians, military leaders, diplomats, corporate moguls, engineers, athletes, entertainers. And don't forget the service workers. Somebody has to maintain the city. And somebody has to be the face of the State. There's an airport two miles from here. People use it to travel all over the world."

"So you work for the State."

"Not anymore, but I did. And many of the people in our organization work for it—just as you do.

"Michael, revolutions don't just spring up from nowhere. They wouldn't be revolutions if they did. People inside the State are the ones who started the revolution. Many of them continue to work for the State, some in positions of considerable authority. But they're not any less revolutionary for being employed by the State. In fact, it's working for the State that makes them valuable to our organization. They provide leverage. And any revolution, to be successful, requires leverage. It requires people working on the inside."

He looked at his watch. "Listen. That's what I wanted to talk to you about before we go in to dinner. You weren't recruited because you're uniquely qualified—any more than I was recruited because I'm uniquely qualified. We thought you might have the right attitude and abilities to be of use to our organization. Whenever we think somebody might have the right attitude and abilities, we probe the waters. We get to know the person so we can try to decide if that person will be useful to us.

"I still believe you can be one of us, Michael, but there's at least one person here tonight who doesn't believe in you."

"Who?"

"I'm not going to tell you. But I can tell you that that person didn't want me to bring you here. That person thinks I'm taking a risk that's not worth taking by bringing you here."

"That person might be right."

"No, Michael, that person is not right. You may not be with us, but I know you'll never be against us. I know you well enough to say that with certainty. Am I right?"

Duda looked him squarely in the eye, the better to make sure his answer sounded credible. "I would never betray you, Plato. Never. I think way too much of you to do that. But that doesn't mean I'm one of you, either."

"All right, I accept that. But I wanted to make sure you understood that one person, at least, is afraid you'll leave us tonight and run straight to the authorities."

"Not a chance."

"I believe you. But there's something else before we go in. The people in our organization conveniently manage to lose their microchips."

"What?"

"If you go with us, we'll have your microchip surgically removed. It'll be done before you're returned to the city."

"What? That's insane, Plato. The scanners will find me out in a month. I'll go through the wrong doorway—or I'll take my next physical—or—"

"We'll implant a dummy, Michael. It'll still show up on the scanners, but it won't record any useful data for the State to use to track you."

"How in the hell do you—"

"I told you we have other people in our organization, Michael. People from all walks of life. None of us in the organization still has a functioning chip. Not a chip that functions in the way the State wants it to function, anyway."

"How do you get away with it?"

"I told you, there are almost a million people here in what you know as the Forbidden City, Michael. There are almost ten times that many people down in the city where you live.

"The State's True Believers, as we like to call them—I think you call them 'Crusaders'—make up about ten percent of the country's population. They *are* the State. Some of us are against them, obviously. But most citizens just go along, don't they? The Normals. They don't care what the government says or does, as long as they can keep eating and sleeping regularly, and their needs are more or less provided for—"

"And they can go to the soccer games on Sundays."

"What?"

"Never mind. I was just thinking of somebody. I see your point."

"Good. But Michael?"

"Yes."

"If you do get a dummy implant, you need to know that if the State does find you out, you'll never be seen or heard from again. It does happen. We've lost some good people because the State found a reason to be curious about them and did some investigating."

"Like Caleb Brewster?"

"Who?"

"The boy my partner killed in the old city last year. He was just a boy, and she killed him. But he still had a readable chip. A normal chip, if that's what you call it. A chip that was doing the State's business."

"Probably just hadn't undergone the procedure yet. There are more of us than you realize, Michael. And we're thankful for that. But we are still vulnerable. You need to know that. We lose people all the time. It's an occupational hazard. That's why I wanted to make sure you understand the risks.

"It's also why I wanted to let you know that you don't have the full confidence of the people who are here tonight. Not all of them. And it's time to go to dinner."

"I'll ask questions, Plato. I'm not going to keep my mouth shut for anybody—not even you."

"Ask all the questions you want. I mean that. I want you to be satisfied that you're finding out everything you want to know. As long as you promise not to sell us out."

"You have my word on that."

"You've barely touched your drink, my young friend. And it's time to go to dinner."

24

As they were leaving the room Plato referred to as "the library," he said to Duda, "You'd have full access to all these books, Michael."

And Duda said, "I've never been that much of a reader."

"You've never had the chance, have you? Or the encouragement. In this country the reading selection is extremely limited, unless you know the right people. You already know that; I've pointed it out to you. And now you know that I'm one of the right people."

"You've expanded my horizons, Plato. It's the reason I love you."

"And reading the right books can expand them a lot further, my young friend. And I can help you find the right books—books the State would go out of its way to make sure you *don't* read."

They had passed through what seemed like a very large foyer—larger than four of Duda's apartments arranged wall-to-wall in a square—and then through an equally large sitting room, and finally they entered a large, rectangular dining room. Two men and one woman were in the dining room, the men dressed similarly to Plato, the woman wearing a dress. Duda recognized the woman. Everybody sat down at the table as the two newcomers entered. The long table was set for five people, all at one end. The woman sat at the head of the table.

"Can we use first names?" the woman said, and without waiting for an answer she extended her hand to Duda. "I understand your name is Michael. You can call me Margaret."

Duda nodded politely. He was suddenly very nervous. "I've seen you on television, Margaret. Without hair, though. And in the uniform of the State."

"Well, the hair is something we take care of with a little trick involving a skullcap—and a Budenovka just like yours. The dress is even easier. I never wear the uniform unless I have to appear in public."

"You're in a different place now, Michael," Plato reminded him.

"A place I haven't even seen on television."

"I can't believe you actually watch the television, Michael," Margaret said. "It seems as though nobody does—except for the entertainment shows, of course. Everybody down in the city watches those."

"I'll take responsibility for Michael's television-viewing habits," Plato volunteered. "I'm afraid I've corrupted the young man."

"We can always use more bad influences like you, Patrick."

The other two men were named James and Alex. When Alex greeted him, Duda felt fairly certain who one of his doubters was.

"Do you need your drink freshened up, Michael?" Margaret asked him.

"I'm fine, thank you."

"What about everybody else?" she said. "Any of you need anything?"

"I could use a Scotch," Plato said. "A little ice."

The other two said they were fine.

Margaret gave a signal of some kind, and a man in a white serving jacket entered the room. She ordered Plato's drink and the man left. A minute later he returned with the drink, and only a minute or so after that a second white-jacketed man came in with a bottle of wine and circled the table, filling each wine glass in turn with a deep red liquid that was translucent for all its rich color. The two servers left the room.

"I won't ask you if you had a pleasant trip out from the city, Michael," Margaret said. "I'm sure you didn't."

He smiled at her in reply and finally sipped his drink. "I didn't know this place was here."

"Most people in the city don't know we're here. And it's a lucky thing for the State they don't."

There was a pause then, and finally James said, "Well, we seem unwilling to talk this evening. So let me ask you a question, Michael. Would you say there's unrest in the city these days?"

"Yes," Duda said without hesitation.

"And why would you say that is?"

"Because the cops are going around beating the hell out of people."

"You're a cop."

"I am."

"Have you been beating the hell out of people?"

"No."

"Why not?"

"I don't believe in it. I don't think anybody benefits from cops who beat the hell out of people. Not even the State."

"Why not? Doesn't the State have the power?"

"Not if the people get mad enough."

James smiled at him, and Alex stepped in. "Would you say the people are mad enough now?"

"I doubt it. If the electricity stays on this winter, and they have enough food, they'll be all right. People will put up with a lot."

"A lot more than they should," James said.

"They're a lot of sheep," Alex muttered, and Michael was reminded of his own musing about the people on that night the previous year when Plato had questioned him about the role of the police. "But if we had our way, they'd still be sheep."

"If we had our way, they'd be better off than they are now," Margaret said.

The two white-jacketed men came back in the room with a large silver serving tray and served up green salads. One of them also set out an assortment of rolls in a basket.

"Please serve yourselves the bread," Margaret said. "This is not a State dinner."

"Well, in a way it is," Plato grinned. "The State just doesn't know about it."

Following the others' lead, Duda took a roll and started in gingerly on his salad.

"Explain yourself, Alex," James said. "Are you saying the people don't deserve to be free just because they're 'sheep'?"

"I'm saying no such thing. I'm saying all of us would be better off if they were free—if we were all free. But they don't know that. And they would never fight for it."

"Do you think he's right, Michael?" James asked.

"Yes. They don't know what they don't have." He spread his hands and arms slightly as if to take in the table. "I've never eaten like this before. I don't even know what these things are."

"Well, there are three more courses," Plato said. "So don't gorge yourself on bread. You'll eat more in one meal tonight than you eat in three or four days down there."

"My point exactly," Duda said. "If I don't know these things, and I'm a cop, what do you think the ordinary commoner knows?" He looked at James. "Yes, sir, I'm saying I think he's definitely right that they don't know what they don't have and don't even know what they'd be fighting for."

"They were starting to fight for that Long bastard," Alex said. "And he's nothing but a gangster."

"But that's exactly the kind of thing that works with most people, Alex," Plato said. "Emotions. Stir 'em up. Make 'em angry. And give 'em somebody to be angry at. If you can make them angry enough, and then give them a target for their hatred, you'll get them to fight."

"They were ready to fight before the virus came along," Duda said.

Margaret suppressed a snort, holding a cloth napkin up to her face. "What do you know about the virus, Michael?"

Duda shrugged. "I don't know. The same as everybody else, I guess. It seemed to come out of nowhere, and suddenly it killed a bunch of people off. And then just as suddenly it went away.

"The State blamed the whole thing on ... *you*."

They all looked around the table at each other as if unsure what to say—or perhaps whether to say anything at all. "Well—you are the Deviants, aren't you?"

Finally Plato spoke up. "All right, Michael. Let's say we're the Deviants, as the State calls us. Do you think we were responsible for the virus?"

"You were still my partner then, Plato. Was there something you weren't telling me?"

"Think about it, Michael," Margaret said. "You're in the government. You have a group of people who are angry and start trouble. They're gaining momentum. Do you attack them? Do you go into their neighborhoods and arrest them? And if you do, then what happens?"

"Their fellow citizens see what's happening and start to get worked up too," Plato answered for her. "Especially the young people who are easily excited—easily riled up."

"Their numbers start to grow," Margaret picked up the story again. "How do you stop them without causing a ruckus? How do you defuse their movement without expending your own resources, destroying your own properties, and probably creating even more resentment?"

Duda stared at her, only beginning to comprehend. "A virus might come in handy, don't you think?" Plato filled in. "It could target a certain group of people, who would then be conveniently carted off to medical centers."

"And never seen or heard from again," Duda finished.

"Problem solved," James said. "And so neatly, too. No bloodshed. No violent destruction. No infrastructure wrecked or soldiers lost."

"Think about how easy it all was," Plato added. "Every person at that rally in the People's Central Park could be easily tracked."

"Along with some annoying members of the press, a few celebrities, a few engineers and tech people and troublesome scientists, and even a government figure or two who seemed to lack faith in the State," said James. "Round them all up, cart them all off to makeshift 'medical centers,' and they're gone in no time."

"To be commemorated with a huge collage in the People's Central Park," Margaret said. "Those are their real pictures, by the way. Do you think there's a chance they'll ever be remembered for the right reason?"

Alex said, "Don't look at us that way. None of us had anything to do with it. All of us are in the Outer Party. We don't get to make those big decisions."

You just get to blow people up, Duda started to say, but he thought better of it. It was too early in this conversation for such a remark. There were other things to ask about, other things to learn.

"If there are other disruptions in the food supply this winter, and more power outages, do you think the people will be angry enough to consider rising up again?"

It was Alex who had asked the question, but Duda didn't get a chance to answer it. The waiters came in with their serving platter again, dispensed bowls of soup, and removed the sullied plates and silverware. Then they were gone again.

"It's a consommé," Margaret said to Duda. "A palate cleanser. It should set your taste buds up for the main course."

"And to think," Duda had sufficient confidence to say, "for many people in the city this would *be* the main course."

"A fitting time for you to answer my question," Alex reminded him.

"Are you saying you would starve people to make them angry? Intentionally starve them?"

"Absolutely not."

"I don't think you understand how our current system works, Michael," Margaret intervened. "We have one person who is essentially in charge of our entire food supply, our Secretary of Agriculture. He has people working for him all across the country, but still, how many of them can there be? For the sake of argument, let's say there are a thousand of them. He has to take the input from all those people and decide what will be grown and where and how it will be distributed, relying entirely on the competence of those who inform him."

"And their honesty," James added.

"And their devotion to their work," Plato added. "Many of them have other concerns besides seeing to it that the people of ..., say, Shwe are well supplied with wheat for the winter."

The three of them all laughed at what appeared to Duda to be an inside joke.

"And don't forget the bribes they must take, the corporate leaders they must pander to, and the dirty deals they must negotiate with other countries to supplement their personal wealth," Margaret chipped in.

"And in the case of our current Secretary of the Agriculture, there's also the mistress he must keep satisfied," Alex reminded them.

And they all laughed again. Duda even smiled faintly, though he didn't really know what he was smiling at. But they seemed to be enjoying themselves.

"There are no market forces here," Margaret explained. "People who know nothing about your wants, needs, or interests are deciding what you'll eat, and how much of it, Michael. Do you honestly think they can make it through a year without miscalculating?

"They blame us, of course. But we are their 'virus.' We are their scapegoats. There's never a question of whether there'll be shortages of this or that. The only question is how the people will react."

"Long will be back," Alex said. "We don't know when, but he'll be back. And although we mock him as a reckless gangster, he's an intelligent man. He knows how to appeal to his peers. He knows what's important to them. And if they're unhappy enough, he can influence them. That's why I asked the question."

"What do *you* think?" Duda asked Plato. "You're almost as much a man of the people as I am."

"I think we're a lost cause," Plato answered. "I think we stand and fall firmly on principle, and principle means nothing to the people of the world."

"Oh, stop it," James said. "That answer is too easy. It's the answer of a defeatist. And you're no defeatist."

Plato looked at Duda. "I talked to you about this when we were partners. I just didn't tell you I was part of this movement. But I told you about our philosophy without telling you it was my philosophy.

"We believe in the inherent dignity of the individual human being. That every person has rights as a human being, and that government's job is to protect those rights.

Do you remember back about a year or so ago, when I told you the next time you visited Anna that you should ask Austin about 'natural rights'?"

He remembered—except that Austin hadn't been at the café that night, and when he asked the cook that question he'd been told to mind his own business. "I remember," he said.

"That was a kind of signal," Plato said. "A signal to Austin. Basically, I was telling him that I trusted you. I'm sorry now he wasn't there to answer the question.

"Well, better late than never. I'm answering the question for you now. And do you happen to remember when I asked you about our motto as police officers?"

"To protect and to serve. I was thinking about it just a few minutes ago."

"And do you remember that I asked you *who* we were supposed to protect and serve?"

"And I said 'the State.'"

"You remember."

"And that was the wrong answer. I should have said 'the people.'"

25

T he waiters came in just then and whisked away their soup bowls, and within a few minutes they were delivering the main course. In the meantime, Duda suddenly felt thirsty and finished off his entire glass of bourbon. Then he took a long sip of wine and asked one of the waiters to bring more. He looked at the meal he was being served. "This is beef?"

"A filet of sirloin," Margaret informed him. "Those are a type of seasoned potato, very tasty, and the green stalks are asparagus."

"I've seen that before."

The waiter came back and filled his wine glass all the way to the top. When he was gone, Duda asked Plato, "So what's wrong with your philosophy? What's wrong with principle?"

Plato was in the middle of a bite of his steak, so he finished chewing before he answered. "It doesn't move people. People are not moved by an idea."

"It's moved them before," James said.

"But that was a long time ago."

"And people then were still people. They had to be taught to believe in something, and they were taught to believe in it. And embrace it. And die for it. It took years to teach them, but they learned."

"And then it died too," Alex said. "And then the State came along."

"And the people are not moved by a principle. They're moved by their stomachs. And the temperature gauges in their apartments," Plato said.

"And a loudmouth who blames the Chinese and the Russians for their problems. And he can coax a groundswell out of them in the blink of an eye."

"Stop it, you two," Margaret said fiercely. "Don't forget that the State also lives by a principle. Don't you dare leave that out." She looked at Duda. "The principle of equality."

"But that's a farce," James said. "This meal is proof of that. Did you eat like this in the city, Michael?"

"No. Of course not."

"And there you have it," James said. "Equality. If you can keep it hidden. Don't be such a defeatist, Plato. I implore you. Or you either, Alex."

He looked at Duda. "What would you think of a system in which you were free to choose things for yourself, Michael? If you want steak, you eat steak?"

"If you can afford it," Alex said. "Can you afford it?"

"You can afford it much better than the people can now!" Margaret interjected, again fiercely. "You don't need to be fooled into believing such things don't even exist."

She looked at Duda. "Why is it that people down in the city don't even know this"—she gestured around her—"don't even know this exists? Why is that, Michael? Why can't they be entrusted with that knowledge? Why can't they see it on the television, even, or read about it in books? Why can't they find out about it on the Internet? Why does their viewing have to be restricted?

"And what about their travel? Why can't they even visit such places? Why do they have to get permission— from somebody like me—just to visit other places in their own *country*?"

"Resources are scarce," Duda answered her. "They have to be used prudently."

"Doled out by the indolent Secretary of Agriculture," James said.

"When he's not on top of his mistress," Alex added.

"Or beneath her," Plato said.

"I know you're not sure about us," Margaret said. "I see it in your eyes. Patrick has told me."

"You kill people," Duda blurted out. "You murder people. I was almost murdered by you myself."

"State officials," Margaret said. "Corporate honchos and rich celebrities and famous athletes who live like royalty. Would you like to know what they think of *you*? I just told you: They don't trust you to know what you don't know. That's how much they trust you."

"Not just those people, though. Other people die too. Ask Plato. He's witnessed it."

"Collateral damage. It's regrettable, but it can't be helped."

"Remember the virus," James added. "Try to remember that the State kills too. And it doesn't even tell you."

"It's the price of getting involved," Margaret said. "Freedom comes with a cost."

"And so does living as a pliant Normal," Plato said. "Only they try not to let you see the price you're paying. They try to hide it from you."

"So you're telling me resources are *not* scarce? Are they lying about that?"

"We're telling you they don't have any business depriving *you* of those resources while they have full use of them. We're telling you you should be able to make choices for yourself—just like they do."

"It really all comes down to that," James said. "Are they better than you, smarter than you? Do they know your needs better than you do? And do you trust them to make decisions for you? Let's say resources are scarce. All right—do they know better than you how to make wise use of them? Do you really believe they do?"

"Because if you do," Margaret said, "you should *meet* this Secretary of Agriculture you're placing so much trust in."

"If he's not on top of his mistress," Alex said.

"Or beneath her," Plato added.

There was a pause, and then Margaret said, "Eat your food, Michael. You're eating very little. We brought you out here to feed you a good meal—so you could see what you're missing that these wonderful planners don't want you to have. Enjoy it. At least have one good meal before you go back and serve the glorious State."

They all ate and drank for a few minutes, and there was no conversation at all. Duda was silently wondering how the food would sit on his stomach. Such was the price of affluence: It might give him a tummy ache. But it tasted wonderful in the meantime.

Finally, he held up his wine glass. "This is really something," he said. "I've never had wine before."

"The wise State knows better than to trust you with it," Margaret said. "You might get ideas. That you're actually entitled to such pleasures."

"Better to get you drunk on the cheap swill they make available to you," James said.

"What you don't know won't hurt you," Plato said.

"Ignorance is bliss," James said.

"I've never heard that one," Duda said.

"Old saying. Very old saying."

"Eat," Margaret said. "Let the young man eat."

They ate. The waiters came in to check on them and filled the wine glasses. Duda raised his glass to the waiter in a gesture of appreciation.

"I'm worried about Long," Alex said, finally. "I'm worried he'll get them to rise up and follow somebody who's no better than the government they follow now."

"Eat," Margaret said.

"I'm sorry. I'm just distracted."

After that there were only a few pleasantries about the meal. The waiters returned with dessert—some kind of sweet pastry, again like nothing Duda had ever experienced. They had desserts in the city, from time to time, but they were bland compared to this stuff. Then there was coffee, and then more wine, but this time a sweet wine. Margaret called it a "cordial." She asked Michael if he'd like to try a cigar. He'd never even heard of them. He accepted the offer.

He was watching the way they rolled the cigars in their fingers, savoring their smell. They seemed to go so well with the cordials.

"Don't you think it's odd that you're not even permitted to smoke cigarettes in the city, Michael?" Margaret asked him.

"But people do it. Many people do it. I'll bet they smoke these things, too. I just haven't seen them."

"On the black market. They can probably get cigars on the black market. They can get a lot of things on the black market, can't they?"

"She's opening up the conversation again, Michael," James said.

"I'm so sorry," she said—but she was not sorry. "I can't help myself. He needs to see. He needs to think about these things."

"I have to take Michael to see Dr. Peters," Plato said. "We're supposed to be there at ten."

Margaret sighed. "You'll have to leave soon, in that case. I hope we haven't bored you, Michael."

"Not at all. I have to admit, I've never been bored in Pl—in Patrick's company."

He was instructed to put on the blindfold again before they went outside. The ride to see Dr. Peters was a short one, and Plato sat beside him in the back seat of the limousine and didn't speak at first. Finally he said, "Did you enjoy your dinner, my young friend?"

"I've never eaten like that before."

"How about the company?"

"Very engaging. I've seen Margaret on the television before and would never have thought ... not in a million years."

"She's the most passionate among us—in case you couldn't tell. And the most idealistic. The woman is a national treasure. And the State doesn't even know why. She's a traitor to them and a national treasure to us.

"There are people who take enormous chances for the cause we believe in, Michael. People who die for it."

Behind the blindfold Duda was thinking about Anna.

"You'll be one of the lucky ones," Plato continued. "You probably won't have to do anything extreme. Unless ..."

"Unless you need somebody killed."

"It's possible. It's not likely. But you will have to talk to people. Cautiously. The way I did with you. Nothing more than that.

"I've never participated in a bombing myself, Michael. Did you know that? I've helped to plan them—and not even much of that. Nothing like my reputation. I've helped with logistics.

"I've mostly become a scapegoat. It's what happens. The State has to have people to blame, and it has to show those people on the television sometimes. Or the Internet. You're a cop; you've seen the pictures."

Duda said nothing, still tucked away behind his mask, but he was reminded of the bombing that first night they were together as partners.

"Think of somebody working in an office," Plato continued. "People all around, constantly around them. They're constantly under pressure. Constantly scrutinized. They believe in freedom, but they can't even talk about it for fear they'll be punished. Think about *them,* Michael."

"I don't even know such peo—"

"There are *millions* of them." He said it with the same kind of passion Margaret had shown, a passion he'd never exhibited with Duda, and it took Duda by surprise. "They are enemies of the State, Michael," he said evenly, after a long pause. "*We* are enemies of the State. Just by talking, just by expressing ourselves, we make ourselves enemies of the State. You don't even need to plant a bomb to be a traitor to the State. All you have to do is say the wrong things."

"Then what's the point of it? What's the point of it if it's nothing but talk?"

"Because it hast to start somewhere. It starts with an idea. Then there's talk. And then … maybe …"

The car had stopped, and Dan, the driver, was getting out. "You don't have to do this, Michael. I won't think less of you if you decide not to do it."

Dr. Peters was a short, portly man with a bald pate and a fringe of gray hair. Like the others who had welcomed Duda that evening, the doctor was wearing causal dress clothes, not the uniform of the State. And like the others, he appeared to live in opulence—opulence he shared with his wife. Their home was not a mansion like the one Duda and Plato had just come from, but it was far more luxurious than anything Duda had experienced in the cold city.

Dr. Peters took them to his "study," as he called it. "Patrick has explained the procedure to you?" he asked

when they were all comfortably seated—with yet another drink in their hands.

"Sort of."

"Well, it's really simple. We take out one chip and replace it with another. A very, very simple surgical procedure. Takes about half an hour, start to finish. That includes the time for the anesthetic to take effect.

"The microchips the State puts in people are really just very basic GPS tracking devices. They're not as sophisticated as our compatriots think they are, and as the State is very happy to let us believe they are. They can't record your voice or take pictures.

"What they do accomplish is tracking you wherever you go. And the data they provide is synced with a huge store of information to provide a fairly complete picture of your life and movements. For instance, if Patrick here and I were still chipped the way they intended, the data could be synced to inform our surveillants that we were here together at this time. It wouldn't explain *why* we're here. The State's super spies would have to extrapolate that from the data collected."

Duda was remembering many instances when he and other cops used the data from these chips to "extrapolate," as Dr. Peters called it. He was thinking in particular of the night following Caleb Brewster's murder.

"The chip we replace the State's chip with contains essentially worthless data: data loops that basically just operate like flashing lights. They're 'colorful,' in their own way, but they also basically tell the surveillants nothing useful. They can't track anybody with one of these implants. All they get from them is noise.

"It's conceivable one of the State's chips could malfunction and be turned into one of these." He held up the tiny chip for Duda to see. "In fact, it happens. It happens with about two of every hundred chips, and the failure rate is growing. Across the country, about a thousand Normals a day are found with these defective chips. So if you should get caught—if you should fall under suspicion and you think your only option is to lie about the chip, use that knowledge to try to get yourself off the hook. It might work—though I have to warn you, it probably won't.

"The problem is the scar. I'm a good surgeon, but even I can't perform this surgery without leaving a trace of a scar. It's a tiny scar, but a decent surgeon—even one trained by our government—can detect it."

He held the tiny chip between his thumb and forefinger for Duda to see. "When our operatives disappear on us—and I have to be honest with you and tell you that it does happen—it's almost always because of this little thing right here."

26

That winter was milder than the previous winter, but Hooligan nonetheless complained about the cold. "We can't go to the beach in wintertime," he said, referring as always to his youth in Castro, speaking of it in the present tense as if he were still living it, as if he hadn't left it behind. Then he would catch himself and switch to the past tense. "We didn't swim then; the water was too cold. But we could go and light a fire and cook shellfish and get drunk. We had the best parties. Right on the beach."

He was immersed in a reverie, lost in warm memories of youthful drunkenness at parties on the beach, but then he seemed to snap out of it and abruptly ended the story, though he clearly had more to tell. The excited tone of his voice and the way his eyes were shining told Duda he still had more to tell. But he also seemed to have become a little more introspective lately, ever since the unfortunate incident with the kid outside the club, and now he was more self-conscious. "Sorry. I know I talk about it too much."

"Maybe if you didn't think about it so much," Duda offered helpfully.

"Sure."

"Were the people happy in Castro?" It was a strange question for him to ask his partner. He rarely asked him for any depth of analysis that wasn't related to soccer or the weather, the only two subjects Duda was sure interested him.

"Happy? I don't know; I guess. They seemed happy."

"Weren't there shortages there?"

"Well, yeah. But everybody has those. There's just not enough to go around." He thought for a minute. "At least we weren't freezing. Freezing is terrible. The heat is bad in Castro, but it's not terrible. A guy can live with the heat. If you have to have shortages, it's better to have them in the heat."

It dawned on Duda then that this was probably the most interesting thing Hooligan had ever said to him.

The constant chatter about soccer and the complaining about the cold in New Leningrad were annoying, but Hooligan's sudden reticence to do his duty had the potential to become a problem. One night they were on their usual beat in the entertainment district when a young man—a boy, really—started hollering at them outside the entrance of a club. Duda thought immediately of Hooligan's previous skull-cracking experience, and he felt his partner recoiling even before they stopped to address the boy. "Let me get this," he said.

"Fascist pigs!" the boy was shouting. "Cops are fascist pigs!"

"Let me get this," Duda repeated to Hooligan. "Don't reach for your nightstick. Just stand a little behind me."

"You guys are all fascist pigs!" the boy shouted.

"He's drunk," his friends were saying. "Please don't hurt him. He doesn't know what he's saying."

"I think people always say what they mean when they're drunk," Duda responded. "It's when they're *not* drunk that they hide their feelings."

He stopped a few feet away from the boy. His hands were by his sides. "Do you know what a fascist is?" he asked the boy.

"They're pigs. They work for the government and they beat people up."

"True. I've seen it happen." Strictly for his partner's benefit, he tried not to make it sound as though he was referring to a specific incident. And, in fact, he *wasn't* thinking specifically of that incident. Unfortunately, there were others besides that one that he could easily recall. Too many others. Mattock alone had piled up more corpses than Duda cared to remember.

"So are you gonna beat *me* up?" The boy had opened himself up a little as if he were issuing a challenge. Duda pictured Drone in this situation, and it almost made him smile. If the kid wanted to see somebody wield a nightstick, he needed to pick this fight with Drone.

"I don't think so," he said.

"Why not?" The boy suddenly seemed offended that Duda had no intention of beating him up.

"I don't know why I would."

"Because I called you a pig. A *fascist* pig."

"Yeah, but I don't beat people up. I thought you said fascist pigs beat people up."

The boy appeared to be flummoxed. He didn't know what to say. His friends were urging him to go back inside the club. He was trying to put on a show for them but it wasn't working out.

"I only beat people up if I have to," Duda said. "I really don't like beating people up. It's no fun for me."

The boy looked stymied. He wasn't sure what his next move should be. "So you're not gonna beat me up?"

"I don't think so," Duda said. "I just don't see a need to do that."

"But you're a fascist pig!"

"Well all right, but I don't beat people up. You said fascist pigs beat people up. I wish you'd get your story straight."

The boy just looked confused. He was searching for his next retort but he couldn't find it. His friends slowly turned him back toward the entrance to the club. They were chattering about the music inside, trying to distract him. He looked very unhappy, but he followed along.

"G'night," Duda nodded to a couple of the boys' friends. One of the girls mouthed the words "Thank you" as they continued gently coaxing the defeated warrior back inside the club.

In the meantime, Duda and Hooligan were slinking quietly away. "Are you all right?" Duda asked his partner.

"What?"

"You're sweating. You'd think we were in Castro."

The attempt at humor didn't appear to have much effect. "I'm all right," Hooligan nodded weakly. But he was not all right.

"I'm a little worried about my partner," Duda said to Hyde the following morning. Then he told him/her about Hooligan's behavior around the young heckler outside the club. "He was sweating," Duda said. "I don't know what he would have done if he'd had to handle that situation himself."

Around the compound it was rumored that Hyde attended gatherings of an evening at which men dressed as women formerly dressed, in the old days, and women dressed as men formerly dressed. Duda noticed a tiny lipstick smudge at one corner of Hyde's mouth that suggested he/she had attended one of those gatherings the night before. "He recently handled such an incident and did just fine with it."

"He killed that kid."

"I know. That's the incident I'm referring to."

"But I think it bothered him."

"Bothered him? He's a cop, Duda. He did his job."

Killing people is part of his job? Duda wanted to say, especially in light of his conversations with Plato over the last year. But he didn't say that because he didn't want to get into a philosophical discussion with Hyde about their job responsibilities. "I just worry that he might be having trouble accepting it." Listening to himself, he realized he just couldn't make this sound the way he wanted it to sound.

"He has to accept it, Duda. The kid gave him trouble; he hit the kid over the head; the kid died. And that's the end of it."

The kid didn't really give him trouble, he wanted to say. And that might be why Hooligan is struggling to accept what he did. It bothers him.

That was what he wanted to say, but he didn't say any of it. Instead he contemplated a wisecrack about Hyde's smudged lipstick, thought better of it, and left.

27

A week or so later came the first night Hugo Lansky Long commandeered the State's airwaves—not during the early evening educational programming but later on, during the entertainment programming between eight p.m. and midnight, when people were actually watching. A popular musical act was performing when the picture simply changed, quite abruptly, from the musical act to a portrait of Long on a neutral background. The audio migrated with it. Only Long's head and shoulders appeared in the camera shot. It was fairly obvious he didn't want to give his location away.

"Good evening, fellow citizens," he began. "I think you know who I am. I promise I'll take only a few minutes of your precious time, just three minutes of your time. Because nobody appreciates your time more than I do. Nobody knows better than I do how hard you toil in your labors for the State, and how much you enjoy your small reward of a few minutes' relaxation in front of the television of an evening. I am you, fellow citizens, I am you!"

"That's why I'm calling on you to rise up with me. Rise up against the government that oppresses us all. Rise up and join your voice with mine in protest of our oppression."

At this point Long's image was displaced by a series of images of people around the world living in luxury and ease: people in extravagant clothing, with extravagant hair and jewelry and face paint, doing extravagant things, things the common citizens could formerly only dream of doing in VREs. They could no longer dream of doing them at all now that such fantasies of luxury had been stripped from the VREs' repertoire. The State *hoped* they would no longer dream of them, at any rate.

Interspersed with the images of luxury and ease were other images depicting the ordinary lives of the Normals: a woman huddling beneath her blanket in her frigid apartment, a man toiling in an agricultural field, a protestor lying prostrate after being beaten senseless in the People's Central Park.

The images passed in a slow but meaningful procession as Long's voice provided the soundtrack. "The State tells us it is helpless to provide a better standard of living for us all. It can't keep our bellies full or our bodies warm. It tells us the world's meager resources are being spread thin, as thin as they can possibly be spread, so that all the world's people may share equally in those resources.

"But while many of us do with so little, sometimes with nothing at all, the world's elite enjoy the lives of royalty, of kings and queens! They swim in luxury at your expense. We provide the labor, fellow citizens, but who enjoys the fruits of that labor? Who enjoys so much of the world's bounty while we enjoy so little?

"Do you see them, fellow citizens, do you see them? Look at them now; see them again. See them and remember, always remember. Do not ever forget. We hear from our government that we must bear the burden of providing all the world's people with equal shares of the world's limited bounty, but elites in China, in western Europe, in Africa, and yes, right here at home, live in luxury.

"It's time for this exploitation to end! I am calling on the State's workers to take a hiatus from their labors this coming Monday. Don't serve your masters; serve yourselves. Stay home, or join us for a protest rally in the People's Central Park, here in New Leningrad. Those in other urban centers should find out the location of your local rally from your local National Workers Alliance representatives. We're easy to find if you look for us. We're far more numerous than you may realize!

"The State has held us down long enough. Workers of the commonwealth, unite! Unite to end exploitation and oppression. Unite to bring social justice to our nation. To overthrow our slave masters and take charge of our own lives.

"Now is the time, fellow citizens. If not now, when. If not us, who then? Join us on Monday at ten a.m.!"

The series of images ended as the speech ended. The television returned to State control. The popular musical act was followed by a comedian who earned his generous entitlements at the expense of greedy capitalists and other such arcane oddballs who had made the world a terrible place before the glorious socialist republic came along to redeem it, and who now served the republic only as fodder for comedians—or, in dramatic productions, as villains to be conquered by the State's heroes and heroines. The comedian was followed by an actor who had just starred in such a heroic role, in a film in which the protagonist flirts with selfishness and greed before learning the valuable lesson that sharing with the world is the essence of moral goodness. His performance brought audiences to tears. Neither the comedian nor the dramatic actor disclosed that he lived in the Forbidden City. In fact, the television studios that produced all of the State's programming were in the Forbidden City. Most of the audience certainly didn't know that and probably wouldn't have cared. They just wanted their entertainment back.

Long's speech was of course the talk of the nation the following day. Both government television stations had been taken over, a feat nobody currently living in the commonwealth could recall ever happening before. How had Long pulled it off? The country's technical specialists confabbed about it in water cooler sessions, speculated on it, and shook their heads in bemused respect. In public they reviled him; in private they revered him. Getting such a stunt past the State's security experts was no easy task. Even those who disapproved of Long's message respected his wherewithal in disseminating it. Most Normals had at one time or another entertained fantasies about somehow cheating their government. There were the absolute loyalists, of course (the country's Drones), but they were vastly outnumbered by the Normals who, even the most timorous among them, had at least fantasized about subversion, at least in some minute way. And there was a large percentage of the population that proudly considered its participation in the black market as a means of subversion.

Few of them were truly serious about subverting the government, though—subverting it in some serious way that would actually put them personally at risk—subverting it the way Hugo Lansky Long had dared to do. For most, what Long provided was a vicarious thrill, an episode of wish fulfillment, short-lived but oh-so-savory. But there were those few, those few who might not take the initiative themselves but would follow the one who did, and it was on those few that Long's whole movement relied. Those few would help him goad the others, help him loosen the State's hold on them. Were they happy with their lives? Truly happy? If not, did they blame the State for their unhappiness? It was critical to Long's project that they be both frustrated and willing to take out their frustrations on those who ostensibly provided for them, those who had established and now maintained the system of rights and obligations that sustained them all. They first had to acquire the perception that the government was causing them misery, then—and this was most important—they had to suffer enough to seek retribution. They had to feel such pain and bitterness and anger they were willing to risk their lives by acting on it. Driving them to such a breaking point was a monumental task. But Long felt up to it. And he was willing to risk everything, his life of course included, to make the effort.

He had contemplated a campaign to reveal the fraud behind the Dev1 virus. The State had murdered its own citizens to suppress a rebellion! But he knew exposing the State's treachery would never get the Normals sufficiently riled up to rebel themselves—although it would help to stoke the flames of rage in those who were already committed to him, so he would absolutely exploit it at the big rally on Monday. But to grow their numbers he'd need to create fresh miseries. He'd have to induce greater suffering, and he'd have to convince the Normals the State was either directly or indirectly responsible for it. He could not let the State simply pass the blame off to the Deviants, as it so often did. He had to convince them to attribute their suffering to the selfishness of other countries that were reneging on their contract with the rest of the modernized world. They had agreed to share, and they were not sharing. If he could convince the Normals of that, he could also convince them their own government was complicit in the oppression by its failure to punish those other countries. He would achieve his goal of blaming both the other countries and his own government. Properly manipulated, his compatriots would support him in overthrowing tyrants at home before unleashing their collective force against tyrants abroad. It was certain he would begin to build this case at the protest in the People's Central Park on Monday.

In the meantime, the State attempted to build its own case. The night after Long interrupted the citizens' evening entertainment, the president did the same thing at almost the same time. She came on not in the middle of an act but between acts, and, smiling her usual fawning smile, addressed them in her usual fawning tone:

"My dear and esteemed fellow citizens," she said. "Last night we were all unexpectedly treated to a regrettable outburst from a known terrorist who managed to take over our airwaves for the briefest time. The State is fairly certain this voice of the Deviants used outside help from a foreign nation to take our own engineers by surprise. You probably noticed that the act of terrorism was brought to a swift end and normalcy quickly returned. We will always act swiftly and decisively to prevent such maverick individuals or organizations from spreading misinformation that might confuse and mislead you.

"Let me remind you that the State employs the world's leading scientific experts and acts only on the latest scientific knowledge to administer the affairs of state. No organization in the world is capable of looking out for your best interests the way we in your government do. It's challenging work, as we all know, and it sometimes confronts us with both external and internal threats to the prosperity, stability, and peace of our nation. Many of the external threats are merely accidents of fortune, as we all know. Natural threats, such as those posed by historical mistakes or malicious forces in history whose consequences are unfortunately still with us, often simply cannot be avoided. We work with our allies around the world to manage these consequences in ways that ensure the best possible outcomes for all the peoples of the world. Internal threats, as you are well aware, most recently from our experience with the terrorist acts that manifested in the Dev1 virus, can sometimes be more challenging simply because they are deliberate. Unlike our faithful allies, the perpetrators of such malicious acts intentionally aim to do us harm. I remind you that if you are aware of any such intentions to perpetrate one of these acts, or if you are merely suspicious of a neighbor or coworker, you should waste no time in reporting the neighbor or coworker to the appropriate authorities. By doing so, you might very well be saving countless lives of your compatriots. And the State will forever owe you a debt of gratitude. The State never forgets its friends.

Finally, last night's interloper announced a gathering in the People's Central Park on Monday. According to the terrorist, similar gatherings are to be held across the country. Please remember that these gatherings, if they take place, will do so without the permission of the State, and any gathering of more than five people requires the State's express permission. This is the law, and you are all well aware of it. Therefore, all such gatherings, should they in fact be held, will be in violation of the law and will invite appropriate consequences. Those consequences may be painful.

"Now enjoy the rest of the program, please. And remember, it's the generosity of the State that makes such programs possible. To protect the State's interests is to protect your own interests, and to ensure that our way of life continues. Thank you, and good night."

The night after the president delivered her address, Duda was sitting with two of his new associates discussing what they termed "the Long problem." "We should take him out," one of them said.

"And how's that supposed to help our cause?" Duda wondered. "I've thought about this thing a lot, and I really don't see the point in taking him out. Forget about the moral argument; I've given up on making those."

"I think the guy can build a following. He was starting to build one before the 'epidemic,' and he can build one again. He's charismatic. Give him credit; he knows how to attract a following."

"You sound like an admirer."

"Cut the nonsense. A follower I'm most definitely not. What I am is a realist."

"Benjamin is right," the third member of the group said. "Don't start trouble, Michael. It's one thing to admire the guy; it's another to respect what he can do. And I agree that he can do plenty. The guy's a charismatic leader. Tell me P. Henry hasn't lectured you on those."

"And lectured and lectured and lectured. I'm just not a fan of murder. And it seems like that's all we do."

"We're adherents of a cause too," Benjamin said. "It comes with the territory."

"So if you believe in a cause you are obliged to murder people?"

"I didn't say that."

"What else could you be saying?"

"All right, so we're obliged to murder people. We've murdered people who oppress us. These are not nice people, Michael.

"Sometimes I wonder why you joined this cause. You seem to oppose everything we do."

"But not everything we stand for," the third man in the discussion said. "We stand for individual rights and personal freedom. He's not against those."

"Of course not," Duda said. "That's why I'm here. In fact it's the only reason I'm here."

"You wanna stand for those things; you just don't wanna get your hands dirty."

"If that's what you say. But tell me, what exactly has this movement accomplished so far?"

"This 'movement,' as you call it—I don't like calling it that—is growing. Our message is getting out. It appeals to people. They realize it favors them. It's better than what they have now."

"And what they'll always have, as far as we can tell. If all we keep doing is killing off bigshot politicians and movie actors and sports heroes. We haven't had any influence on the government. None."

"You wanna influence the government?" Benjamin said. "Let's get Long. Let's arrange a little accident for the man."

"Here we go again with the killing people. What good is killing Long going to do us, anyway?"

"It'll keep him from building too much of a following."

"Sorry, Michael," the third man said. "But I'm still with Benjamin on this. We don't want Long to accrue too much power."

"He hates the government as much as we do. Maybe more, the way things seem to be going. We run around killing people and nothing happens. Except maybe some innocent people die. Otherwise, nothing changes.

"He, on the other hand, gets the people worked up. Gets them behind him and against the government. Exactly what I thought we wanted."

"Except we're not a mob, Michael. We're not a populist movement. We don't want to overthrow the government so we can replace it with more of the same thing. And believe me, Long represents more of the same thing. He wants control of the schools and the businesses, just like the State has now."

"But he says he'll favor the workers— 'the people,' as he calls them. As he calls us, I guess."

"And how's that different from what we have now? Everybody who takes over a government says he's doing it for 'the people.'"

"But then he runs the schools and the businesses, just like his predecessor did. Everybody works *for* the State. That's not what we want at all."

"Right," Benjamin said. "We want the State to work *for* the people. The people run the schools and the businesses. The state works for them, not they for it."

"All right," Duda said. "So we should kill Long and turn the government over to 'the people.'"

"You don't sound very convincing."

"I'm just wondering when all the killing will end."

28

The National Workers Alliance's moratorium on work, the Monday event announced on national television by activist Hugo Lansky Long, was less than a rousing success, but probably more of a success than many government officials would have liked to see. Official government estimates, those that became public, placed the number of strikers at twenty-five thousand nationwide; estimates by Duda's freedom fighters, based on numbers culled from their scattered members in major urban centers across the commonwealth, ran roughly ten times that high. It was always hard to ascertain these numbers in a closed society, one that placed such tight restrictions on expression in the interest of making communication easy for the State but difficult for the people. But the Deviants had ways of finding and disseminating the information they wanted, especially via the relatively large network of spies and sympathetic informants they had inside the government. Information certainly circulated much better than the government wanted it to circulate. In an ideal world— the State's ideal world—only the information it supplied would reach the eyes and ears of the population at large. But as hard as the government worked to keep its citizens properly informed—that is, to make sure they knew what it wanted them to know and didn't know what it didn't want them to know—it still could not constrain the lies and distortions that continually threatened to undermine its authority.

This was the aspect of participating in the cause of freedom that most thrilled Michael Duda. As frustrated as he was that his freedom fighters seemed endlessly stymied, endlessly working toward a goal they seemed destined never to reach, he loved knowing he and his associates could subvert the government's oppressive will with regularity. The government frustrated them, but they frustrated it in return. It would not be misleading to say the pleasure Duda derived from thwarting his oppressors, even just intermittently and in only minutely satisfying ways, compensated to some degree for the loss of his romantic interest, Anna, and his mentor, Plato. The one thing he was now sure of was that he needed something in his life besides the dull routine of serving the State—especially now, when he recognized that serving the State was not necessarily serving the people and sometimes even worked at cross purposes with serving the people. It was a bit easier to put up with the monotony of policing the coffee shops and clubs at night, not to mention the excruciating agony of hearing Hooligan drone on and on about the soccer leagues, when he knew that somewhere in his not-too-distant future lay some act of subversion, or at the very least a philosophical discussion to keep his mind alive.

The National Workers Alliance, however, as some of his fellow freedom fighters had foreseen, would soon complicate both his life as a servant of the State and his life as a revolutionary, in a way that made life in general both more difficult and more dangerous. His initial discovery of that fact came less than a week after the Monday rally in the People's Central Park. On their normal beat he and Hooligan stopped in at their usual coffee stop, which happened to be the same café he and Plato had always frequented for coffee, just as a conflict between two small competing factions was hitting its peak. The competing factions represented the NWA, on the one hand, and a group that had no official name but might be called "loyalists," on the other. There were five or six young people in each group, involved in what had started out as a discussion, evolved into a shouting match, and was on the verge of becoming a fistfight when the two police officers happened along. Epithets were being hurled, along with threats of grievous bodily harm, and even as the officers wedged themselves between the opposing factions, Duda felt threatened, even though he was not the object of any of the threats—at least not at first. But he could not get to his nightstick because both hands were engaged in keeping the combatants separated, and he realized that in his current vulnerable position even his sidearm might be suddenly taken from him. Moreover, the young people kept after each other, and Duda realized he was at risk of serious physical injury himself. Not since the night Drone had been injured at the satyr had he feared for his safety as he feared for it now; nor had he felt more exposed even then.

Worst of all, though, the edgy Hooligan, attempting to restrain the loyalist side, seemed suddenly to lose track of himself, as if he were cresting some wave of self-control that broke suddenly into wild abandon, at which point he seized his nightstick and unleashed a merciless attack on the young people on his side of the scuffle. Shrieks of pain and terror ensued, and they shrank away from him, four of them fleeing the café altogether, leaving two allies prostrate on the floor.

Even the opposing combatants had shrunk away momentarily, surprised themselves at the sudden furious eruption from the out-of-control police officer, who, after administering the savage beating to the loyalist side, whirled to face the NWA side. "No," Duda said, then, "No," finding himself in the bizarre position of actually spreading himself to protect the ones he'd been restraining just a moment before.

"See!" one of them finally shouted. "See the brutal force of the State!"

It seemed to Duda an odd juncture at which to make such an observation, given that all but two members of the opposing force had already departed the café, and those two seemed in no position to make assessments of any kind. Duda now found himself latching onto his own nightstick and joining forces with his partner to assail the disciples of Hugo Long. He used the nightstick to threaten the young people with menacing gestures, but he struck no blows. Hooligan, on the other hand, remained beside himself. By the time this second group could effect its escape, two more bodies were inert on the floor.

Backup was slow to arrive. The ambulance took nearly half an hour, during which two of Hooligan's victims expired. The café was deserted except for a few kitchen workers in the back when the ambulance came to scoop up the remains. Hooligan was by then sitting quietly himself, sipping the coffee he had entered the café to consume in the first place. Duda and the café's server tended to the wounded. Neither of them said very much. The battered survivors of the struggle said even less. Both were, however, conscious when the ambulance arrived. One was in a daze, though, and Duda had a bad feeling he wouldn't make it through what remained of the night.

"What took you so long?" he inquired of the ambulance personnel.

"Busy night. Lots of these fights starting up, it seems like. You shoulda seen the last one. It was at a club, and the bastards were drinking. People shouldn't talk politics when they're drinking."

"Maybe they shouldn't talk politics at all."

He was in a daze. He had lost his Budenovka in the melee and found it trampled and torn but put it on anyway. Then he sat down opposite Hooligan, who seemed not to notice him.

"We want to close, now that you two chased everybody off," the server said sullenly.

"Is there any coffee available?"

"Down the street."

It was cold that night, and soon after they stepped outside again the side of his face, just below and to the left of his left eye, began to hurt. At some point in the fracas he had taken a blow to the eye socket. He couldn't even remember what had happened, but at least he wasn't bleeding. He'd have a bruise there in the morning, though; he was sure of that. It would look as though he'd been in a boxing match. He might even have an orbital fracture. He was just glad the eye itself seemed unaffected. He rubbed the injury gingerly as they meandered down the street.

Hooligan, meanwhile, said nothing—absolutely nothing. He seemed to remain in the catatonia that had taken him over after the fighting in the café stopped. Duda wandered along in silence, discreetly looking his partner over, checking for signs of ... anything. He didn't even know what to look for. All he knew was that Hooligan was broken, and he had no idea how to fix him. In the morning he would talk to Hyde about it again, and this time he would show more urgency.

In the meantime, as they walked along Duda became aware of something else. People were looking at them. The Normals always paid attention to cops, usually just keeping track of them so as to steer clear of them, but tonight they seemed to be scrutinizing them, as if their attitude toward them had changed. Nobody said anything, at least nothing Duda could hear, but he had the strange sensation he and his fellow law enforcement officials had evolved from public nuisance to public spectacle. Was it paranoia, all in his mind? Was it something that occurred to him because recent events were making him more aware of who he was as a representative of State power and State authority? Maybe that was it. He wanted that to be it. But he wasn't at all *sure* that was it; he was sure only that he felt relieved as the streets started to empty and people went home for the night. He was glad there was nobody to confront that night, no loiterers to be chased inside with a few firm commands. The streets emptied, voluntarily emptied, and he was left alone with a partner who also seemed to have emptied. Something in Hooligan had emptied out, and it took with it even the part of him that loved soccer and hated the local weather.

Duda resolved to visit Plato as soon as he had the chance. He had the feeling that was the only thing that might bring him any comfort.

For now, he had to talk to Hyde about Hooligan. He was anxious until their shift ended and they returned to the compound, and all the more anxious because in that time, nearly five full hours, Hooligan said not one word—not a single word. Duda was relieved to get to the compound but still anxious as well because he feared Hyde would brush him off again, as he/she'd done when he broached this topic the first time. He/she would say killing people was part of Hooligan's job when necessary (Duda was fairly sure, at least, Hyde wouldn't ask why *he*, Michael Duda, wasn't also killing people).

But Hyde was more sympathetic than he expected. After the official debriefing he/she asked Duda to stay and meet with him/her in private. "So this started with the encounter at the café last night?"

"Well, that's when it started last night. He'd already had that episode I told you about before."

"I remember."

"Something's wrong with him, boss. I think killing that first kid a few months ago destabilized him somehow."

"He's been like this for that long? Why didn't you tell me?"

I tried to tell you, Duda wanted to say—but that, he was pretty sure, would be a tactical mistake. He had to keep in mind his objective, which had become, for all intents and purposes, to get rid of Hooligan as his partner.

"That's when this started," Duda shrugged. "He got very quiet after that, and he actually seemed to want to avoid conflict. Every time we've had anything like a confrontation, for example, he's fallen back and let me take the lead."

"But not last night."

"Well, at first. I could see the poor guy sweating right there beside me. Even as I was trying to get control of the situation—which just wasn't going to happen. He was okay for a minute or two, and then he just exploded."

"A minute or two?"

"I don't know, boss. That situation was tense. It seemed like we were engaged with those guys for an hour before all hell broke loose. But it can't have been that long."

"Like something snapped inside him?"

"Like something snapped inside him."

Hyde shook his/her head. "He killed three more people."

"Three?"

"Three."

"He's been fine as a partner, for the most part. It's just when this stuff happened, this violent stuff—"

"The stressful stuff?"

Duda nodded. "Maybe this guy wasn't cut out to be a cop, boss. I hate to say that—because I really do like the guy—but, I mean, come on."

"This is where he tested out. Same place you and I tested out. I guess we're all meant to be cops."

I don't know if I trust those tests, Duda wanted to say. I mean, you don't even know if you want to be a man or a woman. Do they have tests for that?

But of course he said none of that. His objective was still firmly in mind. And his objective didn't include getting under the boss's skin.

"You don't have to say it," Hyde said. "I take those tests with a grain of salt myself.

"Look. I'll take him off the street for a while. Put him somewhere where I can keep an eye on him. Maybe have him evaluated."

"More tests?"

"I know, I know. You got a better idea?"

Duda did not have a better idea. In fact, he'd had exactly that same idea. He was relieved. He'd be missing out on the soccer scores, but he could live without those.

29

It was the following Saturday afternoon before he was able to see Plato, and Plato was not happy with him. "You can't come running to me every time you need to talk," he said. "I'm sorry, Michael, I truly am. But we can't have the kind of relationship we had before. It's just not possible. That's the price we pay for doing what we do."

"Part of the price we pay."

"All right, part of the price we pay. Is that why you came out here, to complain? You put yourself, your driver, and me at risk—just to air a grievance?

"How long have you been at this now? And how long has Daniel been at it? And me—how long have I been at it? We've both risked more than you have, I assure you."

"I'm sorry. I did not come out here just to air a grievance. There's something I need to talk to you about. Something that has everything to do with our cause."

"Let's hear it then."

"Things are getting tense in the city. I mean tense like they've never been before. Like I've never seen them."

"The NWA?"

Duda nodded, realizing as he did that he would probably get another lecture for telling Plato something he already knew. "I haven't seen it like this. And I'm not sure how to respond to it.

"There's been trouble," he explained, "I mean trouble like we didn't have before. Not like a satyr." And he told Plato about the scuffle in the café, including the part about how he worried he might be overwhelmed in the struggle. He had feared for his life. What was almost as bad, the Normals didn't seem sympathetic. They gave the impression they didn't care if he got carted off to the morgue or left under his own power when the fight was over. Some observers actually seemed to be pulling for the morgue. "This is political stuff," he said. "I mean, we've had that before, but I just didn't expect it to be quite so intense. There's just this ... this anger in the air. And some of it is directed at us. But not just at us ... at *something*, you know what I mean? Like people are just angry at the world, but they want to take it out on us."

"I know."

"I'm sorry—"

"No, it's all right. Yes, I already knew about it, but it's okay that you brought it to me. You don't have to apologize for it."

"So what do I do? What do *we* do?"

"We're in trouble, Michael. We should have taken him out, but we didn't. And it's my fault as much as anybody's. *More* than most people's. I was against it when I should have been for it."

"You didn't know."

"That's not an excuse. It doesn't help us now."

"So what do we do? Can't we take him out now? I swear I'd volunteer for the job, if you thought it would help. That's why I really came out here."

Plato smiled at him. "Always the eager student," he said. "Always eager to learn."

"Learn to kill."

"Somebody has to do it. But it's too late now—with Long it's too late. He's got too strong a foothold. Much stronger than I realized.

"It's my fault," he repeated. "I should have known."

"I'm sure it's not just your fault."

"No, but I was ... well, never mind. We're in uncharted territory, my young friend. We're competing now with a populist movement like none we've ever seen."

"None the State has ever seen?"

"Oh no. Every generation presents new challenges. There have been challenges before; there'll be challenges again long after you and I are gone."

"Then why do we *do* this?"

"What else *would* we do, Michael? Tell me that. Remember your life before you got involved with us?"

"There was Anna."

"Who turned out to be one of us."

"And there was ignorance. Blissful ignorance. The State raises us on blissful ignorance."

"And look at everything you've learned."

"And how miserable it's made me."

"Are you really miserable? Do you wish you hadn't joined?"

"No. Of course not. I just wish ..."

"You wish the world would listen to us, and everybody would be happy."

"Something like that. I just don't get it, Plato; I really don't. What we offer the world is freedom. Who doesn't want that?"

"You might be surprised."

"I suppose so. I just can't imagine ..." but he could not articulate what it was he could not imagine, though he could certainly feel it. He felt it very powerfully.

"And so you come to me with ideas of assassinating Long. Long the snake charmer.

"Try to look at the bright side. He's our new challenge. You should come to me if you have ideas about him—what to do about him, I mean."

"But we can't take him out."

"Not anymore. I don't think so. Let me put it this way: I don't think it will help our cause if we take him out. I think it will just turn more people against us. You know, the Normals aren't really against us, most of them. They may not be for us, either—but they're not against us. I think it's best to keep it that way."

"His followers have passion. They're committed."

"They are. That's the problem."

"And I don't understand why they aren't committed to *us*. You know, Plato, I think that's the crux of the whole thing, for me. I just don't understand why they're so committed to him, and they won't commit to us."

"What we're offering them is a principle, an abstraction. Not a person to be their messiah. People won't commit to a principle. I think somebody said that the first night you came out here."

"I think it was James. And I think I wanted to ask him then what the hell he meant, but I was too nervous at the time."

"Long gives them somebody to be angry at—several somebodies, in fact. He really knows how to make 'em angry, especially at people and things they can't see. The Chinese, for example. That's one of his favorites.

"And he gives them himself as a replacement for the State. He gives them a savior. It's a simple tradeoff. Together they'll all get revenge on everybody they hate— some people in the government, the Chinese, the Russians, maybe even some of their fellow Normals.

"And their lives won't be one damn bit different from what they are now.

"We, on the other hand, give them an abstract ideal. Not a person they can see and hear and believe in— somebody to take them to their promised land. We give them a principle they can use to guide themselves, and nothing more. Just a right to guide themselves."

"And they've never had that before, so they're afraid of it."

"Oh no, they've had it before. Or at least their ancestors had it before. It has lived in this world. And the world prospered because of it. Prospered as it had never prospered before. Prospered as it is definitely not prospering now." Plato's voice trailed away in sort of a dreamy sigh.

"But that's it, Plato!"

"That's it? That's what?"

"That's what I don't understand. The world realizes this ideal, and then—poof—it's gone. What happened to it? How can people give up something so perfect? That's what I don't understand."

"Because they don't know it's perfect, Michael. They don't recognize it when they've got it. Life is still hard. Things don't seem perfect, not by any means. They don't understand.

"And there are always people selling them something better. Promising them something better. A different abstraction, but one that sounds like something concrete, like heaven on Earth. I guess I never told you what happened the last time people had freedom. It was way before my time too, but I've read about it plenty, and I've seen videos and pictures and movies. And I've had discussions with people who know more than I do— though nobody who lived through that time. Everybody who lived through that time is probably dead now.

"And it was a populist movement that destroyed freedom then, too. Maybe it's always a populist movement.

It was just the same then as it is now: people hating other people blindly, indiscriminately. Other people—people like Long—feeding that hatred. Because that's what somebody like him does. He feeds people's hatred to promote himself—and whatever it is he's selling them.

"Back then, though, some big corporations supported the populists, and everybody else yielded before them. They demonized everybody who wasn't with them and cleared a path to domination for themselves. The big corporations were mostly located in one city out on the West Coast, but they had a monopoly on the communication technology, and that gave them so much power nobody could stop them. Because, remember, communication makes knowledge possible, and knowledge is power. Always, always, always remember that. It's the reason those who seek dominion over others always try to cut off the others' communication. It's the reason they impose censorship. It's the reason the State separates us from each other and moves us around and controls what we see and hear and say.

"You may not believe this, but there was a time long ago—fifty years or so ago—when every person had a communicator like the ones only cops and a few others carry now. And there weren't just two television stations—there were many stations, and the State did *not* control what people saw. And the Internet was wide open then. And of course the books ...."

"Freedom" Duda said.

"Freedom. And they gave it away, on the promise of something better. It's always the same thing, like offering the people a drug that promises them ultimate happiness—heaven on Earth—but in the end it just makes them weak, vulnerable. It makes them like prisoners: All their basic needs are met, but they have no freedom of movement or choice. They are prisoners, Michael—Normals."

"But why? The people let it happen! You've said that before, more than once, but you still haven't really explained *why* they did it. Why they do it. Why the hell would *anybody* give up freedom?"

"Because, for many people, the promise of security trumps freedom. And then somebody—somebody like Long—comes along and promises them both: security and freedom, an impossible combination.

"There's no more to it than that, and there never has been. People will always be people, but there will always be some among them who will claim it doesn't have to be that way. They'll claim history is moving forward … toward something, some preordained goal."

"Toward them."

"Yep. Now you get it. Shows you what a self-centered lot we are, we human beings. A wise man, somebody who believed in freedom just like we do, once commented that each new generation thinks history stops with that generation, that they're the ones who are finally going to get the evil world straightened out. As if nobody before them ever had that same idea.

"Then all they need is somebody to hate, somebody to blame for preventing the world from achieving perfection in all the thousands of generations before them. Then they can clear that somebody out of the way and push on ahead with their movement, whatever their movement is."

"And people buy it."

"Of course they do. People want to believe. What's more appealing than believing somebody else is the cause of your own failure? And what's more appealing than believing *you* can accomplish something nobody else, in all the millennia before you, has been able to accomplish? It gives them a sense of purpose."

"But they won't believe in us."

Plato shrugged. "We're not selling them a perfect world. And we're not giving them a savior to take them there. All we're selling them is freedom. And some of them don't even want freedom. Just tell them what to do and they'll be fine. Give them some comfort—just a smidge. And give them just a little security. They'll get by on that."

"So here we are, selling them something they don't want. We're destined just to go through life killing people without accomplishing anything."

"Like Sisyphus with his boulder."

"You told me that story. Not very encouraging, Plato."

Plato just smiled at him. "Have a drink with me, my young friend. And then have some dinner with me."

"And that's why we live—what we live for. For drinks and dinner."

"There are worse things in life. But that's not all we live for, Michael. The fact that you and I are here together right now, talking about this—in a time and place when there's considerable risk in being together talking about this—that fact alone proves we live for something more. We too need our sense of purpose. Maybe everybody does."

They had two drinks apiece—Scotch for Plato, and for Duda bourbon, for which he was acquiring a taste though this was only the second time he'd had it. A bit later they had dinner, a less elaborate dinner than the first one Duda had enjoyed in the Forbidden City, but sumptuous nonetheless. With dinner they had wine. "Maybe we *could* live just for this," Duda said. "Live for pleasure. What other good is there in the world?"

"Now you sound like Long, my young friend. You're offering the same thing he's offering. It'll work in the short term, but it won't work forever. It's new to you. You'd always enjoy it, believe me you would. But it wouldn't sustain you. Not forever. And that's assuming there would always be pleasures like these around to enjoy. Remember, somebody has to work to provide these pleasures. You should always appreciate that fact. It's something none of us should ever forget."

They had coffee together after dinner, and they smoked cigarettes together. The cigarettes improved the taste of the coffee, and for the moment it was difficult for Duda to comprehend that there was more to life than just these pleasures.

Then again, as Plato had reminded him, there was the work it took to provide the pleasures.

"Tell me what to do about Long, Michael," Plato said. He sat back in his chair and blew a dense cloud of smoke into the air. "What should we do about Long?"

"I've already told you what I think. Take him out."

"He's too big now."

"He'll only get bigger. And one day *he'll* be the one in the limousine we're trying to bomb."

"You might be right, Michael. I'm afraid you just might be right."

Douglass was Duda's new partner. He was the youngest partner he'd been assigned so far, the first one younger than Duda himself, and after Plato the most interesting. He called himself "the African," and he was, in addition to being well read and well informed, an ebullient lover of life. Much like Plato, he looked for the positive in everybody they met on the job, and he handled tense situations with the same level head and calm demeanor Plato had always demonstrated. Duda enjoyed working the streets with him. Just as Plato before him had done, Douglass helped to ease some of the stresses of their work just by being the kind of person he was.

Unfortunately, there were more stresses than ever now, so they were kept busier with conflicts than they would have liked to be. Tensions seemed to be mounting all around them, and as much as they wanted those tensions to ease, they felt there was nothing they could do about them. Nothing, that is, except try to keep their own cool under pressure.

Hugo Lansky Long continued to grow in popularity, acquiring more and more followers, but his growing popularity had an additional unanticipated effect—unanticipated by Duda, at least. It seemed to stimulate additional social fracturing, factionalizing, even among the "loyalists" who had no interest in following Long. The commonwealth was of course built on the premise that all people and therefore all groups were "equal," equal in all respects. No social hierarchy existed, no differences in social status or value. The progressive commonwealth was nominally unique: a society in which no social divisions existed. But in reality, of course, there were divisions aplenty, divisions the Normals recognized in daily life but officially ignored, primarily because the State had commanded them to ignore the divisions since they were tiny tykes in the learning centers. And the State media continually reinforced the proscription against social division once they achieved adulthood. What they saw they were told they did not see because it did not exist. Like the gangs that represented competing urban islands in turf wars that never officially took place, and like the black market that fed the illicit appetites of the people with only the implicit sanction of the State, the social divisions had always been there, but Duda hadn't really seen them, or at least he hadn't really felt their presence—perhaps only because he had been commanded not to feel their presence. Now, with the rise of the populist Long, they became not merely apparent but pronounced. Fissures appeared among the various groups in the commonwealth's social foundation, and those fissures widened, in Duda's perception; they widened to the point of threatening the entire foundation.

They surfaced many evenings on the streets of the urban center, often accelerated by booze and/or drugs, and Duda and his new partner found themselves perpetually extinguishing the flames of potential social conflagration. The groups squared off and had to be separated, and Duda was grateful for Douglass as his partner. He could only imagine the havoc Hooligan might have wreaked. Douglass and he worked together to dispel tensions with humor, most often (Douglass was very good at humor), or with the voice of calm and reason. But on other occasions they arrived only in time for the aftermath, to oversee the cleanup and ensure the wounded were properly shipped off to the nearest medical facilities.

They also found themselves targets, some nights, as Hooligan and Duda had been the targets of the young man who injudiciously shot off his mouth at the wrong time and found himself on the receiving end of Hooligan's nightstick. They were called "fascist pigs," most often— apparently the epithet of choice among disgruntled Normals—and one night they narrowly dodged a few flying objects sent their way. They made no arrests. Working with Douglass, Duda was able to avoid physical confrontation, but he also feared they wouldn't be able to go on avoiding it forever.

There were more rallies, at which hundreds and now thousands gathered, most often in the People's Central Park. Duda and his new partner avoided being assigned to these rallies and were thankful for their good fortune. The SWATs and the Special Ops people had no such good fortune—though it was likely they didn't look at fortune in quite the same way and considered themselves the fortunate ones. Hundreds of them set upon the park. Most survived, but a few didn't. Drone, Duda would later learn, was among those who didn't.

"Long is smart," Douglass remarked. "His timing has been perfect. He started recapturing his former momentum just as winter was ending, and now that spring is in full bloom, so is his movement. You can bet he'll capitalize on favorable weather this summer. More rallies are ahead of us, my friend."

"And they're worse than satyrs. The revelers at a satyr are generally bolstered by booze and drugs, but these people have passion and commitment in their blood. Those things are worse—for the cops. Let's hope our luck holds and we keep avoiding those assignments."

The State's higher authorities also noticed Long's surging popularity and his plan to capitalize on the coming summer. Their response was to perpetrate another biological attack. The Dev2 virus was called a "resurgence" of the Dev1 virus. It attacked in late spring and left a trail of fresh corpses. But perhaps the State's own good fortune was waning. The subsequent lockdown was widely disobeyed.

"Please," the president pleaded on national television. "Our experts have determined that we won't be able to subdue this virus without your complete cooperation. Working together we were able to defeat the previous virus. We have to follow the same strategy this time around. It will save millions of lives. But we need to work together."

And Long commandeered the airwaves again to respond: "You realize the Dev1 virus was a trick played on all of you. It was nothing but a smokescreen so the State could round up dissidents and execute them. Thousands died not because they were infected with some virus but because they were infected with enthusiasm for the NWA. What that means is that we're *winning*. They're afraid of us. We must keep the heat on. Defy the lockdown order whenever you can. Take to the streets. You'll be protecting your fellow revolutionaries. It'll be much harder for the State to kidnap and dispose of them when we're there to *stop* them. Resist!"

Most did not resist, of course—they went dutifully into lockdown as they'd been ordered to do—but many did resist. They took to the streets, usually employing stealth, to smash the windows of supply centers and clubs and rob them of their contents. From the supply centers they took everything from food items to clothing and paper goods.

From the clubs, naturally, they stole booze. They were prepared to do violence when necessary, and two officers Duda knew from the compound died in one ambush.

"I don't know what to do," he said to Plato. It was midsummer, and he had ventured another visit to his mentor to seek his advice. Plato was not angry with him this time, or if he was angry, he didn't show it. "My partner thinks like I do. I mean, I have a lot of faith in him. But how will he react if we confront looters? I don't know. We've faced some pretty sticky situations. I'm really not anxious to have to shoot somebody, Plato. But these are not the old days, when you and I would come across some kids screwing around, and in five minutes you had them leaving peacefully. I'm not sure even you could confront these people now without violence."

"You should listen to yourself," my young friend. "And remember what you've been saying to me for as long as we've known each other. About this movement, I mean. Our fight for freedom. 'All we do is kill people,' you say. How often have you said that to me?

"We already know how you feel about your duty as a police officer. But do what you have to do to protect yourself. Your disloyalty to the State doesn't extend as far as getting yourself killed over a robbery. Our fight isn't about letting people do whatever they want to us. In fact, it's really the opposite of that. So if you find yourself confronted by violence you can't avoid, do what you have to do."

Duda breathed a sigh of relief. "Thank you. But you know how I am about violence to begin with."

"Some cop."

"Hey, I was mentored by the master."

"Who convinced you to join a cause that can only function by killing random people."

"They're not random."

225

"Oh. Now *you're* the one making lectures on morality."

"I was most worried about my partner anyway."

"Why? I'd never tell you to kill your partner. I used to *be* your partner."

"No, I like my partner. He's a lot like me—but he's even more like *you*. A non-violent guy. Not very cop-like. But if we run into trouble, real trouble, I want to make sure I handle it the right way. I don't wanna blow anybody's cover—least of all yours and mine."

"You don't need to worry too much about that, Michael. Your partner's one of us."

Duda was stunned, and his expression clearly showed it.

"For the guy I've touted as my best pupil, you surprise me sometimes, Michael. Didn't you realize we've been engineering your career for you ever since that poor little girl discovered you?"

"Anna."

"Yes. She was the one who drew you in, and then the rest of us went to work on you. You had to be screened, the way all of us have to be screened. You know how it is: We trust nobody until we're sure a person can be trusted. Then we got rid of the True Believer for you and—voila!—you were assigned to me as your partner.

"Not everybody was convinced about you, though. I trusted you, but you had your doubters. When I came here they went and got the young man—what was his name—?"

"Wing?"

"That may have been it. We got him for you as a roommate. And you almost blew that. Do you realize how close you were to being disposed of that night? You were very close, my young friend. Very close."

"Is Wing all right? I felt bad the way that turned out."

"I'm sure he's fine. I don't keep close tabs on every member of our organization I cross paths with. It's not a good policy to know too many people in our line of work—if you know what I mean.

"And it's a good policy not to keep close track of them unless you have to. As far as I know, Wing is fine. But there are many things I don't know. And that's all for the best."

"How do you do all this?"

"We have people in high places. You've met a few of them. They take greater risks than any of us. Because they believe in what we stand for. There was a time, my young friend ..." but his voice fell away.

"One of these days," he said, finally, "when we both have some hours to kill, I'm going to take you back into the library, the room you were first introduced to in this house. There I'll show you things that will astonish you. I'll teach you as much as I can about a country founded on the principles we believe in, a country that flourished because it permitted a citizenry grounded in those principles—and any country grounded in the principles of freedom for the individual will flourish—a country that lost sight of those principles in the space of a generation and left us with ... this. This."

He shook his head sadly. "And when I say 'this,' I mean the 'this' you live with in your daily life. Not this house. This house is a remnant of better times. That's why we bring you young people to this house—so you will know. You will know, and you will realize. We're not lying to you. We're not building castles in the sky. The world we dream of has existed before and can exist again ... we hope.

"I'll never see it. This is the closest I'll ever come. I'll see it here in this house, and in those artifacts that one of these days I'm going to show you: books, pictures, videos. You'll see them, and then you'll understand. And maybe your generation will be the generation that *does* see it. Maybe. And maybe not, my young friend. Maybe it'll be the next generation after yours. Or the next. Who knows?

What history tells us is that it doesn't come along very often. And when it does come along, it is easy to let go of and hard to recover.

"Anyway, you don't need to worry about your new partner. He's been screened—better than you were screened before you came to me. Or maybe he just already knows more about what he wants than you did. Anyway, you can trust him. And maybe you can teach him. You're moving up in the hierarchy now; you have to take some responsibility."

31

One of the responsibilities he would take on in the waning days of that summer was his first genuine act of terrorism. At any rate, the State would see it as an act of terrorism, and Duda, disinclined as he was to participate in such acts, found it difficult not to think of it as an act of terrorism himself. But he knew it was a responsibility he could not shirk, not if he wanted to call himself a true freedom fighter, so rather than try to put a label on it he tried hard not to think of it at all.

His accomplice in the act was of course his partner, Douglass, who invested little commentary in the act either before they committed it or afterward. When the assignment came they accepted it. They discussed tactics and logistics, but little else. Neither of them raised the question of whether what they were doing was right or wrong. They did as they were told.

Both had committed minor acts of subversion before that night, a few of them together. The assignments had been simple and even seemed innocuous, though they were not innocuous, not at all, and there was an element of risk in each of them. Steal a document. Pass on some information. Look the other way—and ensure others were also looking the other way—while somebody else committed the overt act of subversion. (For instance, one night they'd helped a computer expert break into one of the State's data facilities, then stood guard for him while he did a bit of reprogramming of one of the State's computers.)

But they had neither committed themselves nor stood by while somebody else committed an overt act of violence. Not until they were instructed to visit a particular address in Sector C, their normal beat, at a particular hour, on a particular night. The address was on a side street in that district, the entertainment district, a street with which they were obviously both intimately familiar. They walked it together most nights they were on duty.

Their target that night was the son of the scion of one of those infamous high-tech companies of which Plato had spoken to Duda, one of the companies that had participated in undermining the old republic. The company's role had been to facilitate the rise of the socialists while inhibiting the ability of the republicans to communicate and thus undermining their society. Its primary weapon in this subversive activity had been censorship. As a monopolist in the electronic communication of that era it had wielded enormous power over the dissemination of information, not merely within the old republic but internationally; and its capacity to control not only the flow of information but the distribution of resources including money, the medium of exchange at that time, had enabled it to topple the old government in a very short time, less than a decade.

It had additionally relied very heavily on the extraordinary diffidence and apathy of the citizenry— the Normals of that epoch, if you will—to complete its subversion of their culture. Few of them thought deeply about their world, consumed as they were by interests in personal gratification. The Internet in the initial decades following its inception had supplied them with plenty of those. It was not until the socialists had quietly taken over that most of the country's citizens recognized the Internet's true value to those in power. It was a tool, an invaluable tool, in establishing and maintaining the authority of the State.

The company's founder—very young when he founded the company, and very wealthy soon afterward—had been a young man of very high ideals and a very limited sense of history. With prodding from a cadre of intellectuals, assorted other radicals, and fellow corporatist idealists, the young man had not merely willingly but eagerly participated in undermining what he believed and was told was a "corrupt" society dominated and domineered by capitalists whose sole goal in life was to accumulate material goods. In their quest they trampled on the heads and the rights of a plebian horde they viewed merely as fodder for the indulgence of their personal whims. The young scion, with great encouragement from the intellectuals and assorted other radicals, had come to see it as his sacred mission in life to destroy the old order of things and replace it with a magnificent—nay, a glorious— socialist commonwealth.

The son, on the other hand, was a tool. The father had been a tool too, but the son was a different kind of tool. Whereas the father had been a man of high ideals and great imagination, if a somewhat defective understanding of human nature, the son was—like quite a few other children of wealth and privilege, unfortunately—just a friggin' tool. When the socialists commandeered the means of production, the father, by then elderly but still energetic, had pitched a fit. Recognizing he'd been had by a really rather small cadre of political schemers and their useful idiots, he initially recoiled in horror and followed his instincts, battling to regain control of the empire he'd built, then handed over with all the aplomb of a parent handing over the car keys to a teenager. In this case, the teenagers who took command of the car had all the brilliance of a burnt-out light bulb, but they had the passion and the ambition of your typical group of idealistic zealots. In about the same length of time it took the scion to undermine the republic, the zealots and their useful idiots ran his creation into the ground. It didn't matter to them, though. The Internet had been an extraordinary enhancement to communication the world over. They sure as hell didn't want it for that. In short order they converted it into the clumsiest, most inept, most corrupt bureaucracy somebody else's money could buy. The perfect socialist creation, in other words.

The father, completely shattered by the rather rapid dissolution of his dream creation, finally crawled inside himself and died. That is, he withdrew from the world and turned to reclusion, confining himself to his palatial but isolated domicile, where he could sit and watch the occasional whale spouting water in the gray waters of the bay down the hill. The son was retained as a figurehead of the industry, comfortably ensconced in a token position where he could be easily manipulated to do the zealots' bidding. He had a title, and he certainly had comfort, but he had no more true authority than the custodian who cleaned his office every night.

He did have a willingness to please his overseers, though, to keep himself comfortably situated with almost no effort required of him, no responsibility, and no worries, and he had something else: a predilection for sex with young boys. He liked them in their teens and even younger, in ripe pubescence, and he liked more than one at a time. He also liked keeping this predilection a secret, for political reasons. The State's elites could get away with pretty much anything, including murder, but it was sometimes inexpedient to publicize their activities. The politician who had a serious drug habit, for example, didn't have to worry about moral condemnation, but he did have to worry that someday his habit might become a political burden. So it was with the corporate figurehead and his taste for children. It did not need to become public knowledge.

The freedom fighters had had had little cause to concern themselves over this man until recently. He was, after all, a mere stooge for those with more brains and ambition than he had. Lately, though, he'd been put to uses that were inimical to the freedom fighters' interests—the tool was being used to do some actual damage—so they had determined it was time to dispose of him. His death would have nothing even remotely resembling the political impact the Secretary of State's death had had, but it would nonetheless send a message, and there was never any harm in that. It would also put the State in the position of having to replace him, and to do that the State's movers and shakers would either have to find another useful idiot—the right useful idiot—or they'd have to take a chance on installing somebody in his place who might have the desire and the capacity to do them actual harm. Either way the freedom fighters would benefit.

The mission was to be carried out just after midnight on the appointed late-summer night. Douglass and Duda were assigned a basic but vital peripheral task: They were to occupy the target's bodyguards until the mission was accomplished. And so it was that they appeared to be idly strolling along on their beat that night, making their usual rounds, when they happened on the limousine that had brought the counterfeit mogul to his usual weekly rendezvous. The two cops knew the car, but they had also known better than to disturb it on any of their previous visits. Tonight they broke with that tradition. While a third accomplice ensured that the surveillance cameras on that block were malfunctioning at the time, Duda wrapped lightly at the driver's side window of the idling limousine.

The car's occupants were savvy, and the driver lowered the window only far enough to permit conversation. "I don't want to trouble you," Duda said through the small opening, "but your car's motor is running and you're wasting precious resources."

"And I don't wanna trouble you," the driver replied. "but you guys usually know better than to mess with a State limo. No matter what it's doing. I think it might be best if you just go on your way and leave well enough alone.

"And have a lovely evening, Officer."

"I really appreciate.your advice. But I'm afraid I just can't take it this evening."

"Then I should let you know I've got a very large handgun pointed right at your chest. If I lower this bulletproof window just a few inches I can blow a hole in you the size of a grapefruit."

"I appreciate that. And I should let *you* know my partner has attached a small but very potent explosive device to the underside of your car. If anything happens to me, you'll go out in a blaze of glory—so to speak."

"So to speak. So what do you want?"

"First I want you to put your gun down to your right side—in plain sight. And very slowly. Wait. And at the same time I want you to lower this window—wait— keeping in mind as you do that dying in a fiery explosion is not a pleasant way to go. Keep in mind too that I am not kidding. Not in the least."

The State's bodyguards were always mercenaries, and they were *never* True Believers. There would be repercussions for them, but nothing so bad as being maimed or killed in an explosion. *Especially* considering who it was they were protecting: a man who was by no means highly esteemed by his peers, and who was, in fact, something of a joke. With his own pistol trained on the driver's face, Duda saw the window lowered and the driver's weapon gently set aside. This did not, however, slow the beating of his heart. "All right," he said. "now lower the glass between you and the passenger compartment. Lower it all the way. I'm going to get in behind you. And please, please remember that my partner has you in plain sight. If you try anything at all, he'll send all of us to the reclamation center in a heartbeat. I don't know about you, but I'm too young to die."

A few seconds later he was sitting behind the driver with his gun pointed at the base of the man's skull, in just the same way Austin had sat behind him that long-ago evening. He made sure the driver's companion was also disarmed—both of their firearms now in Duda's possession—and then he signaled Douglass, who moved into position well ahead of the limo but in plain sight of its occupants. He had his pistol in one hand and the bomb's detonator in the other. He waved the detonator so the car's occupants could see it.

"Understand this, gentlemen," Duda said. "We have no interest whatsoever in harming either of you. None. All we need from you is about ten minutes of your time. That's all. You don't even have to go anywhere. Just sit right here, nice and comfy, and in a few minutes you can be on your way. I absolutely guarantee that. If nothing happens to us, nothing will happen to you."

"And if something does happen to us," he indicated Douglass standing out in front of them with the detonator, "it will also happen to you."

"You guys know who our cargo is," the man in the passenger seat said.

"We do."

"And for him you'll risk your lives."

"We will."

"The guy's a nobody, a nob." the driver said. "He's a pervert. He doesn't make any important decisions or have any major responsibilities."

"We know that."

The man in the passenger seat shook his head. "Terrorists must be gettin' hard up. You'd think you guys'd have better targets to kill. What happened to takin' out all the bigshots? This guy's no bigshot."

"In name only," the driver said. "He's a nobody."

While they were having this pleasant conversation a fourth accomplice had entered the building and was in the process of dispatching the nobody. He caught the man in the act and was thus able to take some nice photos to distribute around the commonwealth for posterity. As soon as his work was finished, he called Douglass, and Douglass waved a signal to Duda. "All right then," Duda said. "See how easy that was? My partner is now going to watch us all very closely as I climb out of the car. And remember, nothing will happen to either of you gentlemen as long as nothing happens to us."

"Where's the bomb?" the driver said.

"Under the right front fender. Right against the engine compartment. Magnetized."

"But you'll take it with you."

"Are you nuts? You gentlemen will have it as a keepsake."

"*You're* nuts," the passenger-side bodyguard said. "We won't make it to the next block."

"Please don't get excited," Duda said. "Please don't. I gotta tell you, I get really nervous doing this kind of work. The bad part is over; let's just part company as friends. All right?"

"Friends," the man snorted. "You guys are terrorists. You'll kill us."

"No, we won't. We have no interest whatsoever in killing you two. And that's the truth. We got our target. You two can go in peace."

"You have our word," he added.

He meant it, too. The bodyguards left the neighborhood that night unharmed. So did the two police officers. And so, as far as they knew, did the assassin. They would never find out for sure because they would never meet him.

32

I n its commitment to the principle of perfect equality among its citizens, the bedrock principle that was the ostensible cornerstone of the entire edifice of the nation, the State had dedicated itself to erasing all differences among both groups and individuals in society. Nobody could be treated differently if nobody *was* different. That was the theory. Hence the effort Plato had pointed out to Duda in the café that night, the effort to breed a species of human beings who were all essentially the same, virtually indistinguishable one from the others. The effort was far from complete, but with each new generation it progressed toward what the State's founders would have considered the ideal. And because it was a long-range goal, one that would take a number of generations to achieve, it was easily concealed from those most affected by it, the common citizens themselves. Members of the Inner and Outer Parties, the cultural elites who did all the commonwealth's planning and made all its decisions, were not subjected to the hybridization that was being used to homogenize the common people. They procreated and raised families in the same way their ancestors had done, maintaining the integrity of their families to ensure the State would have proper leadership in future generations. They justified their doing so on precisely that basis: As genetic superiors, they and theirs were needed to conduct the complex affairs of state that would determine the State's own course of action in all domestic matters and also govern its interactions with the other advanced nations of the world—all those that were engaged in the joint effort to direct their shared planet to a prosperous and secure shared future.

In attempting to level the commoners, though, and by doing so erase all differences among both individuals and groups, they ended up with an unintended and unanticipated outcome. They had sought unity, but what they found instead was division, division every bit as problematic as the division they had wanted to eradicate. What they had not reckoned on was that for all their leveling attempts, each commoner remained a discrete human being with discrete perceptions of the world and discrete experiences. Therefore, the commoners remained not merely individuals but unique individuals. That was problematic enough, but what was even more problematic was that these individuals were attracted to some of their fellow individuals but repulsed by others. They were prone to seek out the company of those who were like them and avoid the company of those who were not. Those who were like them had similar psychological and social characteristics and developed generally similar beliefs. Their characteristics appeared to have formed through genetic transmission (a process the State's experts despised), but also through perception and cognition. And those who were not like them had different characteristics and beliefs, developed through the same processes. The State's elites were mortified at the results they had obtained. They began to recognize that they could not simply breed a pliant herd of domesticated animals to serve them—serve the common good, that is—and were forced to use other means to achieve their goal of perfect equality and perfect harmony.

In former times, exploiting racial differences had been the favored means of maintaining political and social control. Keeping the various racial groups at odds with each other at least prevented them from joining forces to attack those in authority. But the long-term goal was still the social leveling the experts believed was possible, leveling they thought would lead to perfect harmony without animus and with far less expenditure of energy than was currently required. Since the whole society would have common goals, goals established of course by the cultural elites, it would no longer be necessary to use coercion to achieve those goals. Everybody would want the same things, and they would all work together to get those things.

But there was such a long way to go, as they discovered to their disappointment and chagrin. Other means had to be used until they could get the commoners properly bred and trained. Simply shaving heads and dressing everybody in uniforms wouldn't get the job done. They used the law to pressure their citizens, proscribing free expression and the formation of most types of social, religious, or political groups, and of course moving the citizens around frequently to keep them from forming strong bonds. Still, it wasn't enough. They needed an ominous police force and a powerful, threatening military to remind common citizens that social harmony came at a cost—a cost the common citizens would have to pay.

This strategy had been somewhat effective for a fairly long time, at least two generations, but now it was starting to fail, and Hugo Lansky Long was both aiding and abetting its failure. Long skillfully used the State's own tactics against it, first stoking the fires of hatred among disparate groups, then consolidating the hatred to unify the groups and turn them against the State. What he did was precisely what the State had done to turn the Normals against the Deviants. But he used the tactic much more effectively than the State had used it. Most Normals were largely indifferent toward the Deviants; in fact, they tended to conceive of all Deviants as involuntary members of one big group: the hapless homeless. In their minds, the Deviants weren't really a threat to them. They were more to be pitied than feared. But the State was omnipresent and, as far as the Normals were concerned, omnipotent. The State ruled their lives. So when Hugo Lansky Long decried the State, they knew precisely who their enemy was.

Clever strategist that he was, Long blamed his country's woes on foreign powers that were abusing the Association of Nations' universal pact to share equally in the world's resources and contribute equally to the world's well-being. And the State was letting them get away with it. The foreign nations were using bribery and other forms of corruption to dissuade the commonwealth's political leaders from attending to their duties to their own citizens. Such was Long's argument, repeated time and again, first at secret, then semi-secret, and finally openly public rallies, and articulated as well in fliers that were distributed all over the country. This argument enabled Long to kill two birds with one stone. He could undermine his own government and incite hatred of distant foreign nations all in one fell swoop. And he could do it without being held accountable. Until he had actually taken control of the commonwealth, he'd have nothing to answer for and nobody to answer to. He hoped by that time to have accrued enough power to justify war with those foreign nations—but not a military conflict. He would attack those nations using threats of war but no actual violence. To make his threats credible he'd have to bolster his country's military. But that was something he planned to do anyway. A powerful military could be used as a bludgeon even in times of peace. An implied bludgeon can often be more effective than even a real one, for it can have a deterrent effect. A real bludgeon loses its deterrent effect and must therefore live up to its assumed potential. An implied bludgeon may never have to prove itself.

But a powerful military also served a vital unifying function. People marching shoulder to shoulder in the name of a great cause tend to maintain cohesion. No matter their personal differences, those personal characteristics that in ordinary circumstances would surely divide them, they would as members of a great military force put aside their differences and march in step toward a common goal. The State had tried to level them in the belief that it could erase their differences over time and bring them together in peace. Long understood that their personal differences could never be ablated, and that the only way to minimize those differences was to provide a common enemy, a distraction. The State had used its foreign allies, along with the hated Deviants, of course, as a foil only because it had to. Long converted "allies" to "enemies" because he understood human nature much better than the experts of the State understood it; and he knew the way to inspire domestic cohesion was to turn citizens' anger outward. Forget the Deviants; they would be too easily dismissed as irrelevant. China, on the other hand, with more than a billion people of its own to take care of, was somebody you needed to worry about. Long knew the State's bizarre objective of "sharing" the world with other nations was a pipedream. By the time the State figured that out he'd have conquered it.

His own real long-term goal was to use his political leverage to expand the black market, and thus vastly increase his own wealth, by indulging the hedonistic whims of his constituents at home. Under Hugo Lansky Long's rule, the commonwealth could become one enormous satyr, a sybaritic stronghold of the ravenous and the acquisitive, but with a powerful military and the willingness to use it if necessary (though of course he hoped the mere threat of using it would suffice). Long saw himself presiding over a magnificent pleasure dome that was also capable of dominating other nations virtually on a whim. The commonwealth's membership in the Association of Nations could be discarded. The National Workers Alliance would forge a new nation of steel that was also a workers' paradise.

The Normals were a bit hazy on Long's long-range plans—all right, more than a bit hazy. What they knew was that he was offering them something better than what they had now. And what Normal—in fact, what human being—wouldn't want that? Long avoided making extravagant promises while at the same time criticizing most everything the State provided—or, in his telling, failed to provide. He gave them specific targets for their growing resentment by naming names, the names of people high up in the government. Many of the names they barely knew—for they paid little attention to the government— but they knew enough or learned enough to detest the names, to hold the names responsible for the hardships in their lives. That was all that mattered, to be endlessly reminded that their lives were more difficult and more deprived than they should be—than they deserved to be. It followed all too naturally that Long was their messiah, their deliverer in the making. All they needed to know was from whom he'd be delivering them. That would suffice to let them know at whom their hatred should be directed.

Long also criticized the government's frontline employees by category, singling out, for instance, the police and other first responders primarily by raising questions about their performance. Why did it take firefighters and ambulances twenty minutes to half an hour to arrive at the scene of a fire or accident? A building could and often did burn down in the time it took firefighters to reach a fire. An injured person could die—and again, often did die—in the time it took the ambulance to arrive. Why did it need to take so long? And then there were the police. How could the police justify their brutality? Long would prompt his followers to wonder. Why were they never held accountable? The police literally *murdered* Normals and got away with it. Were they not fellow citizens as well officers of the law? Did they not have an obligation to treat their fellow citizens with at least a modicum of respect? Long demanded answers to these questions, and in demanding them himself inspired his followers to demand them as well.

But he didn't stop there. He also incriminated those who provided various commodities and services to the Normals. How could food be in such short supply so much of the time? Why were there so many power failures? And why, in a country that boasted so many "experts," were there ever times when people's plumbing didn't work and they weren't guaranteed access to clean running water? The targets were so easy to identify. All he had to do was pick something the people complained about and he had himself a target that would draw his followers' ire. He could fume about it at a rally and the people would respond. The crowds grew. Their enthusiasm grew. And they were angry.

But they were not angry at *each other*, and that was vitally important. They were angry together, at their elites, the central planners who were failing them all. The appropriate connections were thus established, and Long continually reinforced them. Other countries were failing the State, and the State was failing its people. To solve their problems and make a better world for themselves, they had to work their way back to the source. They had to go through the State, first, and then get to those foreign powers.

"It's remarkable," Douglass said. "We need to give the man credit. He *knows* how to get people worked up."

"Even more important, he knows what to get 'em worked up about and who to get'em worked up at."

"Yeah. Us."

"It's an art form," Duda said.

"But actually, in principle, it's pretty simple. You single out the common complaints and then rant about them. What could be more straightforward than that?"

"It's a hell of a system."

"If you really think about it, he's got everybody in the country mad at everybody else in the country, and they don't even realize it. They just know they're all mad at the government."

"It's a beautiful thing. Let's just hope it doesn't get us killed."

33

By late that fall, Hugo Lansky Long had the Normals sufficiently aroused that they had definitely become a force to be reckoned with. The evolution had been rapid, as Long had capitalized on pleasant summer weather in most of the urban centers—not to mention the State's usual ineptitude, which was about as predictable as lunar phases. Secret meetings had become open meetings in the space of only a few months, and NWA literature was being circulated among the Normals with impunity in plain sight of the authorities. But what was far more telling, Long had started a trend in dress and coiffure that openly defied the commonwealth's strict conventions. Women were growing their hair long and wearing makeup. Men too were growing their hair long and sporting beards. Under the barter system that had been used in the underground economy for decades, items of colorful dress, and equally gaudy accessories, began cropping up like beautiful wildflowers in a spring meadow. Only one conclusion could reasonably be drawn from these developments: The State was losing control.

Between the State and the people there had to be a mesh point, and the military and the police were it. The police were the first line of defense against change, so it was their job to cite violators and make arrests if necessary. In the first month after this edict came down from on high,

Duda and Douglass had issued no citations. Hyde called them in and took them to task. "You can't claim ignorance on this," he/she said. "These renegades are popping up everywhere. They're overrunning the damn city."

Noticing the remnants of Hyde's eyeliner from the weekend, Duda almost popped off, Yeah, we see that. However, he restrained himself in the interest of maintaining the relative invisibility he and his partner enjoyed. "But this stuff has always been around, boss," he said. That wasn't much better than saying Hey, your eyeliner's showing; but it sounded a little less smug.

"Not in public," Hyde snapped. "These people are flaunting the rules. They're openly mocking us."

"I think you're taking it too personally, Chief," Douglass spoke up. "Does it really hurt anything?"

"Let me remind you that it's hurt about thirty people from this compound so far." He was referring to the eighteen injuries and twelve fatalities the police of their precinct had sustained at the hands either of Long's followers or of those opposing Long's followers. Around the compound these last few months were known as the Bloody Summer.

"Are you asking us why it hasn't hurt us? Are we supposed to get ourselves hurt? Is that the idea?"

"No. I'm not asking that at all. I'm wondering if you two really take your jobs seriously."

Duda went to see Plato. Plato's beautiful residence was being cleaned out. The entire library had already been packed away and shipped off, and much of the furniture and other appointments of the house were gone too.

"I thought it could last forever," Plato said wistfully. "I don't know why. In our world, nothing lasts forever."

"Where's it all going?

"You'll find that out eventually. Soon enough, I'm afraid. You'll find it out before I wish you had to find it out, anyway.

"The books are the most important. We cannot ever lose the books, Michael. The books are our connection with the world we want to reestablish. The books are our bridge to history. That's why we got them out of here first.

"When the fascists rose to power fifty years ago, the first thing they went after was the books. Please remember that. Never forget it. It always works the same way. They try to destroy your connection with the world so you have nothing left but them. Then they force their new religion on you and that completes their rise to power. That's when all the other stuff begins: destroying the family, moving people around, cutting off communication. Etc. It all becomes possible when they get rid of the books and cut you off from your past. That makes it possible for them to destroy any other present than the one they have determined for you. It's a ruthless process."

"I believe you."

"And that's why I beg you to carry on. You and all the others like you. Save it all. Save everything you can."

"I really wish you wouldn't talk like this. You sound like a man on his death bed."

Plato smiled a weary smile. "I'm not dying," he said. "At least I hope I'm not. But I want to make sure you're prepared just in case anything ever does happen to me. I pass things on to you and you'll pass them on to the next generation. There are many more of us than you probably realize, but there still aren't enough. Obviously. If there were, this wouldn't be necessary.

"I assume you came to see me because things are getting worse in the city."

Duda nodded.

"Well, that's why we're leaving this place—as much as some of us hate to leave it. But Long knows the Forbidden City just like you do—in fact, he was doing business here a long time before you ever came out here. When the time is right, he'll turn the people's attention this way. Nobody wants to be here when that happens.

"We're clearing out, as you can see. Don't worry, I'll make sure you're with us. We'll be making quite a little journey, but we won't be going alone. In the next year or so you'll probably meet a lot of other people who believe in freedom. But I'm not going to tell you just yet when that's going to happen.

"The loyalists of the State are packing their belongings too, some of them. Only the hardcore fanatics are likely to be around by the time Long and his people come surging in. I don't know, and to be honest, I really don't care. I'll be long gone myself by then. And so will you."

"But you have no idea when that's going to be?"

"Next few months. That we're not sure about. We estimate he's got about twenty percent of the population solidly behind him by now, and that percentage is going to grow. It doesn't sound like much, but remember, the elites of the Inner and Outer Parties only make up about ten percent of the population—actually, less than that.

"So that leaves the homeless Deviants, who are a small percentage and really count for nothing; it leaves us, and unfortunately our numbers aren't large either, relatively speaking; it leaves most of the Normals, the Normals who aren't with or really against Long—they just don't want trouble—and they account for probably half the population; and it leaves *you*. By 'you,' my young friend, I mean the State's coercive power—the military and the various police forces. And you will be the pressure point. You'll be in the crucible. When the action starts, it will start with you, I'm sorry to say."

"And I'm sorry to hear you say it."

"You're feeling the pressure already, but it's going to get worse. Much worse. We think there are two possibilities: He'll move in the dead of winter, hoping you and yours will be demoralized at having to do battle with him and the cold at the same time. He knows *most* of you are pretty apathetic yourselves. There are some amusing bets about what percentage of you will just capitulate, shake hands with Long's people, and switch sides.

"But a better possibility, we think, is that he'll wait until spring, mid- or late-spring, just when the weather's starting to come around again. We know he will *not* move on the cities in other parts of the country—the warm weather cities, for example—before he moves elsewhere. He'll coordinate his attacks—everybody at once. Otherwise, the State would zap him before he gets a good start and a lot of those Normals would decide they'd be happy to have their old lives back.

"He's not a foreign power. He does not have a lot of heavy armament to work with. He does have some that he's imported from other countries or stolen from the State's military, but it amounts to very little. He knows he doesn't need a big army. He'll be doing battle with his own people. We know he's been providing military training—actually, for more than a year now. We also know he's probably already imported some mercenaries; he has plenty of international connections from his black market days. Still, the man's not going to have, or probably need, a giant, well-trained army. He's counting on guerilla warfare. And he's counting on fairly light resistance, and that's probably what he'll get. We honestly think he'll strike hard and fast with his best people, try to take out the State's best, and then everybody else will pretty much fall in line. We really think it's going to turn out that way.

"Think of all the Normals you deal with on a nightly basis. What percentage of them to you think have the stomach for a fight to save the glorious commonwealth? For that matter, what percentage of your fellow police officers have the stomach for such a fight?"

Duda just grinned at him.

"That's what I thought you'd say. Honestly, if the political apparatus would let him, he'd get himself elected and take the country over that way. But the political apparatus won't allow it, and besides, he doesn't want to waste time on politics. What he wants is to be the man in charge now, right now. He figures once he secures that, he'll have it made. I wonder if any man in history has ever been more sure of himself than this guy is.

"But he's got a reason to be confident, at least somewhat confident. He knows things are bad all across the country, and he sees the rats leaving the ship. He knows he's winning. Maybe the best thing about bad government is that once all hope is lost, most of the rotten politicians follow right behind it. Long knows a lot of these devout socialists are going to seek safe haven. They have no taste for war; their glorious dreams of utopia are shattered, and they'll just want to get the hell out of here.

"And that brings us back to you. You're the front line, my friend; you and others like you. You're the mesh point between Long and the glorious State. You're not at the head of the line, but you're close. It'll be ground military personnel, then cops trained in military tactics, then you. We know things have already started happening—which is why we're prepared to get you out of there as soon as the time is right. I promise. It may be two weeks, and it may be two months. But when the time is right, we'll come for you."

"And Douglass?"

"Of course. Douglass too. All our people who are in the police force or the military will be moving out just as fast as we can get them out."

"The military?"

Plato smiled. "Please, Michael. You've met several of our people who are in the top echelons of the government. You really think we don't have anybody in the military?"

"I guess I shouldn't be surprised, should I?"

"I'm going to tell you roughly where you'll be going, even though I'm not supposed to. But let's face it—and this is the good thing, my young friend—you're not going to be a high priority for anybody right at the moment. Within a few weeks, I suspect, they'll be trying to get you cops organized and hastily trained for the big push they're sure to see coming. But you won't be at the front of the line. You've got the military troops, and all those True Believers lining up in front of you. The State will focus on getting those people ready to throw themselves into battle. They're in a bind, and they know it; and it's too late to change that now. But they'll have some kind of words for you. Probably something utterly useless. Mostly, I suspect it'll just be something like, 'Look out, people, here it comes!' And in the end, the cops who are left behind will be fending for themselves. But you won't be left behind.

"The only things you'll have to watch out for are one: getting caught up in the initial fray—that's going to be dangerous, probably very dangerous, and you'll be a target then—except that you won't be around because we'll get you out of there before it starts; two: getting taken out by one of your own True Believers—they're going to figure out pretty fast that their ship is going down, I think, and if they see you running away they may take pleasure in popping you—but again, we hope to have you out of there before that happens; and three: getting picked off by some random Deviant.

"We're sending you to the old city, Michael. That's where you'll be going when the time comes. There'll be thousands of you there—maybe even a hundred-thousand of you, all together in a predetermined place. It's a university left over from the days before the Great Society program started, and it's out in a wooded area far from the city center. We checked the place out thoroughly, and it even has a library that somehow escaped the socialists' attention when they took over. They were so busy building their own cities, I guess they didn't have time to clean out or tear down everything in the old ones. So there will be books, but there will probably also be a lot of competition for them. And you won't be there long anyway. As soon as we can get people out of there we'll be clearing them out. And I'm not going to tell you where you'll be going next. Sorry. All I can say is, you'll be participating in what we're calling an underground railroad. That's a concept that has a distinguished lineage.

"With that many people gathered in one spot, the Deviants are going to become suspicious. They may panic and try to do something to you out of desperation. Who knows? It's impossible to say for sure, and that's all the more reason you should be prepared. For pretty much anything. We're still in uncharted territory, I'm afraid.

"Well, that's about the size of it. I can't tell you anything else because I really don't have anything else to tell you. But I'll say this: When the time comes, I'll let you know, I promise. I'll let you know by the usual means. And the time will be coming, Michael. I can't say when, for sure, but I can say this: Within a year, you'll be out of here. That's a promise.

"Oh, and there is one more thing. You'll be leaving very fast, probably in the middle of the night. When you go, you'll be responsible for one other person. That person will be Douglass. Your job will be to make sure he gets safely away when the time comes. For you two, it should be very easy. You should be at work when it happens, and somebody will tell you, 'Hey, let's go,' and that will be your cue. Remember to look for the sign. Remember too that a lot of people who aren't with us know the sign now, including many of your fellow police officers, so you'll have to be vigilant. You'll have to use discretion."

He grinned. "I'm not making things easy for you, am I? Telling you to trust us, but don't trust anybody?" He chuckled. "I wish I could just send Dan for you with the limousine, but I'm afraid that just won't be possible.

"Other people will have it rougher, unfortunately. They'll have to do more scrambling around. You two should be on your way very quickly."

"But you can't tell us where we're going. After the old city, I mean."

"Sorry. I can tell you this much: Your undercover days are over. You'll no longer be involved with the State in any official way—except as its mortal enemy. Your main concern with the State will be not getting caught or killed by it. I suspect that won't be much of a concern for some time, but the day will arrive when whatever skirmish is coming will be over, and who knows what will happen then?"

"Maybe you'll get your shot at a free society after all."

"Maybe, Michael. Maybe I will."

But Duda could tell he wasn't very confident that would happen.

34

For the next two weeks their greatest difficulty was staying out of trouble. In anticipation of what were referred to as "riots," the police had been instructed to crack down on troublemakers of every kind. The idea behind the order was to remind Normals that the State, sufficiently provoked, could be quite serious about maintaining order; and maintaining order might very well entail cracking skulls. The Crusaders naturally took their command to show they "meant business" as a chance to conduct some "mean business" by wading into various minor skirmishes and turning them into major skirmishes. One particularly nasty skirmish, which Duda and Douglass avoided only by a last-minute twist of fate, was a massive satyr into which a large force of police officers charged with orders to hold nothing back, to treat the revelers as "the enemy" and not merely disperse but brutalize them. The party-goers were meant to feel the wrath of the State, and feel it but good. It was known that the attendees were almost exclusively followers of Long, and therefore the objective was to send a message. The cops were to leave a lasting impression.

They did. Eighty of the merrymakers died in the raid, and hundreds of others were wounded. Twelve police officers also died, as it was discovered that some of the party-goers were armed with guns themselves—most of the police fatalities resulted from gunshot wounds. The affair eventually earned the name the 19 November Massacre. The State publicly lamented the occasion as a regrettable but necessary police action taken to restore order. Hugo Lansky Long, who now seemed capable of taking over the State's airwaves at will, decried it as an unforgiveable act of State oppression. To counter the anticipated whitewashing of the incident that he knew the government would engineer, he had his own video cameras on the scene to record the barbarities. And of course he broadcasted on national television the most gruesome images his cameras had captured. Douglass and Duda discussed the incident and decided that without question Long and his followers had won the day. They suffered more casualties, but in the court of public opinion they prevailed.

Nor did the State fare well in the November Roundup, which had begun before the 19 November Massacre and continued for a week or so afterward. Even most police officers, Duda and Douglass among them, were unaware of the November Roundup until it was well underway. They found out, at about the same time the general public found out, that a special unit had been assembled from among the most committed Crusaders to go about the city arresting certain key dissidents who were Long followers, identified mostly from footage taken at open rallies. They were to spare no excess in rounding these followers up, the goal again being to demonstrate, publicly demonstrate, that the State was more than capable of summoning brute force when brute force was needed. News footage showed dissidents being beaten, dragged, pulled by the hair (just to show the foolishness of growing hair), and pinned down in humiliating submission. The Secretary of Homeland Security provided the voiceover for these spots, reminding citizens that such violence really wasn't necessary. He left it to them to figure out what he meant by that, but they all knew what he meant by that.

The State had also worked hard to recruit gang members from among the unemployed, those who slept by day and worked in the underground economy by night. But their efforts had not been fruitful. The gang members were Long's people, closer to him than anybody else in the commonwealth. Instead of working for the police, some of them formed their own unit to retaliate against the November Roundup. And retaliate they did, rounding up a dozen of the Crusaders who had participated in the November Roundup and publicly executing them—on primetime television, of course.

The response was martial law. The State imposed a curfew that went into effect at eight o'clock every evening. Anybody caught on the streets after that time was to be arrested. Douglass and Duda, on their usual rounds on the first night of the curfew, came across two girls in an alley soon after their shift started, nearly two hours after the streets were to be cleared. The two girls had been sexually assaulted; they were afraid to say by whom. The officers managed to spend the first half of their shift that night delivering the girls to a medical center and following up on their case. Justice would not be served; they knew that—not in these times. But they went through the motions anyway, as much to keep themselves off the streets as to render assistance to the two young women.

They were on their way out of the medical center sometime after midnight when an armored police detention vehicle swept up alongside them. The man in the front passenger seat flashed the sign of the L and told them to get in the back of the van. When they asked where they were going, he said only, "Freedom."

Duda remembered Plato's advice: Trust us, but don't trust anybody. Many people besides freedom fighters know the sign of the L. This could be a trick. But would the State waste time and energy rounding up freedom fighters when it had Long's people to worry about? Besides, he liked the way the man in the front seat had said "Freedom." Other cops might know their sign, but they wouldn't know what it stood for. Not really. At any rate, they wouldn't express it the way the guy in the front seat had expressed it.

Seeing no better choice, they climbed into the van. Along with two other cops from a different precinct and four apparent Normals, they were taken out of the city.

There was very little conversation on the way to the old city, and they followed a route none of the passengers in the back of the van was familiar with, to a place that seemed even darker than the rest of the old city except that a large number of wood fires were burning there. Human shadows milled about in the darkness—many, many human shadows. The van crept along one narrow drive and turned onto another, then another, human shadows lining the entire route. There were, Duda gathered, many thousands of people in this place.

The van stopped at last in a line of similar vehicles before a large, stately building far more ornate, far more aesthetically pleasing than anything to be found in the utilitarian urban center. A sign out front said Administration Building. They followed their two escorts up a long sidewalk to the front door of the building.

Inside, throngs of people were milling about a large foyer that reminded Duda of the foyer in Plato's house in the Forbidden City. The room was noisy with conversation, most of which sounded quite amiable. There was laughter in the room, and it struck Duda that apart from the television programming, he'd been hearing less laughter lately. Was it just the usual depression that accompanied the onset of winter in New Leningrad, or was it more than that? Were the people terrified at the prospect of upheaval and even anarchy that awaited them?

He didn't really care. What lay in store for them did not lie in store for him. What lay in store for him was something entirely different—better, he was sure. It had to be better, didn't it? Could it be any worse than what was likely to happen down in the urban center? He had the powerful sense that, if nothing else, he was on the threshold of a grand adventure. He still didn't know whether to be elated or frightened, so he was a bit of both. Douglass felt the same way; he communicated it without saying a word. Soaking up some of the energy of their new surroundings, they looked at each other and smiled.

They'd been left in a long line of fellow exiles that led into another room on the first floor of the building, apparently a smaller room. Later Duda would notice that the door to the room, left permanently open to accommodate those waiting in line and a steady stream of those leaving, was labeled Admissions Information. "Just follow the crowd," one of their escorts had announced to the eight of them. "You'll need to produce your ID, so it'll help to have that ready. This is it, ladies and gentlemen. This is where you register to begin the next phase of your lives. We're all going through the same thing. Personally, I'm excited about it."

The escorts left them, perhaps to go and fetch another load from the city, and the line inched forward. Duda looked around to see if he recognized anybody, but he saw no familiar faces. There were dozens of people milling about on the first floor of the house, and from the activity on the staircase on the far side of the room it appeared there were many others on the other three floors.

The line crept forward. By three a.m. they were inside the smaller room, where six people sat behind a long counter, each of the six with a computer terminal before him or her. Finally, it was their turn. Duda stood before a woman who asked for his name, looked it up on her computer, asked for his ID to confirm his identity, then welcomed him. She handed him a small wooden token that she said was his "new ID." "Don't lose it," she said. "You might need it for a while."

She sent him to an adjacent room where more people were in line. In this room there were only four people attending to the newcomers, and they were sitting at desks dispersed as far apart as comfortably possible. Each desk had a stack of papers on it. Duda stood in line at one of the desks, and when it was his turn the man at the desk handed him a paper from the top of the stack. "Welcome to freedom" he said. "This is a map of the entire university. I assume you know you're at a university in the old city."

"I was told that's where I'd be sent."

"Good. This map will help you learn your way around. It's a pretty sprawling place. At one time it must have been very beautiful, but I'm afraid it's not much to look at now. We're trampling the place and stripping it bare at the same time. But it can't be helped. We need the firewood. You're right where the x is on the map."

"Administration Building."

"That's right. The map shows you some very useful things: where you can get some food, where you can clean up, where you *might* be able to find places to sleep. We're getting very crowded here. Your stay is probably not going to be very comfortable, but we also hope it won't be very long."

"How long, do you think?"

"We're getting most people out of here in three or four days."

"And where do we go from here?"

"You'll find that out when the time comes. I'm not trying to be evasive; it's just that we've got so many of us to disperse. We're going all over the country, some of us even out of the country. It's a big operation. I wish I could tell you more, but there just isn't more to tell you."

"I understand."

The man smiled at him. "By the way, that's where your token comes in. You'll notice that it has a letter and a number on the front of it. The letter tells you where your assembly point is. You'll find it on the map. The number identifies your place in the order of departure. It's a good idea to go to your assembly point as soon as possible in the morning—you can't go tonight. But go as soon as you can tomorrow. You'll find out about the procedure for leaving. There are people leaving this place in a continuous stream. It's just a waystation."

"I understand. Thank you."

"We appreciate your patience. We ask everybody to remember that we're all getting out of this hellhole soon. And we're getting out just in time. Things are about to get very ugly for the State. We'll all be better off if we can just stay out of the way."

"I'll be more than happy to do that."

"I can imagine. People wearing that uniform are in for a particularly hard time, down in the city. I wish we could offer you a change of clothing here, but I'm afraid that's just not possible. We're not equipped for that. There's also a chance—a small chance, we hope—you might have to use that uniform to get us something from the State before we leave. Or perhaps on the journey to where you'll be going from here. But it's a very small chance; don't worry. Remember, we are traitors. All of us. We all have a long and dicey road ahead of us. We're just trying to think of all the possible contingencies.

"One good thing: You won't be the only one around here wearing that uniform. You're going to see others like you. Everybody here is one of us. There won't be any of Long's people here trying to pick a fight with you."

"That's good to hear."

"By the way, one building that's still perfectly intact is this one right here." He pointed to a place on the map.

"What's that?"

"The library. Well worth visiting. You'll be amazed what you can learn when you get away from the damn socialists. There's no book banning or book burning here."

He rendezvoused with Douglass and they left the building. Thousands upon thousands of people swarmed the campus. They found they had the same assembly point, so they moved in that general direction, looking for familiar faces but seeing none. People were huddled in nooks and crannies all over the campus. Many were crowded around fires, some of which were set in open spaces, the others in empty fuel drums or other large receptacles. The fires, wherever they were burning, provided welcome light. What little electric power there was to the campus—to power the minimal lighting and computers in the Administration Building and a few other key locations, and not much else—was provided by powerful gas generators, the largest of which sat directly behind the Administration Building. Away from that building the campus got very dark even with the fires burning, and the people turned back into shadows.

"Still beats the city on a power outage night," Douglass shrugged.

"Hopefully it's safer, too."

They passed buildings that had been dormitories on the university campus, and others that had been classroom buildings. They passed a building that had been an auditorium. They stopped and asked several people about possible accommodations, but nobody had any good news for them. "Where's your assembly point?" one man asked them.

Douglass showed him his token.

"That's down by the old stadium," the man said. "A lot of people are just sleeping in the stadium. Conditions are awful, but there are several big fires down there. You might be able to stay warm."

They went down to the stadium, but it had little to offer. Finally, they were able to huddle up along one interior wall of one of the old bathrooms. It was still cold, but less cold than sleeping outside, certainly, and at least they were out of the elements.

They slept fitfully for only a few hours and then it was daylight and they were up again, and both miserable. What had awakened them was people using the bathroom facilities to take care of their matinal necessities, some of them having to resort to very crude measures because the bathrooms, like everything else on the campus save the library, were stripped bare. The bathroom was very crowded and there was much grousing, though no fights. "This isn't much better than back home in the city," one man grumbled, and got a good laugh.

The two erstwhile cops were out of the bathroom as soon as possible, then out of the stadium altogether and into the open air again. The morning was cloudy and damp, but not exceptionally cold. Still, people looked miserable lurching around the campus in their winter clothing. And the numbers were astonishing. Everywhere they turned, throngs of people filled their view. People of all sizes, shapes, and ages, most doing nothing but biding their time, spread out around them in every direction.

"How many people you think there are here?" Douglass wondered.

"I was wondering the same thing. Thousands, that's for sure. Maybe if we find something to eat we can take a walk afterward and just look around."

"Sounds good to me. It'll help pass the time, and it might help us warm up a little."

"We should find our assembly point first. Make sure we know how the system works and maybe when we might be leaving."

At the assembly point buses were loading, different types of buses—old city buses, buses retired from the learning centers, a few ancient buses that must have been used on some kind of long-distance excursions, back when such things were permitted, or were perhaps still used by the fortunate few who were permitted the luxury of long-distance travel. It was impressive, seeing the line of buses being loaded with people who carried very few possessions, and others, like Douglass and Duda, carrying no possessions at all. They had only the clothes on their backs to take with them. After two hours of waiting they were able to find out they might be leaving in three days. They were advised to check in at least three times a day, once in the morning, once in the afternoon, and once in the evening. If they missed their turns there would be others, but nobody could promise those second chances would come soon.

They left the assembly point and found food a few hundred yards away, where another crowd was gathered, even larger than the one at the assembly point. This crowd was impatient, like the morning crowd at the bathroom, and Duda felt the inclination to act as a cop and make sure peace prevailed, until he reminded himself that he was not a cop, not here. He stood in the crowd with Douglass and waited. Two people were dispersing small tins of meat. "I'd like some roast beef and a nice red wine," one man said when they were getting close to the back of the truck, and the crowd laughed. Duda and Douglass finally got their tins of meat and left the crowd and opened the tins and ate with their fingers.

"This is the stuff they give the military," Douglass said. "They eat this stuff when they're in the field."

"Hmm. It's better than some of the stuff you get in the cafés in the city, anyway."

When they were through eating they looked for a place to dispose of their empty tins and when they found one they were asked to pitch in and help remove a huge pile of trash that was growing a few hundred feet from the food truck. They loaded garbage onto the truck for nearly an hour as members of a crew of six people, and then the other four members of the crew departed and Duda and Douglass road with the driver of the truck to dispose of the trash. The truck crawled through pedestrian traffic for nearly an hour, crawling up a gradual slope through some pine trees. The crowd had given way and it was just the three men in the truck now. Then abruptly they reached the top of the incline and found themselves on a bluff that looked out over a river valley. Duda couldn't believe all the trees. Even the garbage that was piling up the steep side of the bluff couldn't spoil the view. They unloaded the truck and then stood there for a good fifteen minutes taking in the sights.

The clouds had broken, and for a few hours early that afternoon there was bright sunshine. The clouds were high and scattered as they stood at the crest of the bluff. "I never get tired of it," the driver said. "That's why I volunteered for this job."

"I've never seen anything like it," Duda said. "Except Stalin's Bluff in the city. Have you ever been to Stalin's Bluff?" he asked Douglass.

"Over there," the driver said. And sure enough, perhaps twenty miles to the north, the concrete towers of the urban center cropped up like whiskers in a beard. Much closer the old structures of the old city also cropped up, near the base of the bluff. And the ocean stretched away in the distance.

"Think we'll get to see things like this where they send us?" Douglass asked.

"God, I hope so," the driver said. "I sure hope so. I could stare at this for the rest of my life."

35

For the rest of the day they explored the campus, their new, temporary home, and did not see a single soul they knew or even thought they knew. Swarms of people were everywhere, people walking briskly or milling about, people huddled in dense clusters or curled up in doorways trying to sleep, people rapt in conversation or just studying the architecture or artwork, people lined up for food or waiting to board buses or searching for bathroom facilities. They spilled out of the buildings and filled all the open spaces. They encircled the fires or exercised vigorously or just jumped in place—anything to warm up. The two former police officers did not talk to anybody that entire afternoon; they just kept walking. It was dark by the time they got back to their starting point, and it was getting cold again. This time they were solicited to distribute food from the back of a truck and were able to get in a meal themselves. They were tired, but they were also cold, and it had felt good to be in motion for a purpose while distributing the food. To give themselves another purpose they went back to the assembly point and verified that they were still at least a day away from departure. At least.

They looked for still another purpose, something else to keep them busy, and found it trundling firewood from an enormous but dwindling grove of trees on the outskirts of the university campus to several nearby fires. Time dragged, but the trek to and from the grove of trees was long, and staying busy was much better than not staying busy. Much better. After a while they came across a huge group of people gathered around a bonfire that could be seen several hundred yards away. The people were telling stories and singing songs. Some of them were drinking alcohol. Many of the stories were barely audible from where they stood, or inaudible, and all they could do was feed on the reactions to the stories—heartbreak or joy or laughter. It didn't matter. Most of the songs were songs neither Douglass nor Duda had ever heard before, but that didn't matter either. They were entertained, and occasionally they were impressed. "This song is an old blues song," one woman said, and then she launched into a type of singing neither of them had heard before. She had an extraordinary voice, and the whole crowd listened to the song. When she finished the crowd showed its enthusiastic approval and clamored for her to sing again. Another man played a guitar, and another told jokes at the top of his lungs. They were entertained.

Duda and Douglass stayed at the bonfire until nearly midnight, and then they went in search of a new domicile, preferring to try to find better accommodations than they'd found the night before. Around the back of a building that sat at the edge of another small wooded area—some type of meditation garden, it appeared to be, like the ones in the People's Central Park but without the cameras—they found a ladder that was attached to the wall on the back of the building. The ladder was tucked away behind some bushes and they discovered it only by accident. They climbed it—the building was three stories—and found to their surprise that nobody was on the roof. So the roof became their bedroom for the night. Before they bedded down Duda scanned their surroundings, hoping to see far off into the distance the way they'd done from the bluff earlier in the day; but he could only see the campus, with its myriad fires and the hum of voices. The din of voices was dying as the night progressed, and he heard vehicles moving either to or away from the campus, probably both. The two men used their heavy winter police overcoats as blankets, trying to curl up beneath them, and then they were asleep for the night.

They slept poorly, both of them, and woke feeling miserable just as the sun was rising. Their bedroom had been freezing cold, reminding Duda of the excruciating Winter of a Thousand Hardships that had facilitated the ascension of Hugo Lansky Long. Fortune had smiled on Long that bitterly cold winter, and it had frowned on everybody else. But at least Duda'd had a roof over his head then. This bitterly cold night he had only the stars. He and his partner had curled up next to what appeared to be an old heating unit, but the heating unit hadn't functioned in many years so it put out no warmth; it only provided a bit of a wind break. When they awoke, in the coldest part of the night just before dawn, they got up very slowly, stiff from the cold, loosened up a bit, and then danced around for several minutes to stretch their muscles and try to warm themselves before descending to street level again. At least at street level the air *seemed* a little warmer, perhaps only because they were a few feet closer to dear old Mother Earth.

"I hope I didn't get sick last night," Douglass said. "I'm nervous about what's ahead of us. I don't need sickness to be part of it."

"I hear you," Duda said. "I was thinking the same thing."

They decided they would try the library that day, see if it would keep them inside and out of the cold for a while, and by the time they'd cleaned themselves up and found some food it was nine in the morning. The sunshine was intermittent and the air was warmer than it had been the day before, but still cold. There was just no real escape from the cold unless you could stand right beside one of the fires—and those spots were impossible to find. The library steps were crowded, the rooms inside were also packed with people, and to their disappointment there were virtually no books left on the shelves. Everybody was reading. There was very little noise in the building as everybody sat or stood with his or her nose in a book.

Duda stood along one outside wall of the library while Douglass left him to try to find something to read, and after a long while he returned with a book in his hands. "I'm sorry I couldn't get you one too," he said to Duda. "They're just hard to come by.

"Look at this. It's called *Life and Times of Frederick Douglass.*"

"Your name. He even looks a little bit like you."

Douglass jutted his jaw out to imitate the man on the cover of the book. "I never heard of him," he said.

"Well, now's your chance. I can't think of a better way to kill time in this place. It's a little warmer inside too. A little bit. Is there a place we can sit down? We're not supposed to take any books out of the library."

They found a place where Douglass could wedge himself into a corner, in a pose that was not exactly comfortable but did roughly approximate comfort, and he commenced to read. Duda stood by in silence for a while. Finally, he said he was going outside just to stretch his legs a bit. "I'll go back to the assembly point and check for us," he said.

"You don't need to do that."

"Relax. Enjoy your book. I'll enjoy my walk."

He was halfway back to the assembly point when a voice called to him. He turned to see Austin standing twenty feet away against a large tree. With him was the cook from the café. He walked over to them.

"I'm glad to see you're getting out," Austin said, and he extended his hand.

Duda shook it. "Likewise." The other man also shook his hand, if not warmly. "This place is a mess, huh?"

"By some estimates there are more than fifty thousand people here," Austin said. "But we're getting near the last of them. In a few more days, everybody but a few higher ups will be out. We'll all be headed elsewhere."

"Hopefully somewhere warm. I had a partner who came from Castro. He used to talk about the weather there all the time."

"Consider yourself lucky to be out," the cook said. "There was trouble in the city last night. As a cop you'd have been right in the middle of all that."

"And it's only going to get worse," Austin said.

"What'll happen in the end?"

"The country will have a new dictator," Austin said.

"You think so?"

"Absolutely. Long has completely outmaneuvered them. He's going to hit them hard this winter, they'll lose the desire to fight, and his ranks will grow."

"What then?"

"Good question, I'm afraid. Let's hope they don't come after us. But I don't think they will."

"Why not?"

"You're just coming into power in a country that's been slowly collapsing. Are you going to have time for a few million freedom-fighting guerilla fighters?"

"Eventually he will. If he gets the country stabilized."

"Which he will, eventually. The advantage Long has is that he's not like the academics who drove the last revolution. Those people lived on theories and social engineering. Some cultural revolution. Dreamers. Lunatics. All big ideas, and not an inkling how to carry them out. Not a clue that what they wanted to achieve would never be possible in the first place. They really didn't know what they were getting into—as we're seeing now."

"Bastards," the cook said. "Look how much damage you can do with big ideas."

"Big ideas that have no foundation in reality," Austin amended.

"You can say that again."

"Long is no dreamer," Austin continued, turning to Duda again. "That guy is a cold-blooded realist. He won't need any excuses to rape, torture, or murder. Those things are just part of the power game, and he knows it. He has no illusions."

"So eventually he *will* come after us. Most likely. He's not going to let us just live our lives in peace."

"No," Austin chuckled. "You're right about that. But we'll come up with strategies for subverting him. That's what guerilla fighters do."

"Why?" Duda wondered. "What's the point? I feel like my whole life is becoming a futile chase after something that doesn't even exist."

"It exists."

"Damn it, kid," the cook spoke up. "Sometimes I think you and I need to just go at it. I really do. We need to just draw a line in the sand and have it out. It makes me wonder why the hell P. Henry recruited you for the cause."

"Easy, Benjamin."

"Easy nothin'. He's always been like this. So self-pitying. You'd think he's the only one who makes sacrifices."

"Look at us, Michael," Austin said. "We're twice your age, and we've lived our entire lives chasing after the same thing you're chasing. Do you think we'll ever see it?"

"Do you think it even exists?"

"It exists," Benjamin said sharply. "It's existed before. Didn't P. Henry ever show you the library? I mean, really show it to you?"

"He never got around to it."

"Cut him some slack, Benjamin," Austin said. "He hasn't seen it. You can't blame him for doubting. We've all doubted."

"But not anymore?"

"I don't know," Austin shrugged. "Maybe you just reach a point where it doesn't matter if you doubt anymore. Life's short; it doesn't last forever. What else do you have to give your life to?"

"Well I don't doubt," the cook said fiercely. "Not ever. I've seen it. Books. Pictures. Videos. A world you can't even imagine. All thrown away by a bunch of dreamers. You can't even imagine."

"Maybe Long'll bring it back. You said he's a lot smarter than the people in the government now. You said he's a realist."

"Long is Caligula," Benjamin said.

"Who?"

"Never mind. You need to do some research. You need to learn what's possible, and why."

"Maybe so."

"All I can tell you is Long won't bring it back. Long's not for the people, kid. Long is for Long. Long is a damn boot-legger."

"A what?"

"Never mind. It's like talkin' to a damn Normal. Long was weaned on the black market. Booze and drugs. And all that other stuff. He'll probably keep the people drunk and high, and otherwise diverted, for as long as he can. Then he'll burn out and the next guy'll come along. Wonder what *his* great program will be."

"Maybe the next great program will be us," Duda said. "Or whoever follows in our footsteps."

"Yeah, sure," Benjamin said. "Maybe it'll be us."

"We may never get it back, Michael," Austin smiled at him. "But I like that spirit. We need that. It's what we need to survive."

"I just can't wait for Long to settle in so we can start bumping off *his* people," Benjamin said. "That's all I can say. Give us a shot at the next Secretary of State. The next corporate honcho."

"It never ends," Duda said.

"What's the alternative?" Austin said. "What's the better option?"

Duda didn't have a better option. He shook hands with each of them again as he said goodbye. Then he went to the assembly point to check on the status for their departure.

36

Down in the city the agitation had begun very early in the morning, but it would not reach its climax until very late that night. Long had as expected struck the first blow, sending a small but well-trained strike force to attack the military base in Sector P two hours before daybreak, when most of the soldiers were still in REM sleep in their bunks. Two other strikes on military posts near the city occurred at that same hour, in addition, of course, to similar coordinated assaults on military installations across the country. Relatively few personnel were involved in these surprise attacks, but because of training and tactics their potency was considerable. They knew what they were doing.

Three hours later came the raids on various police compounds, all just after the morning shift change. The military strikes had military objectives, one being, for example, to amass ordnance for future use. The assaults on the police compounds had essentially one objective: to kill. The more cops killed, the fewer would survive to offer future resistance. Perhaps even more important, the more cops killed, the more likely the survivors would be to weigh their options and choose surrender. This was a civil conflict, after all. They could plausibly claim to have loyalties on both sides.

Prior knowledge of the impending incursions had existed in some quarters, and word of the incursions once they had occurred spread purposefully and fast. Now the real ugliness could begin. Long's zealous but entirely unorganized followers took to the streets later in the morning and spread like a virus through the urban centers, burning vehicles, smashing storefronts, terrifying their compatriots into cowering submission. In a socialist paradise with no private property to defend, they concerned themselves only with saving their lives. They took shelter wherever they could find it and let the insurgents have the city. By and large, the insurgents left them alone.

And have the city they did. They continued vandalizing and looting the shops and bars and restaurants and supply centers until late in the afternoon, chanting all the while. "Change things now! Tear it down!" and "The State is wrong! Long live Long!" and "Hear the call: Justice for all!" and "Hear our plea: Set us free!" and "Now is the hour to feel our power!" echoed through the streets, the volume swelling as the multitude swelled, the seething, angry, amorphous multitude fortified by the courage that numbers and intense passion inevitably supply. A group called The Winds of Change imagined itself to be in charge, but in fact nobody but the witless mob was in charge, and the limits of its authority were the limits of its anger and energy, unless some agent of the State arrived to stop it. None did, for the State's agents were mostly otherwise engaged. Long had seen to that. The Special Opers and SWATs made attempts but were everywhere beaten into retreat. The regular cops displayed more discretion and less valor. They hid in their compounds, under siege, and contributed to the common good by saving their own hides.

There was a method in this madness beyond inchoate rage, and Hugo Lansky Long was to be credited for it.

He was keeping the most capable resistance occupied with organized attacks while the raging mobs were left to their own undisciplined devices and could therefore rage all the more because nobody was making an effort to stop them. It would be almost midnight before military units could arrive and stake out territories to claim and maintain in State control. Normals who were not within those territories were on their own, and a decent number of them simply fell in with the rioters, not participating but moving with the flow, and in some cases letting themselves be consumed by the passion.

Late in the afternoon the drinking had begun, and once the drinking began the insurgents became even more unruly. The chants grew louder, the fights grew more frequent and more violent, and any semblance of order—and there certainly wasn't much of that—gradually dissipated. The statues came down then, the revered symbols of the socialist paradise: statues of Marx and Lenin and Stalin and, yes, even Trotsky; of Mao and his henchmen; of Castro and Chavez and Guevarra; of Minh and Il-Sung and Pol Pot; of Gramsci and Milosevic and Tito and Qing and Grybauskaitè. And more—there were others, too, lesser lights in the glorious socialist constellation, but lights just the same, having helped to illumine the way to utopia. Pity their residence there was so short lived. In an ecstasy of revolutionary exuberance they fell, one at a time or in multiples, the icons of a glorious movement toppling like bowling pins into heaps of rubble. And the chats continued.

Darkness bolstered the rioters' courage even more than booze did, and when night fell the collective zeal of the insurrectionists was infused with a powerful measure of personal wantonness, of private lusts being satisfied under cover of a protective shroud of lawlessness and darkness and drunkenness, a lethal combination. The personal attacks began then, beatings and sexual assaults, vendettas carried out with the implicit permission of an anarchic fever that saturated the air. A woman was raped by a gang of men in an alley. A cruel supervisor, unable to escape the mob, was dragged from his office where he had tried to hide and beaten to death in the street. A gang rival was ambushed and succumbed to public immolation as a warning to his confederates. Away from the chanting throng who provided the gathering with the minutest semblance of cohesion and purpose, rapt as they were in religious fervor, the communal celebration of communal destruction—away from the central core of all that collected ardor, hideous shrieks and pleas for mercy and howls of execration and threats of gruesome violence all made their way into the same frigid night air. Terror and rage commingled, and the air throbbed with the violent energy of mass aggression.

37

"I t's in there," Douglass said.

"What's in where?"

"About splitting up the families. To drive them apart. To create separation. To make them loyal to the plantation. The State.

"I read the whole book today in the library," Douglass said. "And it's all in there. It's more than two-hundred years old, and it's in there."

"Just like Plato said."

"Just like Plato said."

Douglass was breathless. Reading that book had reenergized him. If he'd had reservations about their future, reading that book had vanquished them. He was ready now. He couldn't wait to board the bus to wherever it was he'd be going. And he no longer seemed to care where he was going—as long as it was away from where he'd been.

They would not leave until late the following night, which meant they'd be spending at least one more night in the cold. But what bothered Duda was that he and Douglass were being separated. They were on separate buses. "Does that mean we're going to different places?" Duda had asked the woman who told him their assignments.

"I can't tell you that."

"Why not? What's with all this secrecy? I thought we were the people who disclose things. Are open about things."

"It's not that. I can't tell you because I don't know. I'm just in charge of seeing that people get on the right buses. I'm sorry."

Duda looked despairingly at her, and she offered, "Maybe you can go and see John. Maybe he'll know."

"Where is John?"

"He's at the Administration Building."

It was early in the evening, and dark outside, by the time they reunited; but they went to the Administration Building anyway. John wasn't there. "Will he be back tonight?" they asked the man who had taken the time to see them.

"I don't know. Probably not. We're very busy here. Do you both have passes? Do you have bus assignments?"

Duda nodded. "But we're not on the same bus. We want to be on the same bus."

"All hell is breaking loose in the city, gentlemen. What happens if Long finds out we're here—all of us congregated in this one place? Do you want to take a chance on that?'

Although they both doubted very much Long was interested in them right now—he had plenty of other things to keep him busy—they didn't want to sound selfish so they conceded they didn't want to "take a chance on that."

"I'm sorry," the man said, and he probably meant it.

They returned to the Administration Building the following day, but things were even more hectic there than they'd been the night before. They did not talk to John. For that matter they never found out what John looked like. The place was starting to look like a city under siege, everybody desperate to leave and their desperation starting to influence their behavior. When one first arrived, the Administration Building looked like the beacon of freedom. After a few days' waiting it was more like an internment camp.

In the end they said goodbye and got on their separate buses, both expressing the hope they'd end up in the same place, but hugging each other in case they didn't. Duda took a seat next to the window on his bus and sat staring out, feeling sorry for himself. Benjamin would have been furious with him. He was thinking about all the people who were parading through his life, coming and then quickly going, leaving him no sense of commitment, nobody to hold on to. The gloom he'd felt when Anna disappeared was settling back over him. Most of all, he wondered if he'd ever see Plato again.

Somebody sat down in the aisle seat next to him and said, "Hello." Duda turned and it was a girl. "Hello," he said.

"Martha," she said, extending her hand.

"Michael."

"Are you excited, Michael?"

"I think 'anxious' describes it better."

"Not me. I've never felt like this before in my life. Ever. This is like starting life all over again."

"I guess so."

"I just ... in the past year I've had my horizons broadened so much. To think that such a world is possible. I'm so, so happy Dolly brought me in. I just ... I just never thought such a world was possible, that's all."

"You're sure about that? Freezing to death in the countryside and then riding off into the night on a crowded bus doesn't seem like such a great world to me."

"How can you be so gloomy? Of course we can't be sure what's ahead. That's part of the excitement. But almost anything's better than what we're leaving behind. That's the way you have to look at this.

"Like my hair?"

"It's beautiful." He said it to be nice, but he could see that one day it might be beautiful.

"It'll be down to here," she said, turning to indicate the small of her back. "You wait and see."

She was very attractive. "I like that stuff on your face," he said.

"Cosmetics. They make me look beautiful." She said it jokingly, batting her lashes at him, but what she said was true. He was taken with her. He was reminded of the daydreams he'd had while Hooligan was boring him to madness with soccer talk—or with complaints about the climate in New Leningrad. Whatever happened to Hooligan? Duda hoped he was all right, but he wasn't optimistic. Hooligan's temper was likely to get him in trouble in a revolution. It was likely to get him killed.

"Like my bracelet?" Martha was saying. "This is a bracelet."

"What's it for? Is it some kind of ID device or something? Does it have a chip in it?"

"No, dummy. It looks pretty. That's all it's for—to look pretty. And nothing more."

"Ah, I see. Well, it does look pretty."

The bus's electric motor clicked into gear beneath them, and the bus lurched and then glided forward. Duda wondered where they would stop to charge the motor. Would they need to charge the motor? How far were they going? How long would it take them to get there? And what kind of life awaited them?

"This is it," Martha said. "The future begins now. Life begins now." He felt her trembling, and he wanted to be as excited as she was.

The bus eased its way among the shadows and the fires toward the open road. Some of the shadows shouted and waved at them as they passed. Others were stark silhouettes against a fiery background. The bus rolled on, slowly, finding its way among the shadows.

"You like my perfume?" Martha said. "Here, smell it." She held her wrist out for him to smell. The smell was pleasant, faintly sweet, like the smell of the flowers in the park.

"Smell behind my ear." She leaned over.

Duda liked that even better. He liked her being close to him. "It's wonderful," he said. And he meant it.

Soon enough they were beyond all the shadows and on to the open road. Complete darkness enveloped them, and he craned his neck to find the pool of light the bus's headlights made in their path. He heard the gentle murmur of voices all around him. The wheels hummed beneath them. The bus's heater blew warm air that circulated through the passenger cabin, and he started to relax as his body warmed. The smell of Martha's perfume was still in his nostrils, and, feeling her excited energy beside him, he smiled faintly. Looking out through the window, he thought he saw Plato's reflection in the glass.